The HIDDEN Queen

Opening Dedication:

This book is dedicated to all of those people who give second chances, and to those who earn those second chances and actually make change. Too many people are unwilling and have no drive to make love work. Thank you for showing your determination.
Earn your love, worker bees!

The Hidden Queen

Written by Kristen Elizabeth

Table of Contents:

Opening Dedication:..2
Table of Contents:..3
The Hidden Queen   Muse Playlist 5
Disclaimer Notice: 7
Author's Warning:...8
Special Author's Note:..9
Preface… 12
Kinley… 17
Terse… 32
Kinley… 39
Carlisle Lawrence… 50
Kinley… 65
Carlisle..83
Kinley Lawrence… 109
Carlisle..118
Kinley… 126
Kinley… 143
Merik Arden… 155
Kinley… 168
Carlisle..177

Kinley… 201
Kinley… 226
Kinley… 243
Carlisle 256
Valence Trident… 269
Carlisle 280
Epilogue – Winter Lawrence 287
Bonus Chapter 1 – Valence… 291
Bonus Chapter 2 – Halo Trident 295
Author's Medical Corner: 301
Extras: 308
Book 5 Excerpt 312
Books by Kristen Elizabeth 324
Acknowledgments 327
About the Author 329
Author Q&A 331
About this Book 333
Reader's Observing Questions: 336
Special Bonus Note: 340
Final Remarks 342

The Hidden Queen Muse Playlist

(Alphabetical Order)

Book 4 Theme: So Far Away – Staind

1. 30 Seconds to Mars – I'll Attack
2. AFI – Kiss My Eyes and Lay Me To Sleep
3. Ashlynn Post – Silent Cries
4. Besomorph, Coopex, RIELL – Redemption
5. Breaking Benjamin – The Dark of You
6. Bring Me The Horizon – Throne
7. Camylio – Hurting me, hurting you
8. CARLISLE theme: The Show Must go On – 2Cellos
9. Citizen Soldier – Monster Made of Memories
10. David Guetta – Hey Mama
11. Evanescence – Imaginary
12. Evanescence – Taking Over Me
13. Fearless Soul – Find My Way
14. FesS – Sweet Dreams Cover
15. Fun – We Are Young
16. Imagine Dragons - Enemy
17. Journey – Separate Ways
18. KINLEY theme: Butterflies (piano) – Tony Anderson
19. Lauren Paley – Hide and Seek cover

20. Maroon 5 – Sugar
21. MUDSPITTERS – Purple Hydrangeas
22. Nine Lashes – Anthem of the Lonely
23. Neoni – Darkside
24. Pink – Funhouse
25. Rex Mundi ft. Susana – Nothing At All
26. Rosse – coincidence (Slowed/reverb version by Sereine)
27. The Score – Stronger
28. WITCHZ – I'm Fine
29. YOHIO – My Nocturnal Serenade

Disclaimer Notice:

Disclaimer Notice:

All of the art in this novel series is drawn by the author, Kristen Elizabeth.
By no means am I a professional artist, nor do I claim to be, but I've always enjoyed the hobby.
I hope the drawings help you to integrate even further into this novel's world.
Thank you for reading!

Kristen Elizabeth

Author's Warning:

This book contains trigger warnings and material, including:

Abandonment/Neglect
Child Abuse/bullying
Implied grooming/marriage between children
Maiming
Assault/gore
Witch Craft
Attempted Murder/Murder
Infidelity

Please proceed with caution, and if triggered by any of these themes or by the story, please seek the appropriate help or resources. Be safe! Thank you!

Special Author's Note:

This novel saga uses an entirely different Calendar system, with different names of the months and days of the week. So, the Months and Weekdays are as follows:

January – Blizzard's Reign (30 days)

February – Nivis's End (20 days)

March – Seed's Sewn (40 days)

April – Rain's Fall (40 days)

May – Veras's Height (40 days)

June – Veras's End (20 days)

July – Solaris's Gifts (30 days)

August – Solaris's Reign (40 days)

September – Solaris's End (20 days)

October – Moon's Dance (27 days)

November – Folias's Blessing (30 days)

December – Year's Fall (20 days)

Sunday – Sun's Dawning
Monday – Morning's Stars
Tuesday – Seed's Rising
Wednesday – Sun's Reign
Thursday – Sun's Falling
Friday – Twilight's Reign
Saturday – Moon's Height

Spring – Veras
Summer – Solaris
Autumn – Folias
Winter – Nivis

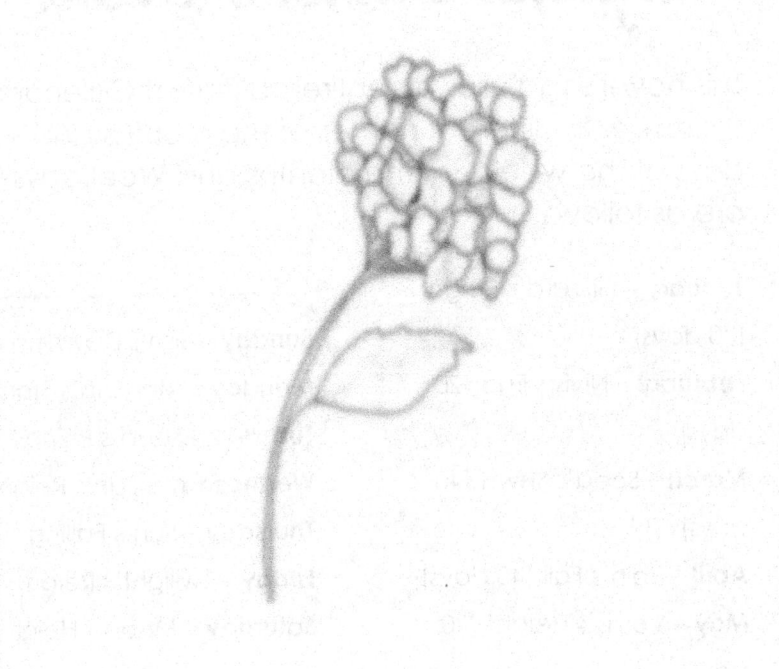

PREFACE

Preface...

Year's Fall, 500 Lawrence Dynasty (LD)

"And so, the Oracle proclaims, that in the month of Year's Fall in exactly one year, a life-mate child shall be born to the Crowned Prince that has been born on this day, the last day of the current year; that she may bring the nations to their knees by his side and rule over them justly. For this child, the only child who could undermine him, is also the very key to a peaceful reign," the scribe told us over my birthing table. "She will be born on the last day of the last month of next year."

I looked down at my son, my arms tired; but I still insisted on holding him. It had been foretold that he would be next *Dark Prince*, and he had been.

In our empire, there were two royal families for this nation.

There was the royal family of the North, the ruling *imperial* family, who had a Crowned Prince or princess bore to them once a generation.

It was meant to be an even distribution, a balance. It was meant to make it fair to both sides.

This child was born with either solid black hair or solid white hair; hair to distinguish darkness or light, positive or negative energy.

.   The child would also be born with golden eyes. He or she would, no matter what *numbered* child he or she was born into the family as, become the next king or queen.

My husband, himself, had been the fourth son of his family, but he was now king, born as the Light Seer King with his solid white hair and his golden eyes. I had been his match; his Dark Seer queen, with my black hair and golden eyes.

This child would now become the future king.

The golden eyes were a huge clue of our ruler;

The Eyes of truth, the eyes that could read through anyone and everyone; the eyes that could see your *true heart*.

Otherwise known as *"The eyes of the Truth-Seer."*

The last living dragon after the Dragon War, hundreds of years ago, had used sorcery to revert himself into a human form, and he had chosen two brides from bloodlines whom had helped him.

These two bloodlines became two separate ruling families in the empire.

Before he had died, he had bestowed his powers into the bloodlines, and enchanted us so that we held authority.

Only the true king and queen were born with these particular attributes, as the spirit of the King and queen found its way into whichever child was of its choosing.

The other royal family, the royal family of the South, would be the only man or woman born with the opposite hair color to the new king or queen, and he or she would also share the golden eyes of the Truth Seer.

He or she was always born with hair that was always the opposite in color to the other, to be his or her balance.

Since my son had been born as The Dark Seer—black hair, meaning that he had the eyes that could see the darkness of the hearts of his people—of course, then the child born as his bride would be born as The Light Seer, with white hair and the eyes that could see the light of the hearts of her people.

It was imperative to get the girl as quickly as possible upon the event of her birth, and to bring her to the palace to raise her as a proper queen.

If we were successful, then the king and queen would marry as soon as she arrived, and they would grow into a power couple. That was how it had always worked.

When I had been born as my husband's true partner, I had been brought to be his infant bride and we had been raised as a married couple.

If the child *didn't* come to the imperial kingdom, it could lead to ruin…either famine, war, attempted coup de tats, droughts, even plagues.

It was only the queen, as well, who—if not brought to the palace and raised to *love* the king—could kill him.

The queen was always brought to the king. It was never the other way around. It was also almost always the queen that was born in the South, while the king was born in the North, so the North ruled as the true power of the dynasty, while the South sat bitter and resented this.

That was why the child was brought in as soon as they were born…because the parents could negatively affect the child and turn them against us.

A Truth-Seer could not read another Truth-Seer's internal thoughts. They were the only ones who could fool one another.

As a Dark Seer, one could see all of the dark thoughts and feelings inside of peoples' hearts. That was the eye of judgement. It was the fiercer of the two linked Seer's.

The Light Seer, however, was powerful in its own right, serving as the eye of mercy.

Where the Dark Seer could see all of the dark thoughts and feelings in a person, the Light Seer could see their pure thoughts and feelings, their love, their purity.

Both were required to rule over this world justly and with mercy.

If they didn't meet and grow to love one another, they could destroy the nation, instead.

Although, so long as one child or descendent of a former Seer lived, however, there could be another born, which was how the royal family had survived.

My husband's father had been the brother of the king before him, as it were. That king—my husband's uncle—had been a Dark Seer, himself, before my husband had been born as a Light Seer. As long as you were a member of the royal family with blood relation somehow, it didn't matter what branch you actually came from.

I looked into my son's golden eyes, thinking of a name for him. "Carlisle Jameson Lawrence," I named him, and his father came and smiled down at him.

"A good name for him," he smiled, giving me a kiss. "Thank you, my queen," he smiled at me, his golden eyes warm as he blushed lightly.

Chapter 1

Kinley...

Veras's End, 506 Lawrence Dynasty

"But why do we have to move again?" I asked, clutching my stuffed animal. I had found it at the last place we had moved from; moldy and dirty and sticky as it was, I couldn't leave it behind.

It was my only friend. All it needed was some love...

Just like me.

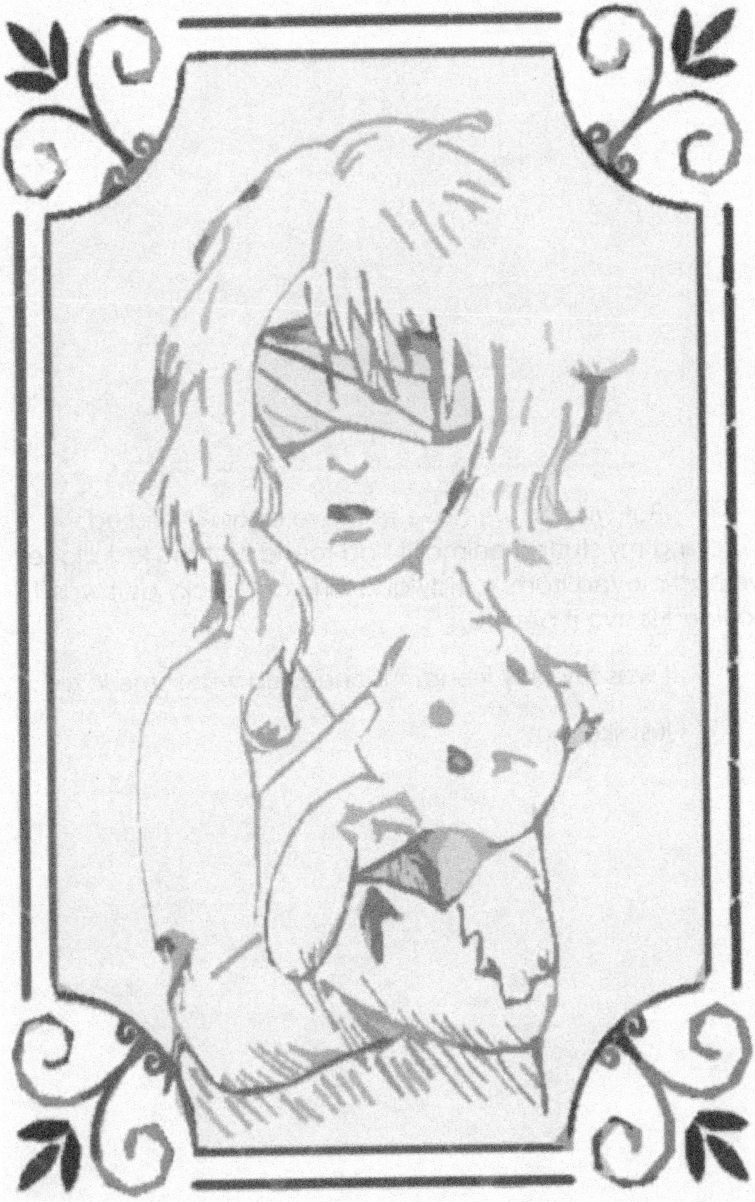

I didn't understand why we had to move around all of the time, why we couldn't stay in one place.

"You're the one who decided to take your blindfold off!" My father shouted, and I felt something strike me. I yelped, cowering. "You know better! You can't take off your blindfold. You are not allowed to see."

"I don't—"

"I don't care that you don't understand. You need to listen and obey, and that's all you need to know. If you do that, you'll stay fed and sheltered."

Pain radiated through my arm where what felt like a boot had struck me, but I lifted the shoe and tried to sense my way over to my father to return his shoe to him.

He grumbled, but took it, and I held onto my rope that kept me tied to the wagon as we began walking again.

Father said that the wagon was pulled by the horse, and that it held all of our things so there was no room for us to ride on it.

It wasn't a large wagon, but I felt his presence leave my side even as I kept walking along and I had to think that he was, in fact, riding on the wagon.

For as long as I could remember, I wasn't allowed to use my eyes.

I didn't know what anything was.

The two occasions that I had taken off my blindfold, I had been so overwhelmed that I'd almost immediately closed my eyes and felt blinded.

The last time that I had taken it off, however, we'd had one of father's friends over, drinking with him...he had seen my eyes before they had closed, and there must have been something bad about them because just like the first time I'd opened my eyes, we'd left that same day.

I remembered feeling suddenly surprised and happy when I had met that man's eyes.

He was thinking that I was special.

Though, I didn't see how that was possible, when father insisted that I keep my eyes covered.

Perhaps they weren't special.

Maybe I was scary?

Father kept most of our belongings loaded on the wagon at all times, just in case.

In *this* case, the man had begun crying out and shouting in alarm, and father had demanded he leave before he grabbed me, carrying me out to the wagon and tying me to it before we left our small little shack.

Father worked small odd jobs as a carpenter, so he could work anywhere.

Whenever we met new people, he told them that I was his servant girl, and I guessed that he must be ashamed of me because I couldn't use my eyes.

If only I had been normal.

He also regularly dyed my hair, so I assumed that he hated my appearance entirely.

I didn't know where my mother was, or what had happened to her. All I had ever known was *this* man.

Perhaps...perhaps, I mused in my mind, my mother had died or had left my father on bad terms, and left me with him.

He seemed to strongly dislike me.

I didn't know how to ask my father for information, either.

We found lodgings just after dark. I knew, because I could see the vague change of lighting through my blindfold and my closed eyelids, no sunlight filtering through to my vision.

"Alright, we'll stay here for the night. I have to go inquire about a job and housing tomorrow, so I need for you to stay here and out of trouble."

I gave a nod. "Yes, father."

He grumbled, but we got our horse tied up in the stable before we entered the building, and we were led upstairs to a room.

"Goodness, when is the last time the girl had a bath?" A higher-pitched voice asked.

That was a woman, wasn't it? I didn't know what that meant, but when I had asked my father why voices were so different, he told me that women sounded higher and softer than men did.

What father had told me a "woman" sounded like, it seemed, was like this.

"How would any lady like to be around you if you can't even take care of a young girl's hygiene? She *stinks*," she commented. "I can give her a bath, if you like."

He grunted. "I guess she *could* stand a bath," he said. "But don't mess with her eyes. She's blind, and sensitive to touch around her eyes."

We stepped into the room, and the woman got me a spare dress and a towel—or at least, that is what she *told* me that she was doing, before she led me to a room off of the main room.

I heard the water filling the tub before she helped me undress and helped me feel my way to the tub.

"Where are you two coming from?" She asked, making conversation. "We don't see a lot of slaves in this area."

"S...slave?" I asked. "What is that?"

"Oh...well, a servant. Normally made to do hard labor. Is that your master?"

"No," I said.

"But you are a slave, aren't you?"

"No," I said, soft. "That man is my father."

21

"*Father?* You don't look anything like him, miss. He has rich, dark, chocolate skin, and you have white skin…" She paused for a long, long moment. "Did he *tell* you that he was your father?"

I hesitated. "Well…"

Come to think of it…he hadn't.

Not once had I ever heard him say that I was his daughter, or call me his daughter to me, myself.

I looked back on it now, remembering that I had heard a "child" call out for her father one day, and that I had asked him what a father was.

He told me that it was a man who had a child with a woman, and that he raised and took care of. I had asked him if he was my father, and he had told me he was sort of like a father.

I had always called him father ever since, but he had never told me that he was my father.

I shook my head. "Actually…*no*. I've just always been with him. He raised me. We move whenever someone sees my eyes. Oh, but he's so good to me and takes care of me," I said, trying to defend him against her harsh tone. "He even feeds me his extra bread and scraps, and he lets me eat mushrooms and fruits from the woods when we travel."

She paused. "Why…" I suddenly felt the girl take off my blindfold. "I'm going to wipe your face," she said, and I felt a warm wetness on my face as she got my face and neck clean. "Can I see your eyes?"

I quickly shook my head. "*Nobody* can see them. That's why we move so much."

"But you're in the middle of a move, aren't you?" She asked. "I won't tell anyone."

"Well…"

"You don't have to be scared. You can't see me, anyway."

"I *can* see," I said. "But something is wrong with my eyes, that's why they stay covered."

She got tense and I could feel something thick hanging in the air.

I tensed up, afraid and nervous.

She seemed to know more, and I wondered if she knew why my eyes stayed covered.

Finally, she spoke to me again. "May I see? Please? I'm sure they are beautiful! You are such a pretty girl."

I...*I was pretty?*

I'd never heard that before...

"What does pretty mean?" I asked, and I felt her shock.

"Well, it means a good thing. Pretty is good."

I mulled it over for a moment.

If she thought that I was pretty, and pretty was a good thing, and she promised not to tell anyone about my eyes...it wouldn't hurt to let her see them, right?

I slowly opened my eyes; the light stung, and she quickly moved the lantern a bit further away to let my eyes adjust.

The first thing I saw was her bright hair.

I didn't know the color, but it reminded me of heat, for some reason.

The strange color that filtered through my eyelids when the sun was setting, a burning color.

"What is that?" I asked, looking at her hair.

She startled. "You...you *can* see..."

"Yes," I noted, a bit flustered. "I told you that I can. But I've never seen that. I don't know what that is." I pointed at her hair.

"My head?" She asked.

A head...?

No...no, I knew what a head was.

I had bumped my head and father had been mad and told me to be careful about my head.

I shook my head, so she tried again.

"...My hair?"

Not right, again. I knew what hair was.

Father always got irritated when I needed my hair brushed, so he usually kept it cut short so that it didn't need to be brushed or kept up.

I shook my head again.

I didn't know the word for it, but it did have to do with her hair.

"What is this?" I asked, taking a strand of her hair. "I know it's hair! What is it?"

She paused for a moment before it seemed to dawn on her. "Oh! My hair is an orange-red, miss. I am named Ginger, for my red hair."

I noted her dark skin. It was a light brown but it was much, much darker than mine, and her bright eyes.

I felt a sudden rush of surprise, the breath leaving me, but it felt weird.

It didn't feel like it was from me. That didn't make any sense, though.

What...what was this?

It didn't feel like *me*.

I didn't feel surprised, so where was the surprise coming from?

"Why do I feel so shocked?" I asked, alarmed. "I feel so heavy," I said. "I...I feel surprised, and happy, and I—" I suddenly felt fear, and I met her eyes again. "W-what's wrong?"

She jumped, eyes wide, and I felt a rush of fearfulness.

"Are...are you okay?" I asked, and she stood.

"You...*you're* the missing...you're the..." She hesitated, rapidly shaking her head. "Never mind. It's nothing, I must be wrong. It couldn't be. Your hair isn't even the right color."

Color! That was what that word was, now I knew.

Her hair was a red color. My hair was—

That's right. My hair was dyed a dark color, but my real hair was very, very light.

"Well, I don't know what you mean, but father dyes my hair."

She gasped dramatically in horror, before she hurried to finish bathing me, and she got me rinsed and dried off.

"Don't...*don't* repeat what I said to your father. You are beautiful, and have very pretty eyes. Don't worry miss, I won't hurt you or tell anyone. You can trust me." She tied my blindfold back in place, and helped me into a new set of clothes and out of the bathroom.

My father wasn't around, and I was glad, even as the girl—Ginger, she had called herself—quickly took her leave, letting me get into bed.

I was the missing...*what*?

I felt lost.

Was I a missing...whatever she was thinking?

Had father...stolen me?

Was I *kidnapped*?

I supposed that it would explain why he was so harsh with me sometimes, but I thought he was just a stern father.

So, he really wasn't my father?

He had told me he was only like a father, but I had sort of hoped he was my father and was just awkward and not affectionate.

Her words played back in my head.

He had dark brown skin, and I had pale white skin. How did that mean that we weren't related?

Did skin color need to be similar to be related?

I didn't know anything about these things! Though, I supposed that if I looked *nothing* like him, that must mean that we didn't share relation.

What did that all mean?

Sometime later, I was getting myself curled up on the pile of blankets that I had found on the floor, where I assumed my father wanted me to sleep.

I hadn't ever slept in the bed with him, and he had always told me that kids were supposed to let the grown-ups have the bed, because as your body ages, the floor isn't tolerable anymore.

I had to sleep on the floor while I was still young enough to handle it.

I heard the door open and shut hard, and I flinched against the irritation that I felt entering the air.

"Here," he said gruffly, and I startled with a small moan when something soft suddenly landed on my lap.

It smelled delicious, though!

I took a deep breath, and brought the softness to my lips, taking a bite of the bread roll that he'd given me.

It was the first I had eaten today, and I was definitely hungry!

"I'm going to bed early tonight," he said. "We will set out as the sun rises, so get to sleep quickly. We need to get out of here," I heard him say darkly.

He was in a bad mood.

Had someone made him feel urgent?

He sounded urgent...

I saw the light through my eyelids go out with a huff from him, and I assumed he had put out the lantern.

I heard the bed shift, and I tucked myself on my blanket as best I could.

I waited and waited, on the very brink of sleep when I noticed his breathing change, and he began to snore.

I...I wanted to know.

I wanted to know, for sure.

Was he truly not my father? Did we truly hold no relation to one another...?

At all?

I took my blindfold off carefully, and I let my eyes slowly adjust to the darkness. There was still a lantern lit in the corner of the room, so that he could see if he had to go use the bathroom, but it wasn't very bright. The flame was sitting low, near the bottom of the lantern.

I stood, and tiptoed over to the edge of the bed.

I leaned in, peering at the only companion I had ever known, and I startled at what I found there.

There lay an incredibly dark-skinned man, with black hair that was thick and curly. He was large and muscular.

She had been right.

We didn't look even remotely the same.

My skin was a pale, pale light color, and I knew that my hair was white because he had told me so. So, my skin was almost white.

I glanced at this man, feeling suddenly like he was a complete stranger. Had I really spent all my life with this man who looked nothing like me?

Did everyone think that I was a slave?

I knew that he told people that I was a servant, but a *slave?* From what Ginger had said, a slave was even lower than a servant. If I remembered correctly, servants got paid money.

I didn't get paid.

I was barely fed.

Clothing me and making sure I didn't starve to death, and making sure that I had a bath at least once a month...seemed like the most tedious chores to him.

So, if we weren't related, and I wasn't a servant, then...what was that his intention with me? Why did he, exactly, keep a girl around who he seemingly disliked who wasn't allowed to even use her eyes?

What was the point?

I startled when I saw a light outside the door, and a few shadows as hushed voices whispered outside our room. I glanced around, panicked.

Were they here to hurt us?

Rob us?

What should I do...?

I quickly put my blindfold back on even as I heard the clinking of keys, and I rushed to the edge of the bed, shaking my "father."

"Father!" I said in a frantic whisper. He roused right away.

"Wha-what? What?" He asked. "Blast it all, why did you—"

"There're voices outside our door, and something clinking..."

He startled, leaping up and swooping over to peer at the door—I assumed.

I felt the breath nearly knocked out of me as he whisked me up into his arms, and I felt a rush of cool night air as he opened the windows.

I gasped as he jumped out of the window even as we suddenly heard the door of the room burst open, and he slid down some bumpy hill—I guessed the roof of the inn?

I clenched and sucked in a deep breath, feeling my entire body sinking and my heart in my throat—on the verge of vomiting—as we fell, and we landed with a hard thud and he took off running.

"Father, what's going on?" I asked, alarmed.

"Shut up, girl. I need to focus, I don't have time to answer your nonsense right now," he said quietly as raised voices started to get closer. "*Shit!*"

We took off in the opposite direction, and I felt him shove me up onto an animal. From the snorts, it sounded like a horse.

He quickly unlatched its restraints, and jumped into the saddle behind me before we took off, and he commanded the horse as we rode, fleeing.

That seemed to confirm things well enough.

If I wasn't sure before, I was definitely sure of it now.

There had to be a reason that he couldn't let me be discovered, and I felt stupid for letting that woman know about my eyes and talking to her. She had obviously alerted authorities.

If I wasn't in danger, or if I wasn't kidnapped...those people would have had no logical reason to invade our room at the inn, nor pursue us...would they?

What was happening?

Fear struck through my entire body.

Was I in danger?

He had never hurt me before, but eventually, I knew that this current relationship wouldn't be able to continue any further forward the way that it was.

What was I supposed to do, now?

Chapter 2

Terse...

Blizzard's Reign, 502 Lawrence Dynasty

"What do you mean, the child was *kidnapped?!*" The ambassador cried, and the knights glanced at one another, alarmed and upset. "She was only born a month ago!"

I dabbed at my eyes, trying to produce fake tears. "My poor daughter!" I cried, trying to sound authentically upset. "We just awoke in the night, and saw the thief taking off with her! We couldn't catch up!"

I threw an arm over my eyes, defeated and destitute.

That ought to do it, I would think...

"Oh, darling, it isn't your fault!" My husband cried, taking me in his arms.

He should win an acting award.

The ambassador glared at us, sputtering, and threw up his hands. "We must return to the temple, and seek an oracle!" He cried, and the knights poured out of the palace.

I waited until they were gone, before slinging my glass of wine out of the window, shattering it on the pavement.

"That arrogant king!" I snarled. "Sending for her as soon as word of her birth spreads! Better if I hadn't had that brat at all."

My husband shushed me, looking at the twin that had been born with the Light Seer child—a normal looking child, with no powers to speak of, thankfully. The child that had our silvery-gray eyes.

All of the members of the Northern and Southern royal families had gray eyes, while the Seers had golden eyes.

"At least we have one beautiful son to love and hold," he smiled.

"I hope Enock isn't suffering too much because of that kid," I said, waving it off. "She was a whiny brat. Her brother is *much* calmer. Far better suited for us, I think."

He sighed, looking out the window as the soldiers poured out of our castle. "To think he would try to demand we send her immediately," he growled. "What a *joke*. We have, for five hundred years, been expected to send our Seer to the Northern Kingdom, just because our seer is always female! When will the *Southern* Kingdom get to rule? When will they have a female seer that they are forced to relinquish to the South? Are we not just as good? We produce Seers of both types, just as they do, and yet…and yet, we are always subjected to be underneath them. They trample upon us," my husband snarled. "Stupid daughters!" He shouted.

I sighed, clinging to him.

He was right.

In the South, the ruler did not have to be a Seer to rule. Of course, not, because the Northern Kingdom always demanded that the *female Seer* be sent to live with the male Seer.

So far, it had always been the female Seer that had been born in the South.

It had been centuries since the *female* Seer had been born in the *North*.

It wasn't fair to our kingdom that we were second rate, when it took a Seer from *both* of the royal families to justly rule over the empire.

"If it means that we can screw them over for a generation, I am all too happy to send off that child," I said. "They look down upon us, but without our Seer, they aren't so high and mighty, are they?"

"What was the prince's name, again? Carl?"

"Carlisle," I sneered. "A *preppy* name. I remember the last female Seer we had. She was born from snobby people, and I hear she is a snobby, preppy lady," I said. "What a joke. Sorry, I know she was your biological cousin, but I am just so infuriated," I sighed. "I do wish that I had a daughter, though. Too bad my daughter turned out to be the Seer." I shrugged.

He barked out a laugh, taking me in his arms. "We can *make* another daughter," he said, and he claimed my lips with his as I moaned heatedly into his open mouth.

"Yes," I moaned, grinding my hips up into his. I pulled my dress to the side, and spread my legs to him. "Yes, let us make another daughter to replace that one, hm?"

"Fuck, yes," he moaned as he slid into me...hard and ready for me.

Solaris's Reign, 506 L.D.

"What?!" I cried, and my husband sauntered over to me, our daughter in his arms.

"What is it?"

"That fool, Enock! He almost got caught! That blasted girl almost ruined our perfect plan to destroy the North!"

He took the newspaper from my hands, reading over the article.

"'Rumors of a maid who saw the missing Light Seer child in the hold of an overbearing, dark-skinned knight, have been running wild in the Central town of Clarke,'" he read aloud. "'The child was said to have dyed hair, with bruises and scrapes over her body, and a blindfold covering eyes that were confirmed to be golden,'" he read.

He gaped at the paper, before he dropped it, anger clouding his face.

"They're not being careful enough. I paid Enock good money to get rid of her, but that fool...but to think he chose to raise her, and didn't keep her locked up somewhere! Of course, a silly blindfold isn't going to work forever! What is he thinking?" I asked.

"I can hardly believe he has actually kept her alive all of this time. Why would he?"

"Well," I contemplated, crossing my arms. "He is one of the best knights of our kingdom, here in the south. Perhaps he couldn't bring his *honorable self* to kill a baby?"

My husband looked away, mulling it over. "Possibly. But what are we going to do, Terse? If the other kingdom finds her, all of our plans will be ruined! We wanted to keep them from getting their hands on her, to be sure that they couldn't have their way this time...but what if that stupid knight blunders everything?"

"I will send an assassin after them, if nothing else," I said, nodding. "I cannot have that girl ruin all of our hard work. Those knights from the North pillaged this castle looking for her, and thankfully, she was already gone, in the care of Enock. If they find her with him, then they will know we are the ones who sent them away!"

"We should have just killed her to be—"

"No!" I cried. "Don't you know what happens if a member of the *royal family kills the Seer?* Legend tells of it happening only once in the past...and that person's entire lineage, their children, grandchildren and greatgrandchildren...all died, in a single night. Luckily, they had siblings who kept the bloodlines alive, but their direct lineage was exterminated. If an outsider kills the Seer, it is different, but if the Seer is murdered by their own blood...that entire branch of the family dies."

He flinched, reminded of that event in our history. It had been precisely the reason we hadn't killed the girl in the first place, but given her to a knight and told him that he could do away with her if he wished...just to get her out of our sights.

"That is precisely why the South is so looked down upon, and why we are forced to send our female Seer to the North as soon as they are born," I reminded him. "Because, one of my great, great, great, great uncles murdered the Seer born to his sister, and he and all of his children and grandchildren died suddenly before the sun had even risen the next day." I bit my nails. "No, no...we could not have killed her ourselves, or directly affected her death in anyway, lest the same happened to us."

"That's right," he said, sighing.

"That—"

"That is why they didn't press us further after realizing that she wasn't here. We couldn't have killed her, or else we would be dead ourselves."

"Exactly."

"Hopefully, they can get back into hiding and remain that way, but he had better be careful in the future. If we hear any further news of her...we will need to arrange for someone else to take it into their hands, and have 'their will in the situation.'"

"And so, we agree," I said, shaking hands with him.

That worthless brat couldn't ruin our plans to destroy the North.

Chapter 3

Kinley...

Solaris's End, 506 Lawrence Dynasty

I felt tears run down my cheek, as I sat in the locked treasure box.

Since that fateful night where we had been chased out of the inn, my captor—whom I no longer referred to as my father—had purchased a large treasure chest to keep me locked inside of whenever we were not resting alone in a room, with his supervision.

I no longer felt safe in his presence; not even marginally.

I hadn't been seen by another person since that night at the inn in Veras's End, and he had been very angry with me for quite some time.

From what I gathered from his grumbles, he had been forced to take me, and it wasn't even *his choice* to begin with...

So, why didn't he just kill me?

I gasped as a particularly hard bump on the road jumbled around my box, and I rubbed my sore elbows and legs, pulled in tightly on myself.

There were air holes drilled into the top of the box, but it was always terrible when it began to rain and I would get wet.

I felt my tummy grumbling, and I restrained myself from crying harder or whining.

Once, in another town, I had whined and someone had been very concerned and questioned my captor about the box. He had gotten into a heated argument over it, and the person had tried to get the knights to open the box, swearing that there was someone trapped inside.

My captor had sped us off through the town, and we had fled.

He threw my box down on the ground, hard enough that I bruised my arms and legs, and demanded that I remain silent at all times in the box. I could only knock if I had to relieve myself. Other than that, he let me out at night to eat a few bites, before I was locked back in the box to sleep.

In the last few months, I'd had to learn to breathe very softly and very shallow breaths, taking in as little as my lungs could make do with.

I didn't have a *lot* of air, and I needed to be sure that I didn't take in too much air so that I had plenty of oxygen.

It is amazing what your body can accustom itself and accommodate to.

I had already adjusted to living in this box.

I sighed softly, feeling my eyes burn again.

Lately, I had tried to imagine that I had parents who missed me.

Perhaps, this man had taken me from a loving family and I had parents who wanted me back.

Parents who...*loved me.*

Were they looking for me? Or were they mourning my death?

Did they think that I was dead?

Would I ever be returned to them?

What purpose did this man have in mind for taking me, to begin with?

I waited and waited, and it seemed to be getting late, because the small hut we were staying in began to get dark, and I suddenly heard the lock jiggling from the key.

He had returned.

He came to the box and let me out, and I took a small breath of air in the room as I clung desperately to my belly, rushing to the room with the toilet, and I gasped as I relieved myself.

I had been holding that in since the night before, and I was thankful I could finally get it out.

I heard the man sigh heavily, before his boots on the floor came closer, and I startled when I heard something hard and full of liquid slosh on the floor.

"You stink. Wash yourself before you come out. I'll be waiting in here with your dinner."

When he had walked away, I took off my blindfold and let my eyes adjust to the dim lamps that lit the room, and saw a container of warm, soapy water. I wiped myself from the toilet and flushed, before I stepped over to the bucket and began using the wash cloth to clean my privates.

He was right...I did stink.

It had been two weeks since my last wash, and I was smelly.

Though, whose fault was that? He was the one in charge.

It wasn't as if I had a choice.

"Um...sir?" I asked, timid. "May I take off my blindfold to eat?"

He hesitated, before he groaned. "Fine."

My heart picked up a beat. "Really?" I asked, beaming.

He had actually agreed?

"We aren't around any people," he said. "But don't look at me with those eyes," he grumbled.

Thankful gratitude soared through my spirit, and I smiled as I finished washing and then jumped in surprise when I noticed the clean undergarments and simple cloth dress sitting by the bucket.

He had...even gotten me fresh clothes?

I dressed myself in the clean clothes, and set my other clothes to the side in a basket that held his dirty clothes as well, before I dumped the dirty soap-water down the sink.

I stepped out into the other room, and found a plate with a small piece of meat, a bread roll and a glass of water.

I was a little worried. Why was he suddenly being so nice? What did all of these gifts mean? Was this a last meal? A way to make up for all the bad before he finally killed me off?

At the moment, I almost didn't care.

I sat with my mouth watering, and took small nibbles of my food to savor it and to try to let it fill my starved belly a bit, even though there wasn't much here.

I kept my eyes down, but I could feel his gaze upon me, watching me intently.

I glanced up at him, and I felt a rush of...*confusion...?*

"What is the matter, sir?" I asked, and he startled, and I felt his surprise.

"You really are..." he mumbled softly. "I told you, don't look at me with those eyes."

"I-I'm sorry..." I whimpered, setting back to my food.

I could feel him watching me again a moment later. He sighed. "I don't know what to do with you."

"What...to do with me?" I asked. Fear hit me—it was my own fear, but his as well. "What...do you mean? What do you mean by, 'do with' me?" I asked, nervous.

"You have seemed to grasp enough of the truth," he said. "You will be five, soon. Did you know that?" He asked, and I shook my head. He nodded. "You will be five in Year's Fall. Since your birth, you were placed into my care. You aren't kidnapped, since I am sure you've been wondering if that was the case."

"Sir...?" I asked, surprised.

"*They* told me to take you away, to get rid you. They didn't care what I did with you, as long as you were gone and out of their lives. Though, I didn't know at the time that you would cause me so much trouble. I had been given the option to kill you, but I was once one of the most respected knights in our kingdom. I couldn't bring myself to kill an infant for no reason, whose only fault had been in being born."

"'They?'" I asked.

"Your parents," he told me, and I startled, feeling my own sadness course through me.

"My parents...*wanted* you to take me away? They even told you that you...you could...but..."

He glanced at me. "You are an unwanted child," he told me. "Had it not been me, you would have been disposed of in another way." He shrugged.

He was very frustrated and flustered, I could feel. He wanted to do the right thing, and that's why he was telling me this. I could tell that he was telling me the truth, but I didn't know how I knew that.

"So...you didn't kidnap me?" I asked.

He barked out a laugh. "Your parents *told* everyone that I did, but that was a ruse to throw off suspicion. They ruined my entire career and my hard-earned reputation to paint me out to be a kidnapper. I am sorry," he told me.

"...Why sorry?"

He sighed. "I didn't choose to take you of my own choice. I was ordered to. Your parents were my rulers, so I had to obey their command, you see."

"Why did they send me away?"

"I cannot tell you that," he told me, though I could hear his thoughts dancing around the reason.

He was purposefully trying not to think about that.

"You...know about my powers...?" I asked, and he looked at me, a rush of surprise in his heart.

"You...know about your powers?"

"Yes," I mumbled. "Every time I have seen anyone with my eyes, I have felt strange things and heard whispers in my head. You knew about?"

He nodded. "I do," he told me. "That is why you are always blindfolded. That power comes from your eyes."

"Why can't I be seen?" I asked. "Are my powers against the law?"

"No," he said, shaking his head. "They are dangerous to our kingdom," he said, once again trying to skirt around the topic without revealing too much.

"Do I have to keep having my blindfold on?" I asked.

"When we are alone, you don't. But I need you to cooperate with me. No talking to strangers. Stay away from other people. Don't answer any questions they ask you. Pretend you don't understand them. If you can do that, you will be fine."

I looked away. "Do I have to keep being in the box?"

He glanced at me. "If you can follow my orders and *actually* listen to them, then no. The box was to punish you for disobeying me."

I sighed, nodding. "I can listen."

"Good," he said, and he handed me another roll and another piece of meat.

I jumped in surprise, gulping down the rest of my food on my plate before I savored the extra food given to me.

I hadn't ever been given *seconds*, before.

Maybe this wouldn't be so bad!

Year's Fall, 508 LD

I awoke in the early hours of the morning, the sky still dark outside, when sharp pains started running through my chest.

I gasped out in a sharp, quiet cry, and grasped my chest as I thrashed, begging the pain to stop.

"Girl! What's wrong?" Knight Enock asked, rushing to my side on the floor.

Shortly after our understanding two years ago, we had grown a bit closer.

He had told me his name, and allowed me to eat more and wash more often, and even keep my blindfold off when we were alone...*as long as I behaved.*

"My-my chest! My chest is *burning*!" I cried, and he pulled the neck of my tunic to the side, inspecting it.

"Oh, *shit*!" He cursed. "No, no, fuck *no*, **no**!" He looked around desperately, grabbing a wash cloth and wetting it in the water basin nearby.

"What—what is it?" I asked when I felt his shear panic through his emotions.

I was now accustomed to feeling emotions and hearing the surface thoughts of those around me whenever I saw them, but I had to be looking directly at them—at their body, at least—to hear it or feel it.

"A seal. Blast it all, it is a *seal!*"

"A seal...?" I asked. "What...what does that mean?"

"It means that the Northern kingdom is trying to locate you. The rumors from a few years ago must have finally reached them, and a mage must have cast the spell to find you. Damn it all!"

I hesitated. "Northern kingdom…but you told me that they're scary people who want to hurt me because I am from the Southern kingdom?" I asked, confused.

"I don't have the patience to explain everything to you, and I'm not *supposed* to!" He snarled, trying to wipe the seal off to no avail. "*Perhaps…*"

He fingered his dagger on his hip, but I didn't understand at first.

As he eyed the seal and then gripped the handle, I could hear the thoughts in his mind and I cried, scooting away from him quickly and clutching my chest, even as he pulled the dagger out.

"S-sir Enock, what…what are you doing? What are you going to do?" I asked in heaving breaths, my chest rising and falling quickly as I panted.

I already knew what he planned to do, but I hoped I was wrong.

"I'll have to cut it out, of course!" He said. "If the Northern Kingdom finds you, that will be a problem for the Southern kingdom…and I will be hunted down and assassinated in no time for failing to carry out my mission. You will be killed, and quickly."

"But I—" I tried to get out, but his holding up the dagger cut me off, and I felt the blood drain from my face. "P-please, sir Enock, please…please don't do this," I sobbed.

A sudden knocking pounding at the door startled both of us.

"Open up! There were reports from the neighbors of sudden screams and shouts and cries! Order up by the order of the knights in jurisdiction of the town of Hamel!"

"*Blast!*" Enock said, pulling out a sword. "I don't have *time* for this! It will be no time before they find you with that damn *thing* on your chest! I *have* to get it out of you!"

My fear took precedence over his own, and I realized that if I didn't use this moment to escape my warden, I would have this seal cut out of my chest by force and I would forever be bound to him.

Chapter 4

Carlisle Lawrence...

<u>Nivis's End, 502 Lawrence Dynasty</u>

"Mommy," I asked, tugging on my mother's sleeve. She looked down at me, worry etched into her tired face. "Where is my princess?" I asked.

I felt her worry shoot through me, and sadness and anger. I heard horrible curses about the South, but she smiled at me quickly, trying to put her thoughts away.

"Oh, my darling prince. She has been lost...*stolen*, if the claim is true. But worry not, my prince! We are searching for her, quite thoroughly. I am sure she will be found in no time!"

I looked around the room, hearing the worried and frustrated thoughts of those who I saw, and I heard the anger in my father as he paced furiously in front of his throne.

He was convinced that it was a trick.

His own golden eyes met mine, and he smiled at me as I felt a rush of peace.

"Don't worry, my son. We will find your princess, and bring her here to you as quickly as we can."

I wondered about it.

I was the Dark Seer prince of the Northern kingdom, next in line to become the king.

I knew this, because it was what I had been taught all of my life.

My princess would be the only person on this earth whose thoughts and feelings would be a mystery to me.

Even my own parents, who were also Seers, I could hear their top-layer thoughts and feel their feelings.

Only a Seer's born partner was exempt from this.

I was, as of this month, supposed to have my princess here with me, to be raised with me.

She would become my queen, my Light Seer princess.

I knew this, because it was what I had been taught all of my life.

We shared the same birthday, only one year apart.

Each set of Seers had a special birthday circumstance, as well as a special appearance.

I knew, because I had been taught.

I was a big boy.

I was just over a year old, and because I had the ability to read minds and had the "Eyes of Truth," my mentality grew at an exponential rate compared to most children my age.

I learned faster;

I was smarter, more cunning…

I had to be, to become the next king.

So, *where* was my princess, you may ask?

When my soldiers arrived to her kingdom to receive her on my behalf, only a month ago…she had disappeared, and was gone.

My mother had cried and grieved, cursing the South for letting my princess out of their sight.

If we didn't find her quickly, according to the information rushing through my knights' minds, she could become a serious danger and liability to me in the future.

It was dangerous for us not to be raised together...

Was she okay?

Was she alive?

When I questioned my mother about this, she said that the girl had to be alive.

If she wasn't, I wouldn't live much past her.

Our souls and lives were linked, our powers a balance to one another.

She had to make it here safely...she just had to.

Solaris's End, 506 LD

"There has been news, my prince!"

"News?" I asked, rolling my eyes.

Like I cared. Everything was dull.

My life was dull.

My feelings, my thoughts...

I was too aware of what people thought around me. It was all bad, all negatives.

I knew what they thought.

They thought that my princess would be the death of me. If she were ever found, she would turn against me and kill me.

She hadn't been raised with me so far as was tradition for hundreds of years, and who knows what she has been being taught in the meantime.

*Would I ever even **meet** her?*

We were supposed to rule together...what kind of king could I hope to be, without my queen of light and mercy?

I scoffed, rolling my eyes again.

"Are you going to answer me?" I barked, and my servant trembled, kneeling.

"The...the *princess*," he said.

I put him under the full view of my eyes, scanning his emotions and thoughts.

Fear plagued him, but a sliver of hope.

Worry...

He held out the newspaper, and I took it from him, reading it.

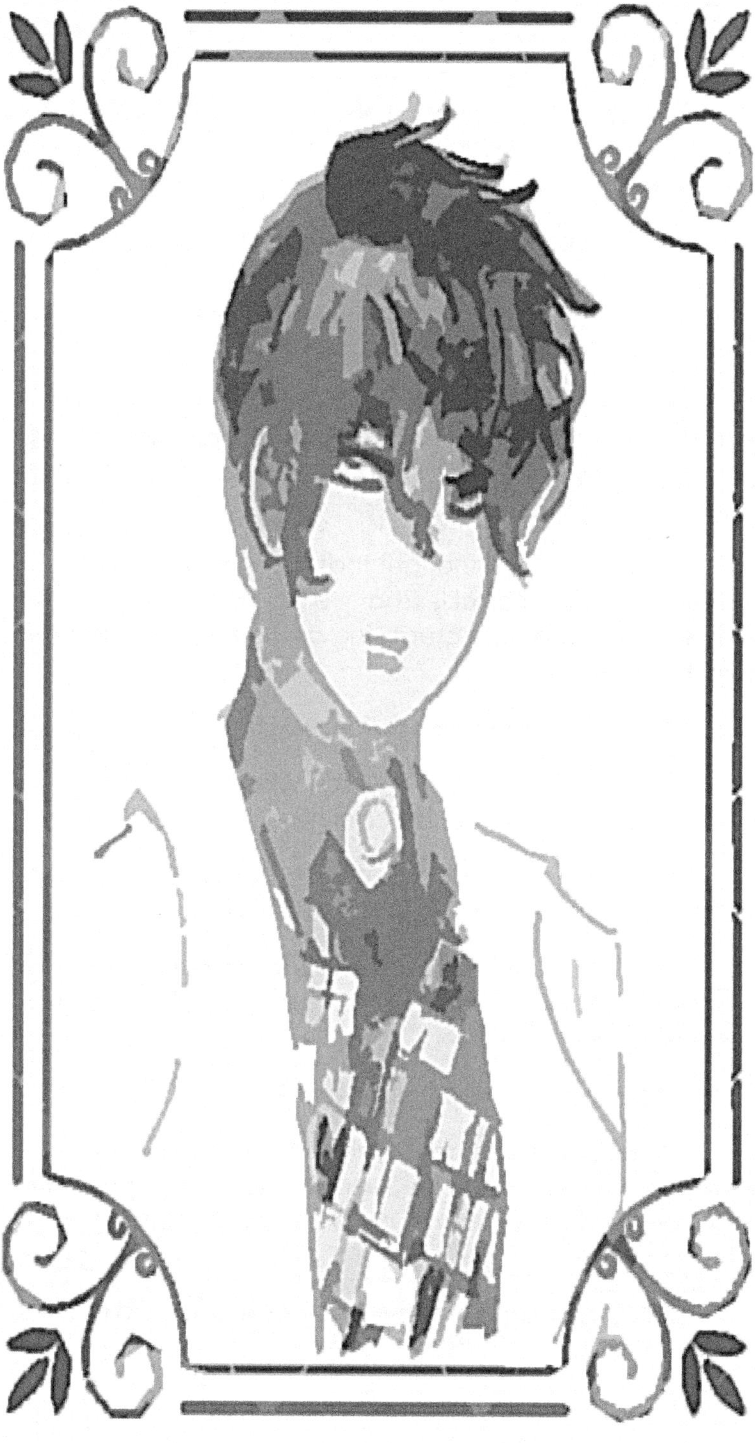

I took in the information.

My princess had been spotted, in a town in the central part of the kingdom, where the south and north met in a combined city jurisdiction.

"So, my princess has been located, but her captor has run away with her again...?" I threw the newspaper to the floor, glaring at him. "If she isn't on her way *here*, currently, then why would you bother bringing this to me?"

He trembled, mumbling out pleas and apologies, and I sighed, plopping down in my chair again and fiddling with a toy in my hands that I had once made for my princess...in anticipation of her arrival.

I once held the thought that she would be found, and returned to me quickly. That we would grow up together after all, and become a great king and queen; the best the world had known.

That hope had fallen rather quickly.

I was almost six, and she was almost five. Where was she, that she could not be brought here?

Now, this article declared that her captor was *dyeing her hair* to disguise her? So, he'd chosen to die, is that it?

I huffed, pondering. Should I just throw this toy away? I was starting to be convinced that she wouldn't arrive in time to play with it.

Would I ever get my princess?

As a Seer, it was absolutely forbidden to marry anyone other than my fellow Seer. She had been foretold to be my princess on the day of my birth, a year before her own birth.

This was an entirely new precedent that had never happened before.

Folias's Blessing, 507 LD

"And you are telling me that with this spell, upon her seventh birthday, we can locate her?" I asked the sorcerer who stood with the priests.

The priests hadn't wanted to bring in a sorcerer, but I hadn't left them much choice.

The Paladin Sorcerer, named Sir Axel, was now employed in the castle.

"Yes, your highness," the Paladin Sorcerer nodded, and I sensed no lies. I did sense nervousness that something might go wrong, but that was just because he was the worrying type. "Upon the day of her seventh birthday, I can link the two of you by a seal. The seal will be painful, but we can track it through you."

"Through *me*?" I asked, surprised. "What do you mean?"

"You will be seeing through her eyes, since you will be the caster. You will see and feel what she sees and feels, and we can use that to find her location. We can cast the vision up onto the screen," he said, pointing at a giant canvas on the wall that our mages used to stargaze and find constellation messages.

"Hm," I said, stroking my chin. "Fine, then. We will do that." I looked to my parents, who clutched one another. "We will finally find my princess."

They smiled. "Yes," they said.

Year's Fall, 508 LD

"Stand here," the head sorcerer said, directing me to stand in front of a podium that held a basin of water, standing in front of the constellation screen in the mage's tower.

It had been just over a year since I had found out about this spell, but if it worked, I would finally have my princess.

It was before dawn, the early hours of the morning, but we wanted to get an early start so that we could see the princess and find her before the day was out, if we were able.

I was a bit nervous.

I was anticipating of the pain, but I was only eight years old. I knew it would hurt, but this may be my only chance to locate my young bride.

"Now, I want you to close your eyes. Extend out your hands, and focus only on your power. Picture a white haired, golden-eyed girl child in your mind. *Focus*," he told me. "*Breathe*. I will prick your finger, and your blood will drop into the basin. When that happens, I want you to call with your mind, calling your Light Seer. Can you do that?"

"Who do you think I am?" I scoffed, cocky, but I nodded.

I did as he told me, and closed my eyes with my arms extended, picturing the girl.

I got an image of what I would *like* her to look like in my mind.

I wanted her to be pretty, and pale.

A pale, doll-like girl would be nice, I thought.

That would be a good compliment to my black hair and rich, bronze-brown skin, and for some reason, that was what I hoped for most. I hoped she was pale and light.

I heard the chanting words, and felt a sting in the tip of my finger, but I kept my eyes closed.

An image was starting to form...

I heard the drops of blood fall into the basin, and I began to call the girl in my mind.

I could feel that she was confused, and didn't understand if she was hearing a real person or imagining things.

I called for her again, louder and more forceful in my mind.

I saw her turn to face me in my mind, suddenly, and I spoke aloud, rather than just in my head. "Show me your face, my Light Seer. I wish to find you! I want you home!"

I felt a sudden spearing pain in my chest and I gasped, crying out, but I forced my eyes to remain shut.

I saw the girl face me full on, shooting out of sleep and crying out in pain, clutching her chest.

She whipped her head around, searching for the source, and I got a good look at her face.

Though her hair was dyed a shade of dark, yellow-orange blonde, her skin was milky white and her golden eyes were bright, filled with tears as she panicked over the sudden pain.

She was drastically underweight, though, and looked emaciated. She reminded me of a stick, almost. Bony, and severely unhealthy.

Not quite the pretty young princess I had imagined and envisioned for myself. I couldn't see anything beautiful about her beyond her golden eyes.

Her body was skinny and her hair was short and choppy...almost as if it had been cut by a knife.

The first thought that crossed my mind was that she was ugly, and only her pale bruised skin and her bright golden eyes had potential.

"Oh...she is beautiful," I heard my mother breathe.

Beautiful...? Was my mother crazy? Well, I certainly wouldn't have gone that far.

She had *potential*, I supposed, but she looked so *unhealthy*. She looked like she would break like a toothpick...

"But her hair...it really is dyed, as the article mentioned. So, she's been intentionally hidden?" My father asked.

I knew that the images in my mind were being displayed.

We heard the knight by her side start cursing; a dark, dark brown-skinned man who was tall and had rich black hair. He obviously held no relation to the girl biologically.

Why was she with him? I didn't understand.

We startled as we listened to her pleading with him not to do it; he wanted to cut out her seal, and I jumped in surprise.

"He would go to such lengths to keep her hidden?!" My personal knight raged in the background. "How dare he impede between you two!"

I gasped in panic when she tried to run when the guards approached them, having been alarmed by the commotion...and he slaughtered them all, before he caught her on her way out of a window.

He slammed her down onto the floor even as she sobbed and begged for him to have mercy, to just let her go.

We heard him mention the Southern kingdom, about how he would just be killed by the royal family for failing his task if she were to be found.

I cried out in pain as I felt the seal on my own chest stabbed and cut through, watching and dry heaving as I watched him cut the seal from her body.

Then he burnt the wound closed, cauterizing it.

I watched him lift her and carry her out of the door, glancing around—and I managed to spot the street corner where they were located.

"Send the soldiers!" I cried, telling them the location. "They are heading West from that location!"

Then, I vomited, losing the contents of my sickened belly at last, before I fell into unconsciousness.

How I had lasted so long without puking sooner would astound and confound me for many years to come.

I awoke sometime later, and found my parents—my mother sobbing, and my father pacing in anger—at my bedside.

"Father? Mother?"

"Oh, Carlisle!" Mother clasped my hand in hers. "I am so sorry you had to witness such...such...*atrocity!*"

My father shook his head. "I cannot believe they went to such an extent...sending away their child, with a man who would be so brutal...did you see how skinny she was?"

I felt my chest burning as their thoughts raced.

I wasn't sure if I was as upset as they were, or if I was just feeling their anger, but I felt weird thinking about her.

My princess, my fated bride...had been maimed and forever scarred, just because of who and what she was...*what we were*.

It seemed odd and strange to me. It also seemed like a lot of trouble to keep wasting resources and money and time on her, trying to locate her.

"*Perhaps I should just let her go*," I said, soft, and my parents gaped at me, shocked horror on their faces.

"What?" My mother gasped. "No," she said. "Prince Carlisle, you cannot *ever* think that thought again!" She scolded harshly. "That girl was seriously abused and malnourished, and you wish to keep her subjected to that? And now, she's been maimed because we tried to find her. Do you want that to be in vain?"

"But...if I weren't trying to find her out of my own selfishness, would she have had to suffer that way?" I asked.

My father shook his head. "They would never have allowed her not to be sent away simply because of what she is, my son. It is not your fault."

"But—"

"I know that this incident feels like you are to be blamed, but it is they who are at fault. That knight was clinging to his own life to the point that he maimed a child to protect himself, for fear of her parents. You are not the one who is to blame, here. I can't even entirely blame him. He just wants to live. The ones truly at fault are her father and mother."

I sighed, nodding. "I suppose."

"Carlisle," my mother addressed, and I gave her my attention. "You have a new purpose in life, my son: find your princess, and rescue her from that terror. You are the only hope she has at a future, a real future. You are the only chance she has to live."

I gulped, but I looked to my personal Keeper knight.

"Valence," I said, and he bowed. "Hear and obey my order; locate my princess, and bring her here safely. As the crowned prince, I cannot leave the kingdom...but *you* can. I have many knights here, but you are the most skilled. Can you do that for me?"

"On my honor and on my life, I vow to strive my utmost to find the missing queen-to-be and bring her to you, your highness," he said, kneeling.

Then he stood, and hurriedly left the room.

Chapter 5

Kinley...

Blizzard's Reign, 509 Lawrence Dynasty

I panted, tossing and turning in my restraints.

Things were bad, again. Very bad.

I was, yet again, kept in the box that I'd had to live in for so long. It wasn't much tighter than it had been, though, at least, as I was still so tiny.

After Sir Enock had cut out the seal on my chest before he had cauterized the wound, burning my flesh, and I had cried and screamed until I had passed out.

I had awoken sometime later to find a bandage around my chest, and the stink of burnt flesh in my nose.

I was much weaker for a while. I found it hard to use my arms or move if it meant moving my chest.

What was the reason for which I had gone through all of this? Why had I been born to such a fate?

It just didn't make any sense to me.

I was just a child who didn't even know what colors were. I didn't know what most things were called, or what to do.

I had grown up so ignorant, so in-the-dark, that I truly had no idea where to go from here.

What had I ever done so wrong to warrant what I was having to go through, now?

It was late into the month of Blizzard's Reign, after I heard the knight muttering to himself whether or not he should just do away with me, that I finally came to an important decision...

The next time that we stopped for the night, and he left me in the box in the room...I would cause a huge scene from my box, and I would pray for a miracle.

I wasn't being fed at all, now, and barely given any water. I only got fed a few bites of rice a day, if I was lucky.

To be punished for having made things so much worse on myself before, when if I had only stayed still, he would have tried to make it hurt as little as possible...or so he claimed.

I wasn't being let out to use the bathroom but once a day, now, and I was no longer being bathed.

It was almost an entire month after the incident with the seal before he finally left me with *one such opportunity*; He left to go get some supplies.

After I waited long enough for him to get away from the room that we were staying in at the inn...I began to scream and beat myself against the box as hard as I could manage to do so. I threw my entire body into the box, almost to the point of rocking the box onto its side...and then, it tumbled, and I startled, crying out louder as my elbows throbbed from the slam.

Oh, no! No, no, no!

If this didn't work, he would come back in and know that I had made such a racket!

He would certainly kill me if—

"What is that? Is there someone in here?" I heard a woman ask, and I began to scream.

"I am in here! Please, *please* help me! *Please!*" I sobbed as shrilly and loudly as I could, doing everything in my rapidly weakening capability to get someone's attention and help before my captor returned and killed everyone and probably me, too.

I heard the keys rattling, and I saw through the keyhole of the box as light lit the room.

"*What—*"

"I'm in *here!*" I cried, banging the box. "Please! *Please* let me out! Please *help* me!" I sobbed, my desperation reaching a peak.

"Oh, my!" The woman cried, and she rushed into the room. "What on earth?"

"My captor keeps me locked inside this box! I had to wait until he finally left me alone, but I need to get out before he comes back! He's never gone long!!"

"I can't find a key…if I could go and get a knight—"

"Please!" I cried sharply. "He's killed so many guards and knights to keep us on the run! What if he returns before you do? I don't have *time!*"

She seemed to be panicking as well. "Stay calm, stay calm…I know!" She rushed out, and I heard her knocking on the door next to our room. I could hear that she was explaining the situation in hushed tones, and I heard male voices pick up and rush into the room.

"Young lady, I brought traveling mercenaries from the room next door to open the box. You hang in there, now!"

I heard clanging on the box, and after a few strikes as I held my hands over my ears and cried, I felt my eyes sting as the box was forced open.

"*Dear heavens!*" She cried when she saw the state of me. "You…you're injured…skin and bones, and you look ghastly! Goodness, me…"

They lifted me out of the box, and even as my legs and arms screamed and groaned with the movement of stretching out fully and cramps racked my body, I gazed up at one of the mercenaries...an extremely handsome man with dark bronze skin and bright green eyes.

"Oh," he breathed, meeting my eyes. "You...you're the missing princess! Your highness!" He cried, kneeling suddenly, and the other mercenary kneeled as well.

"Princess...?" The lady breathed, looking at me. "*Her eyes!*"

I looked at them. "I *don't have time* for this!" I said, beginning to feel nauseous. "If he comes back and I'm gone, he will—"

"Let us move," the mercenary said, taking my hand. "I promised the prince that I would return you to your rightful place. If you are in danger, *I* need to act." He lifted me into his arms, and we rushed out of the room.

The prince...?

Were they not mercenaries, then? Or random city knights?

I couldn't let myself trust them, but I could feel that they genuinely didn't mean me any harm.

"Miss," the other "mercenary" said to the maid who had found me. "*Please*, keep this quiet. Tell the captor that you don't know what happened."

She nodded. "I will think of something. Get her out of here!" She took my hand, kissing it and startling me. "Please be well, princess Light Seer," she smiled.

...Light Seer...?

What was that?

She was obviously addressing me, but what did that mean?

As we rushed out of the hall and into the room, one of the mercenaries glanced out of the window in a sneaky way.

"The knight who was renting this room is coming," he said, quiet. "As soon as he enters, we need to leave through the window and quickly scale down and away from here. We are on the third floor, so it will take him a moment to get to the room and discover her missing. It won't take him as long to get back out, however. We have to time this just right."

We all nodded, and I clung to the handsome mercenary. "Please...please don't let him take me back. He was talking about possibly getting rid of me because I'm so much trouble. I can't go back to him!"

"We won't let him hurt you," he said. "Zonate," he said. "If he confronts us...you are the more skilled of the two of us. I will leave it to you to handle him."

He nodded. "Right. He just stepped inside. Let's do this."

He slipped the window open quickly and quietly, and he stepped outside, glancing down at the entrance to the inn, before he popped back up at the window and held his hand out for me.

"Your highness," he said, and though I wasn't comfortable with such a title, I took his hand and he jumped down to a balcony on the second floor before he held his arms out for me.

I slid off of the roof over the second floor and fell into his arms, and the other "mercenary" was just behind us. Then he got down to the ground floor, and held his arms out for me, which I slid down into easily.

They both got on the ground and the older one turned around quickly as we heard the maid crying and rushing to say she had no idea.

"He's faster than I thought!" Zonate said, scowling. "Valence, quickly, get her highness out of here. I will stay and fight him off."

"Zonate—"

"There is no time!" He said. "If I meet my maker today, at least I'll have given you two a good head-start. Go!"

I took in his graying hair and his bright brown eyes as he pulled out a sword, standing in a defensive position between us and the entrance to the inn even as the younger, handsome mercenary—*Valence*, his name was—took me into his arms and bolted in the opposite direction.

I felt his thankfulness and his respect through his emotions as I looked at him.

I could feel in his spirit that he held no ill-will toward me at all, and that both of them were sincere. They weren't lying...

Did that mean that I really was a princess?

What was a princess?

I couldn't understand what it all meant.

We heard shouting and clanging far in the distance, and I felt his body force forward as he pushed his legs even harder.

His eyes lit up as we approached the docks, and he found a ship that was preparing to set sail.

"Hurry!" He said in a hushed voice. "I've found her. Get the anchor up and set off! *Quickly!*"

He jumped over the boarding board and we landed on the deck of the ship, before he set me on my feet.

I cried out, startled, as I rocked and swayed with the movement of the water on the ship, having never been on the water.

He helped me hold my stance, peering off into the distance.

His face clenched and his pain speared him as my captor came into view even as the sailors rushed to get us moving.

"We are finished here," he said, looking to the crew.

"But, what about—"

"Sir Zonate met his end at the hands of her highness' captor. We must get out of the bay quickly. Full-speed ahead!" He called.

As we got away from the docks, I felt Valence's hands tighten on my shoulders as we watched Sir Enock throw down his sword and curse as we were too far out in the water for him to get to us.

As the land started to fade from view, the handsome young man turned to me.

"Your highness," he kneeled. "I am Sir Valence Trident, a Keeper knight and the personal attendant to Prince Carlisle, the Dark Seer of the North. We will get you to his side where you belong, I promise."

I cocked my head to the side, confused, and he looked at me in surprise at my lack of surprise.

"You mean...you don't know?" He asked.

"I don't know what you're talking about, Sir Valence..."

He sighed, rubbing his temples. "I see. So, you were never informed. Your highness, you are the princess of the Southern Kingdom. Each kingdom produces a Seer, who come together as a couple to rule over the nation as a pair with their combined 'eyes of truth.' You are the Light Seer, and my prince—the one whom sent me to find you—is the Dark Seer. There is a Dark and Light Seer born every generation to rule over the nations."

"Oh," I said.

"Your parents sent you away with the knight because of their hate for the North...due to some very complex history that you will learn about in lessons with a tutor. For now, your highness, may I know your name so that I might address you properly?"

I hesitated.

...Name...?

He looked at me with concern. "Your highness?" He asked.

I looked away. "Name...?"

He gaped at me, and I felt his emotions tug on him as he felt sorrow and sympathy and a sudden urge to hug me. "You don't have a name, your highness?"

I shook my head, feeling ashamed.

What did it say, if I didn't even have a name?

He glanced away. "I see. Well, princess, perhaps we can request his highness to name you. After all, you are to be his bride, so—"

"Bride?" I asked. "What is that?"

He paused. "I mean no disrespect, princess, but perhaps you should tell me what you do know?"

I looked around. "I know that water is what I drink and wash with, blood is inside my body, food is what I eat when I feel hungry, and sleep is what I do when I am tired. I know how to use a toilet and I know what color my eyes and real hair color are...?" I sighed. "I know that a mom and dad are the ones who made me."

"Yes, those things are all good, but is that...the extent that you know?"

"I know a knight is a special rank of soldier, and knights are called Sir, like Sir Enock."

"I thought I recognized him, but that really was Sir Enock, then," he said, contemplating this. "To think they sent you away with such a fearsome knight for a warden...he used to be renowned for his honor and valor, but he was very feared for his skill. It seems it wasn't simple boasting," he said, his expression dark. "My companion was one of the best Knights I had ever met, and he was killed rather quickly. I know that he was getting on in years, but I grew up with him as a staple role model who always was revered as a powerhouse..." He sighed.

"Sir Valence?" I asked. "What will happen to me now?"

He smiled brightly at me.

"You will be able to get the highest education available, your highness! You will have your own maids, beautiful dresses and shoes, anything you could think of—"

"*Food?*" I asked, hopeful, and he froze in his place, a look of shock on his face.

His bottom lip quivered, and he cleared his throat.

"As much as you wish, your highness," he said, his voice thick.

"I won't be in trouble for sneaking extra rolls?"

His eyes filled with tears. "You can *have* all the rolls, your highness, and no one would scold you."

"I won't get scolded for needing to wash myself?"

He turned away from me. "You will be bathed every day," he told me. "You will never want for anything, your highness."

I smiled brightly, not even able to imagine a world such as what he described.

A maid approached us, and she gave me a bow. I didn't recognize the action or its purpose.

"Princess, I am Marron, and I will be taking care of you during our journey to the north. I have gotten a room prepared for you, and supper is cooking. I will prepare a bath for you as well."

"I can take a bath? Here?" I asked, looking around.

She smiled. "Your chambers were gifted by the captain, your highness. You have a water-closet inside the room, as well. It will only take us a few days to get to the north from this port."

I glanced to Sir Valence. "How did you find me?"

"That was completely by coincidence, actually," he said, smiling. "When the prince cast the seal to locate you, he was able to discern your location and which way Sir Enock was heading with you when he fled."

"Oh…"

"So, I found my way to that location and began in the direction that I was informed. I found my way to that inn to rest with my colleague. We heard that a suspicious man with a locked chest had been appearing in the area, so we were following the rumors to see if it was a pirate. Imagine our surprise when you started crying and shouting for help, and the maid at the inn called on us for aide!" He said, scratching the back of his head. "It was fortunate that we were able to find you."

I smiled, and I gave a bow even as he stammered and looked on in surprise.

"Thank you for saving me," I said.

I stood again, taking the hand of the maid as she led me to my room.

When we entered the room, I looked around at the room, taking everything in.

"Is everything alright, your highness?"

"Is it really okay for me to stay here?"

"What do you mean, your highness? I am sorry it isn't better, but you will have nicer things when we arrive to the palace."

"Nicer…?" I asked. "But…I don't understand. This is nicer than my box," I said. "This is nicer than the pile of blankets on the floor…"

She startled, surprised. "Pardon?"

"Can I…sleep on this bed?" I asked, getting excited.

She stared at me, confused, before she held up a hand. "Hold on a moment, your highness. Are you…are you suggesting that these accommodations are…*better* than you are used to?"

I glanced around. "Well, I am usually locked in a box or I sleep on blankets on the floor…I've never slept on a bed before."

Tears ran down her face, and she cleared her throat and wiped her face quickly.

"What's wrong?" I asked. "Why are you sad?"

"I am...I am so overwhelmed, your highness. You...you're a princess! How could any knight, regardless of how the circumstances are, actually think to allow a princess to sleep and live in such poor conditions!?" She cleared her throat, turning. "Please pardon me, princess. I will return with your meal, and then I will run a bath for you."

She rushed out of the room, and I looked out of the window to look out on the deck, where she went to Sir Valence and they spoke to one another for a bit.

From the thoughts I could hear, they were very overwhelmed and saddened by the sorry state I was in and what I had endured, and they were not entirely sure if I could even manage being royalty.

Soon enough, they agreed to carry on with the plan to get me safely to the northern kingdom, and she scurried off to enter into another cabin on the ship, steam billowing out as she entered, and I assumed it must be quite warm inside.

Some moments later, and she left that room, carrying a tray with a cover over top of it, coming toward my captain's chambers.

She entered the room, and I watched as she went to the table and sat the tray down.

She lifted the cover, and I gasped as the steam and smell filled the space of the room.

I cautiously approached to peak at the meal...a strange set of items I had never seen before, with the only item I recognized being a large, delectable roll seasoned with butter and salt.

There also sat a glass of white liquid like water.

"What is all of this...?" I asked, looking at her.

"Pardon?"

"I...I only know bread. What is the rest?"

She gaped at me for a moment, surprised, before she caught herself at my hurt expression.

She cleared her throat.

"This, princess, is a roasted pheasant, stewed potatoes, and steamed cabbage and onions with baked bread."

"And this?" I asked, pointed at the beverage served.

She looked at me in confusion. "Milk, princess..."

"...Milk?"

"You haven't had milk in the past...?" She said. "Hardly a wonder that you are so malnourished," she said, shaking her head. "Good heavens, to think you have been so neglected. It breaks my heart, your highness," she said, and I couldn't sense any lies from her. "It is a travesty."

"Is...is *all* of this really for *me*?" I asked, looking at the tray.

"Yes, princess. If you need more, just let me know—"

"But I've *never* had *this* much food!" I said, overwhelmed. "Can I...really have *all* of this? You won't take it back or throw it away?"

"No—"

"Even if I make you angry and get in trouble? I can eat this?"

She gave me a sad expression. "Simply eat what you can, princess, and we will take care of the rest."

"Where is Sir Valence?" I asked, looking out of the window. I suddenly felt a bit nervous, and she seemed to hear it in my tone.

"Your highness?" She asked, and more fear and nervousness rushed into my system.

"I...I'm scared...Where is he?"

"Scared?" She asked, confused.

My voice raised in pitch and volume. "I-I'm scared!"

She was immediately worried that she had done something wrong, but before I could assure her that she hadn't, she had scurried out of the room, rushing to step below the deck.

A few minutes later, she came back onto the deck with my knight trailing behind her.

He smiled at me, hand over his chest and spoke.

I immediately felt comfort and peace in my heart.

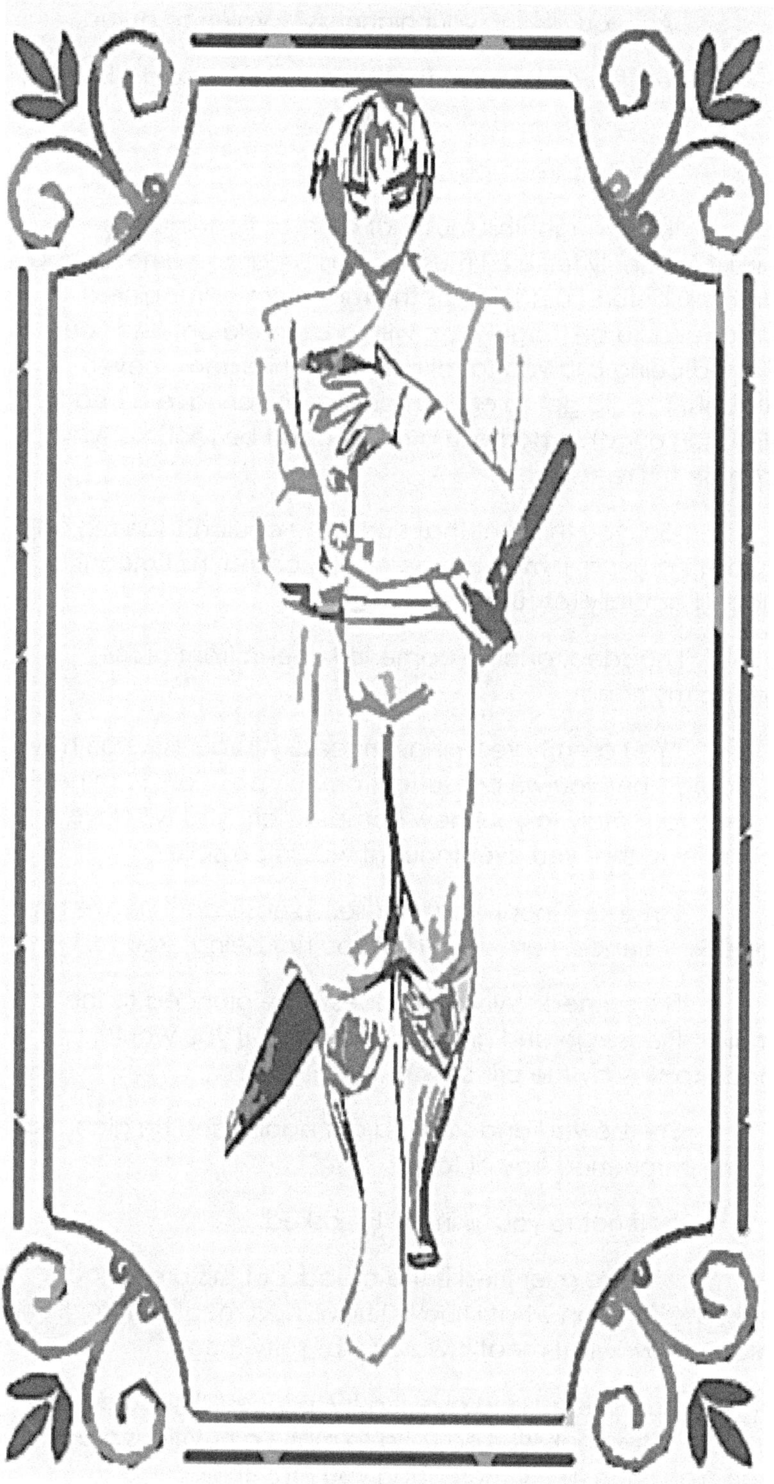

"Are you alright, your highness?" Valence asked.

Relief flooded me. "Thank goodness," I said. "I...I was scared..."

"What scared you, princess?"

"I...I thought this must not be real. I couldn't see you, and it suddenly felt like I must be in a dream. I've never had dreams, before, but this was the most I could imagine a dream could be. I...grew up with a blindfold on, and I only started being allowed to take it off a while ago. I never thought I could get to eat a meal like this or have a *bed* to sleep on or get to bathe in a *tub*. It can't be real. No way can be this real."

"So, you thought that since you couldn't see me and I wasn't around, it must not be real because that meant I hadn't actually rescued you...?"

I nodded, and he came to kneel in front of me, taking my hands.

"You aren't dreaming, princess. All your life, you have suffered...but you will not suffer from this point on. I am here to get you safely to your new home, where you will have everything that you ever thought was impossible."

I smiled. "Thank you. Please...please don't leave my side, Sir Valence. I am scared of you not being around."

He grinned. "Alright, princess." He glanced to the maid. "Please go and grab my food tray, if you would. I need to stay by the princess."

She bowed and scurried out again, and he glanced to my untouched tray of food.

"Is it not to your liking?" He asked.

"All I've ever tried is the bread, but this bread looks even better than what I know. I have had meat before, but I didn't know what meat it was. It was salty meat."

"Go ahead and give it a try, princess," he said, smiling. "The cook worked hard to make a nutritious meal for you. You might like it more than you may think."

I sat down and tried to take a bite, but with the stress and worry and the lack of strength in my body, my hand trembled and shook before I dropped the spoon.

"I-I'm sorry!" I cried. "Oh, I won't do it again—"

"Your highness," he said, looking at me solemnly. "It is alright, princess."

Then, he smiled at me and moved closer, taking the spoon and lifting it in his hand, fixing the bite on the utensil and bringing it to my lips.

I flushed, feeling embarrassed, but I could feel that he truly, genuinely wanted to help and didn't look down on me, so...I took a bite.

I took that bite, and I was overwhelmed by an explosion of robust, amazing flavor.

"Wow..." I said. I slowly enjoyed my meal as he fed me, bite by bite, taking in everything and enjoying it in a way that I had never thought I would get to.

I kept whispering praise and amazement, and he watched me with a humbled expression as he gingerly ate his own food between my bites.

With the assurance that I wouldn't be hurt or scolded for eating all of these amazing things, I couldn't hold myself back.

How had I ever gone until this point without food like this?

I realized, now, that I hadn't truly been living before.

Had I ever even been living before now?

I just couldn't fathom that I had been.

I couldn't wait to see what else was in store, if this was only the beginning.

Chapter 6

Carlisle...

Nivis's End, 509 Lawrence Dynasty

It was the third day of the month, when a knight rushed into the courtyard where I was reading a list of supplies needed to fix the garden.

"Your Highness! Prince Carlisle!" He said, rushing to me. "She...the princess, your highness, the princess was *found*!" He said.

"What?" I asked, surprised, and I sensed no lies in his statement. "Tell me," I said, feeling a bit wary.

The last time that I had been told that there was news, all I learned was that she was taken again and that she was not, in fact, on her way to the palace.

A waste of my time and energy, that bit of news had been.

What was it this time? Had her body been found? Was she dead?

I half expected that to be the case, at this point.

"*Sir Valence*, sire. He found the princess! He sent a messenger hawk, and said that they are only about a day away, now. The bird arrived this morning."

The list dropped out of my hands and I stood there for a moment, stunned and feeling for the first time in a while.

I hadn't felt such an intense rush of my own emotion in quite some time.

Was this truly it? She had truly been found, rescued, and was on the way here? It wasn't false?

I rushed to my father's office, my current task forgotten, and my parents looked up at me in surprise.

"Is it true?" I asked, and they looked at each other. "I just got the news that the princess has been found. Have you two not heard?"

My mother's face lit up. "Oh, that is wonderful!" She said, reading the news in my mind.

It seems that they hadn't heard yet, and the news had been brought to me first.

"We directed the staff to bring any and all news of the princess to *you* first," my father said, sheepish as he heard my thoughts. "She is *your bride*, after all, and you are old enough to take responsibility for the news in regards to her. That aside, I am thrilled by this news!"

"It is said that they are about a day out," I said. "So, what should I do? I will admit that I had never actually expected for her to be found and come here, honestly, so...how do I prepare? What do I do?"

My father contemplated. "We never did go over this, did we? When we received the news that she was missing to begin with, and when we lost her after the seal was cut out, we never did discuss the next steps to complete when she arrived. We didn't want to get your hopes up further, so we just...waited."

"So, what do I do?"

"Alright," he said, glancing at my mother. "When your mother arrived, I was an infant, but we were placed into the same room right away. We grew up together, learning to care for one another's needs from the beginning. We had servants who would teach us to feed one another, change one another's clothes, bathe each other...we were married to each other from the beginning, so we grew up as a married couple."

"Things are quite different in this situation," mother said. "I suppose that the first thing we need to do is hold a wedding ceremony, declaring you two married, and set servants to teach you these things."

"Wait...we'll be married as soon as she arrives?" I was admittedly horrified at the notion.

This girl had been raised with a captor and had, obviously, not been taught proper etiquette and manners and she was already very unhealthy, as I recalled...didn't she need time to learn and get healthy before I went out of my way to marry her?"

"No," my father said. "She needs as much time as your bride as possible, and you are going to be responsible for her."

"Rather than getting her settled into her own room and teaching her to live on her own and confusing her by then marrying you and she together later, and then putting you together in a room after the fact...we need to just get straight to that at the beginning," mother said.

They wanted me to go ahead and bring this girl into my *chambers?*

With me?

At night, without any guards to watch over us?

Really?

What if she was dangerous?

I had to say, I was shocked by this.

I hadn't anticipated that they would be so ready for that option, considering that we didn't know anything about this girl...we weren't raised together, as was dictated by tradition.

Not only that, but I had no idea how to be prepared in a situation like this. How to love.

I hated the thought of love. I hated the idea of loving someone, after all that loving this girl—whom I had never even gotten to meet—had made me suffer through.

I hated her, and I didn't want to love her. I hated love. I didn't want to love her...

I didn't want to love anyone, honestly.

Love was horrible. Love was traumatizing.

How could anyone willingly choose to love and be loved, and trust being loved by others? Trust that they wouldn't be betrayed, disappointed, or abandoned?

"So, the first thing I need to do is prepare a wedding ceremony, and take her hand in matrimony," I said, taking their suggestion in. "But...what if she dislikes that idea?"

"If she is disagreeable to that, then we will have to accommodate her, but hopefully she will not be opposed."

I sighed, glancing at my mother. "Do you mind helping me prepare things for her in my chambers? I...I don't know what she might like. I don't have any sisters, so I don't know anything about girls."

She smiled at me. "Of course, I can, dear," she smiled, and got the attention of some servants nearby. "Please prepare a wardrobe of dresses, nightdresses, coats, riding clothes, and appropriate shoes for a girl the age of seven years," she said. "Also, prepare stuffed animal dolls and a girl doll. Add some girl's décor to the prince's chambers, and a vanity in the changing room with accessories."

"Right away, your majesty," they said, bowing and rushing off to follow my mother's orders.

"You, there," she said, calling over the head maid. "Prepare a handmaiden for a girl the age of seven. A child around the age of ten or so should suffice. Make sure that girl is prepared to deal with a child that will require a great deal of patience because I have a hunch that she will need a lot of time to adjust."

"Yes, your majesty."

"Also, prepare a selection of knights to take on being her personal Keeper knight. We need someone exceptionally skilled, but who isn't too intimidating that they will frighten her." She glanced to a kitchen attendant. "Prepare a set of tableware for the princess."

"Of course, your majesty," they all set off to their tasks.

I hugged her, and she looked at me in surprise.

"I...I'm nervous," I said. "What if she doesn't like me? What if I don't like her?"

She chuckled. "I worried about that too," she said. "When your father and I were entering this age, I wondered if he liked me, or if he was just familiar with me. We just decided to be honest with one another, and we spent a month alone in our own rooms. When we missed one another and told one another the truth, we found that we both really like each other. We loved each other."

I sighed, clutching to her. "I hope she will like me."

She lifted my chin to look at her. "So long as you are honest and warm, caring and compassionate toward her...she will love you," she smiled, kissing my forehead. "My charming prince."

I sighed, hugging her tighter. "Thank you, mother."

I wasn't so sure...I didn't want to be loved, not by this girl. I didn't want to love her...all I felt was aversion to the thought.

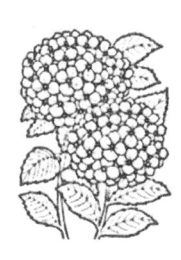

The following day finally arrived, and after a very restless night, I was up bright and early in a brilliant uniform, looking dashing and ready to make a good impression on my princess.

I was nervous, scared that my princess may not be interested in me, but I put that thought aside.

Of course, she would be interested in me, I thought, cocky. *I am a handsome prince. She will definitely like me. I mean, just look at her. The real question here was whether or not I would like **her**.*

I strode through the halls, glancing out of the window to look toward the docks. The ship that had left at the end of last year was docked, and I took a deep breath to calm myself.

My princess was coming.

Father and mother and my brothers had the same thought that I'd had; we all wanted to make an impression. We all wore high-status clothing, the boys all in uniforms of our royal family, highlighting the white and black for the Seers, with trims and accents of blue for the north.

It was about ten minutes before we heard the trumpet, and we heard the announcer.

"Announcing the arrival of Sir Valence, and...and, ahem, The Light Seer princess!"

I glanced to my parents.

"No name...?" I asked, surprised.

Normally, when someone was announced, their name was given. It was surprising that they hadn't done so.

Did she have no name, or was she simply *embarrassed* of her name? I imagined that her name must not be very pretty or elaborate, if a rogue knight kidnapped and raised her.

The doors opened, and I felt myself taken aback by my knight, who took my bride-to-be by the hand and led her slowly and cautiously through the throne room, even as her wide eyes fell on everything.

She clung to him as if her very life depended upon it, and he could hardly move his arm for her grip on him.

She looked absolutely panicked...but why?

Was she really so afraid...?

She reminded me of a rabbit...timid, small, at the bottom of the food chain.

Her hair was not white, but the *roots* were. It must have been a while since her hair had been dyed.

There were fading bruises on her body, and old, lingering scars and rough spots on her elbows and knees.

Her dress—a patchy, worn, brown, scratchy burlap material that I would expect a slave to wear—hung very loosely on her tiny body, and she was barefooted.

My parents and brothers were just as taken aback as I, and my younger brothers giggled at her lowly appearance.

...Making fun of her already, it seemed.

"Look at the girl brother gets to be saddled with," one muttered, and the others cackled under their breaths.

I shot them a glare, promptly silencing them, but I couldn't help but feel similarly. They were just vocalizing what I was already thinking. I had to be with this girl. This...this...depressing loser that was nothing more than a sack of bones.

She looked like a bad joke.

This was to be *my* princess...? My queen?

*She certainly doesn't **look** like a queen,* I thought bitterly.

I didn't want to love this girl.

I hated her already, because I loved her. Her pitiful face, her body...

What a sick joke.

She finally looked at me, and gasped as we made eye-contact.

I felt a bolt of electricity through me, and I felt suddenly attuned to her feelings.

I...I didn't like this.

I felt oddly attached to her, responsible for her, and bound to her right away, and I didn't like it. It made my skin crawl.

I couldn't hear her thoughts or feel her emotion directly, like I could with everyone else, but I definitely felt an immediate bond. I could feel her discomfort and fear, as if those things weren't clear enough by the way she carried herself and glanced around like a rabbit being hunted.

It annoyed me. Didn't she know that she had been rescued?

That she was safe, now? She'd never go without again. What did she have to be so blatantly terrified of?

Shouldn't she be relieved? Thankful?

Begging for forgiveness for making us put in all of that work and effort to find and rescue her?

She glanced to Valence for assurance, who gave her a warm smile and encouraging nod, before she looked at the floor and came to stand before me.

Slowly—*cautiously*—she got down on her hands and knees like an animal and pressed her face to the floor, leaving my parents, myself and I'm certain the rest of everyone else in the room gaping at her in shocked horror.

While I had thought, in a snide way, that this was what she should do, seeing her actually doing it made me feel queasy and even further irate.

"It is my greatest honor for my humblest self to meet someone so important," she said in a tiny, shaky voice.

Her entire body trembled.

I could see right away that she clearly didn't have the makings to be a queen, and she never would, no matter how much training she received. For too long, she had been raised as a thing, not a person, and you could see it plainly in her body language. There was way too much instillment of self-objectification for her to ever be able to rule.

She was basically an animal, lower even than a commoner.

Even most of the commoners I had met held themselves well and with dignity and pride. They had their own value, and they knew it. They respected themselves, and the knew what they had to offer. They knew their place, but they had pride and dignity in their roles.

She didn't have any dignity.

No self-respect.

No self-care, nor self-value.

For her to prostrate herself on the ground this way, face on the floor...? At our very first meeting, at that?

This girl was no princess.

My mother, father and I all exchanged glances. Their expressions were pitying, but I felt much harsher than that.

This was the girl who was born to be my queen.

She was destined to be my life partner, the mother to my heirs...and I would get no exchanges.

This was it.

I had been jipped, it seemed. Slighted. Bamboozled. Tricked. Played. Teased.

Never had a Seer defied their destiny and denied their partner, but in this moment, this regret and humiliation almost made me want to do so.

There had been a Seer to betray their partner once, in our history...but they had still accepted them until the betrayal at the end.

I was a properly raised prince, who had been waiting for my destined partner all my life, and yet, she was so *lowly*. I knew who I needed to truly be angry at, of course. Her parents, who had sent her away to hurt the kingdom...hurt the north. I knew that it wasn't her fault, but I couldn't help but take it out on her.

All they did was seal their own fates and make a mockery of themselves.

I couldn't look too unfavorably upon the Southern Kingdom as a whole—after all, my mother was from the South. A Dark Seer who was born in the Southern kingdom and brought here to the north, to become my father's bride.

My mother finally glanced to me, and gave me a stern expression, jutting her chin toward the girl on the floor.

I nodded with an internal sigh, and took a step toward the girl, going and standing so that I could reach down to her.

I held my hand by her face. "Get up," I said, and she startled, looking from my offered hand to my face.

She slowly and gingerly took my hand, letting me help her stand, and she stood before me on shaky legs.

I gave a slight bow at the waist, showing her my respect. "I welcome you to the Northern palace, princess. It is an honor to meet you. From today onwards, we shall be together, so let's make sure to get along," I said, offering my hand.

She looked from my hand to my face, and back again.

Did she...not know what she was supposed to do? I was lowering myself enough to offer to help her to stand! I was a prince, coming to help her up...but she disrespected me by ignoring it?

Looking at me like I was a fool?

"Give me your hand!" I shouted, startling her and her eyes filling with tears before finally setting her hand in my own.

I hated those tears, acting like a puppy that had been kicked just because she had been scolded.

Sad, pitiful child.

I loved her, but I hated her. Hated her for having to be born where she had been born, for being sent away and abused for so long. Loved her because she was my soul mate, but hated her because of the same thing.

Bruised and calloused with little splits in the skin, much like a slave's hands. It was small and so skinny. She was practically a stick person. A skeleton with skin. I felt sick even touching her...like I would break her at the slightest touch. I felt uncomfortable.

"Is that...really alright?" She asked, timid.

I nodded. "You are a princess," I told her. "Just take my hand and follow my lead. I will do the rest."

She gave me a look of confusion, looking to Sir Valence yet again.

"Go on, your highness. His highness is right."

She smiled at me shyly, and took my hand a bit more firmly as I led her to my parents.

We faced them together, and I looked to my father.

"We are ready," I told him, trying to suppress the frustration boiling beneath my skin.

I didn't want to do this.

He nodded. "Prince Carlisle, the Eyes of Truth's Dark Seer, the Crowned Prince of the Northern Kingdom and heir to the throne...do you so promise to honor, cherish, respect, and love your bride?"

I gave a firm nod. "I do."

"Princess...?" My father trailed off, and she startled.

"Y-yes...?"

"Might I know your name?"

She flushed, even her ears turning red with her blush, and she looked to the floor. "I do not have a name, your kingliness..."

He and I glanced at one another.

Somehow, that was even worse. I had thought that she must be embarrassed of her name, that it wasn't a pretty name...

For her to not even have a name? Why? Slaves had names. Even pets had names.

She truly was treated worse than an animal.

Even orphans had names, didn't they?

Did that knight truly not feel that she deserved at least the respect of having a given name? What exactly had he been calling her all this time?

"Then, as your groom, I will give Prince Carlisle the honor of bestowing a name upon you," father said, and he beckoned for the scribe to come and have a pen and paper ready to take her official name.

"I will name her..." I looked at her, taking her in. I wanted to give her a pretty name, because she had the potential to be pretty...even beneath all the grime and abuse and filth, if I pictured her with white hair and pale skin with golden eyes...she was pretty. I hated to marry her when she was so dirty and ragged, but it couldn't be helped. "Kinley. I deem her maiden name to be Kinley Haze."

"So, she is deemed," the scribe said, before backing away.

"Princess Kinley, the Eyes of Truth's Light Seer, the lost princess of the Southern Kingdom and destined bride of the heir to the throne of the Northern Kingdom...do you so promise to honor, cherish, respect, and love your groom?"

"What...what does that mean?"

I nearly smacked my forehead. I stared, mouth agape, at how little she really knew.

He hesitated. "A groom is someone who will stay by you for the rest of your life as your life partner, who will honor and cherish and love you for the rest of time. He will take care of you and make sure you have all you need. Do you accept that?"

"You mean...he will love me? Can someone like him love someone as ugly and lowly as me?"

His eyes got sad, but he nodded. "Yes," he told her...though I was seriously questioning it myself.

Her eyes filled with tears as she looked at me, her hand trembling in mine.

"I-I d-do..." She stammered, emotional.

Was she not aware that she would be marrying me when she arrived?

Why was she so upset...?

My father—who I knew was able to feel her emotions—looked upon her with pity and a warm smile, so I wondered if she was actually upset or not.

If she was upset, father wouldn't look so happy, right? He'd be trying to comfort her or find a solution, surely.

Was she just an emotional child? More evidence of not having the makings to be a good queen. Queens needed to be level-headed and sure-minded.

"I pronounce you husband and wife, bride and groom. This marriage can only be voided by death," my father said, clapping his hands together. "And so, it shall be!"

The maids rushed over, and murmured encouraging and caring words as they took my bride off to our chambers while she looked like a deer in headlights in an ambush.

That frozen-in-fear expression that haunted my memory.

Before I followed after them, I looked to my parents.

"Do you think that this is really okay?" I asked. "She...isn't what I had anticipated."

"Give her some time," mother said. "She has faced countless abuses and troubles. It will take time to teach her the way of things here."

"The girl has never had anyone truly care for her. Even her warden was someone she cared for in all instances, despite the abuse. I think she is afraid to believe someone can love her. She's never been loved before, so it is a shock to her. Give her time."

Take time? **That** was their solution?

It seemed to me that it was unlikely to happen at all, honestly. I couldn't imagine that girl every learning palace life.

I sighed, bowing. "Thank you, father and mother."

Then I turned, following after the group of maids.

When we came to the chambers that I would be sharing with Kinley, and she gaped at the room.

"Is everything to your liking?" I asked her.

She startled, and I felt a pang of irritation at her fear.

"Is this...your room?" She asked.

I cocked my head to the side. "This is our *shared* bedroom. You are my wife, now. Surely, you don't expect to be sleeping in separate rooms?"

"Wife...what is a wife?"

I gaped at her even as the maids all murmured and looked on with confused and somewhat mocking thoughts.

I sighed, realizing that I had now been legally tied to a girl who knew less than nothing about the world or the way it worked.

At this point, I wouldn't be surprised if I had to hire a tutor to teach her how to *breathe* properly, on top of everything else.

I was stuck with this, and I was stuck with a bride that would be mocked and belittled all our lives together.

I would face endless humiliation because of her, and the thought enraged me.

Not if I have anything to do with it, I thought.

I was a prince. I shouldn't have to endure disgrace just because I had gotten stuck with this ignorant girl for a life partner.

I refused to be embarrassed by this nitwit.

She would just have to learn, or this relationship wouldn't be able to proceed any further than this in the future. I was too amazing to be stuck with a fool.

"It means that we live together, *do everything* together...and when we grow up, we will kiss and hug and have babies," I told her, and she blushed heavily at the thought. I smirked. "You are my wife."

She twisted the hem of her burlap scrap dress in her calloused hands. "I-I see..."

"Your majesty, it is time for her to bathe now. Would you like to learn how to perform this task now, or would you rather wait to learn later?" The maid asked me.

"I will learn now," I said, and I followed as they led her to the adjoined bathroom.

I watched as they began to undress her, and I startled when her body became bare to me.

She was covered in bruises and scratches all over, but the most notable was the jagged cut and seared flesh over her chest, where the seal had been cast and then carved out and burned shut.

All of her ribs showed, and her skin was loose and sickly.

What a horror show...

She blushed as the maids turned her away, and I kept my eyes on her face as they led her into the tub.

I took off my own uniform, stripping down to my underwear and stepping into the bath.

She didn't have any underwear to bathe in the way that I did, but that would be remedied quickly. Once the tailors were able to get her measurements, they would fashion her a wardrobe better than the few outfits we had prepared for her beforehand.

The royal children bathed in wet-suits that covered their private places from one another until adulthood, but since she had just arrived, she didn't have that yet.

Though, I supposed it didn't matter that much. We were married, and I would be seeing it at some point anyway.

I stepped up to her in the water—a bath that was built like a pool in the ground, a sauna almost—and I took the washcloth from the maids and lathered it with the soap that they offered.

"Take her hands and arms, scrubbing lightly over her body, your highness," they instructed me, and I glanced to my trembling bride.

I took her hand and lifted it so that her arm was held up, scrubbing over her arms one by one.

They instructed me similarly with the feet and legs, having me let the girl sit on the edge of the bath so that I could bathe her properly.

I felt the rush of heat in the maids' bellies as they instructed me how to bathe her back and chest, her bottom and her front...all which I tried to do without looking at her too much.

Sick maids, I thought.

Getting hot and bothered watching children bathe...this wasn't anything sexual.

It was just my duty as her husband to help her bathe.

I felt a rush of disgust at their pleasure.

Kinley seemed to understand it in a different way, because she blushed prettily and gave me a timid smile.

Looking at me from beneath thick lashes with those bright golden eyes.

As recorded, I couldn't read her thoughts or emotions the way that I could everyone else. She was the only person with whom I couldn't.

Though, I instinctively knew that as the Light Seer, she was likely feeling all the positive aspects of their thoughts and feelings and was trying to see it in a good light.

I lifted the choppy, shoddy strands of her hair, washing them and gingerly massaging her scalp with the shampoo in my hands and slicking it with the oil.

I watched as the dye faded even further, seeming to wash out of her hair.

It was just a few shades darker than white when I rinsed it, and I was glad that the dye seemed to be temporary. I wanted to see her in her true form as soon as possible.

After I had finished bathing her, I handed her a fresh washcloth.

"Now, just mimic what I did to you, to me."

She blushed, but she nodded, starting with my arms.

When she came to my more intimate places, I held her hands at bay and shook my head.

"Don't worry about that, I will bathe those on my own for now," I told her.

She blushed but acquiesced quickly.

I reached in the water and scrubbed my intimate spots myself, before I turned so that she could reach my hair.

"You may wash my hair," I said.

She timidly set to the task, her touch feather-light and cautious. "What...is this?" She asked, pointing at my hair.

"...Hair?"

"No, I mean...um...uh..."

"The color?" I asked.

She lit up, brightening considerably. "Yes, color, that's it. What is this color?"

I hesitated. "...It is 'black,' princess..."

"Oh," she grinned. "I'm sorry. I don't know many colors but I promise I will try to learn quickly!"

She didn't even know *colors*?

Colors?

Something I had learned by age two?

Embarrassment fueled me, as hatred fueled my rage.

I was so dreadfully embarrassed by her. I knew that it was wrong of me, but I was so embarrassed.

How on earth could I be with someone like this? I was so far advanced and ahead for my age, but her...?

Soon enough, we were both squeaky clean and fresh, and I stepped out, letting the maids dress me.

"There is a problem, your highness," the maid for my wife said, and I turned to give them my attention. "These clothes that were ordered...they were ordered for an average girl of seven, but...they are far, far too large on her."

I gaped at how they hung on her body, and I sighed.

"Go to the closest boutique and have a tailor brought to take her measurements. We need at least something that we can have her wear until she gains the proper proportions for her body and age," I said, rubbing my temples.

She scurried off, and the maids wrapped her in a big, fluffy towel that seemed to swallow her whole.

I laughed softly. She did look cute, being so tiny in that towel.

That, and clean...she had more potential to be pretty and she smelled a lot better.

I glanced to the door as a doctor came in, accompanied by my mother.

"We are here to give the princess a check-up," she smiled, and they approached us.

The doctor took her time examining her, a grave look on her face as she took down her height, weight and size.

"Well?" I asked, feeling the course of negative emotions running through her.

She sighed, turning to me. "She is very malnourished. She is the size of a four-year-old, rather than a girl of seven. I am sad to report that she also has a mild infection in that wound on her chest," she said. "It wasn't treated properly, but a salve should clear that up quickly since it is mild. I am worried by her size, though. Even if she were not so malnourished, her height and bone-frame is clearly not normal. It is obvious she has had an extreme lack of calcium and other crucial vitamins. Also, from the shaping of her posture…it looks as if she were almost…compressed in a tiny space much of the time. This is very odd, indeed."

"So, what do I need to do about this?" I asked.

"She needs to go on a supplemental diet right away to get the proper nutrients, and she needs to be fed small portions with increased meal-times and snack times."

"Can we not give her large meals?" I asked, confused. "Would that not work better to put weight onto her?"

"Simply giving her large meals and expecting her to finish them will not help her gain the weight that she needs. Many people lose weight when stressed, so be sure that she is comfortable and feels safe. Give her foods rich in iron, calcium and other antioxidants. Give her plenty of vitamin supplements and milk. But most of all—be patient with her."

"Thank you, doctor," I said, and as the doctor was leaving, the maid I had sent to fetch the tailor was walking in.

The tailor was in awe when she saw my bride, surprised. "Well, it is no wonder that the clothes I sent over yesterday didn't fit. I had been told to fit an average girl of seven, but this girl is *barely* the size of a girl of five!" She said, sad. "Don't worry, your highness, I will get your measurements and fit you for some clothes to wear until you get healthy."

"Th-thank you, ma'am..." My bride said, and the tailor gasped.

"Oh, my, you're so sweet!" She gushed. "Alright, then," she said, pulling out her measuring tape and setting to her task. "Goodness, what a tiny thing you are." After getting the measurements, she turned to her assistant and they pulled out a case of clothes. "Here are some things that should fit you fairly well for now, princess," she said, pulling out a few tiny outfits.

Kinley gasped, looking over the modest dresses that were brought to her as if she hadn't ever seen anything so pretty.

They weren't ugly, but they were barely good enough for a lower-ranked noble, let alone royalty...

"These...are the prettiest clothes I've ever seen..." She breathed, stroking the dresses. "Can *I* really wear *these*?"

The tailor gaped at her, confusion and sadness filling her mind and negative images of my bride coming to mind.

She didn't understand why my wife showed such pitiful behavior, why she didn't act like a princess.

I was even further embarrassed, but I gritted my teeth and bore the shame for now.

Hopefully she would improve quickly.

As my wife took off her robe to change into a night-gown the maid handed her, the tailor gasped and cried out in shock, covering her eyes.

"What...what on earth...?"

"The princess was abused heavily before arriving here," a maid said. "Please, keep this information to yourselves," she implored. "We do not want anyone looking down upon the princess. Treated this way or not, she is of royal birth, and is the rightful and honorable Light Seer of the Eyes of truth. She is due your respect."

The tailor and her assistant nodded, setting back to writing down the measurements and asking my wife her favorite colors.

"Color...um..." She couldn't seem to pick one. "I don't know colors," she said.

"Why do you not know color, anyway?" I asked, crossing my arms indignantly.

What kind of child our age didn't even know colors? That was just absurd.

"I...I-I was kept in a blindfold most of my life. I only know my eyes are gold and my real hair color is white...your hair is black. Ginger's hair was red, and—"

I sighed, resting my face in my hands, tuning out. "Tailor, show her a color guide," I told her.

The tailor smiled simply, pulling out a catalog of clothes her boutique offered and showing her the colors.

"These are colors, your highness. This is red, and this is blue. There is purple and pink. I offer some green choices as well, and some yellow. But being in the north, most of what I have to offer are blue and purple clothes."

My wife looked over the colors in the catalog, and I noticed her attention on one item specifically.

I stepped over, looking at it, and noticed that she was drawn to a pretty lilac-printed dress with various shades of purple.

"You like the purple the most?" I asked, and she startled, looking up at me as I peered over her shoulder before she turned her attention back to the guide.

"Oh, I...well, yes, this is my favorite of the color choices."

"She favors purple," I told the tailor. "So, give her mostly purple clothes, but also some blue and a few pink choices. If we have any need of anything else, I will call for you."

"Yes, your highness. I will have the order finished by the evening," she said, setting out with her assistant.

I turned to my young bride. "Are you hungry, Kinley?" I asked, and she brightened.

"Am I allowed to eat now?"

I took a good, long look at my wife.

She had been very *respectful*—to the point of dishonoring her own dignity.

She was shy and timid, and was so overwhelmed by what a normal princess would just expect.

Now, she was asking if she was allowed to eat...?

I eyed her like she had two heads, but I nodded. "Yes, we can eat now. The maid that was with the doctor took the list of meal requirements for you to the cook, so they have probably started making something for you by now. It is already past time for breakfast."

She nodded, smiling. "If I am allowed, I would like to eat."

"Alright, then," I said, reaching out for her hand. I showed her to loop her arm beneath my own, letting her forearm rest atop of mine and her hand clasped in my own. "Let's go eat."

I led her through the palace to the dining hall, where my family was already sat and eating.

"Ah, there they are," father smiled at us. "Bathed and measured for clothes that will arrive later, hm?" He asked.

"Yes, father. She has also been seen by the physician."

"Ah, good. Remember, you are in charge of the princess's care, so all of her care falls to you and your charge."

"Yes, father," I repeated, and I pulled out a chair beside of my own for Kinley. "This is your place from now on," I told her. "And this is your tableware. Each of us has our own set."

She looked at her seat and her dishes, which were promptly taken by one of the maids and filled with some food items for her, and a group of pills were brought to sit at her place setting with a glass of milk.

"These are your vitamins and medicines to help you, your highness," one of the maids said. "They were provided by the doctor."

Kinley looked to me. "Uh...how do I take them, your highness?" She asked.

"Set one at a time on your tongue, and take a sip of milk. Swallow the pill down with the sip of milk."

"Okay," she smiled, and she made to sit down but as I pushed her seat under her, she was startled and looked at me, almost having fell out of the seat. "What..."

"I was pushing your chair beneath you as you sat, so that you could sit...you know what? Never mind. You can sit on your own." I scoffed, moving to my seat and sitting as I watched her in irritation while she pushed her chair out, readjusting and sitting before scooting up to the table with harsh scrapes of the chair against the stone tiles.

We all flinched as our ears were assaulted.

Oblivious, she set to taking her prescriptions as I had instructed.

When she finished, she looked to the plate of soft foods before her. They were very healthy, but had been diced and pureed so that she could digest them easier...like a baby.

"May I eat?" She asked.

I nodded. "Go ahead."

"Thank you, your highness," she smiled softly at me, and she took small bites of food.

I was once again reminded of a rabbit.

Chapter 7

Kinley Lawrence...

The food was amazing, better than anything I had ever eaten before, and I could hardly believe all that had happened to me in the last few days.

I had been rather terrified when we had come to see the palace, and when I had seen the prince for the first time...that may have just been hours ago, but it felt like an eternity and a single instance ago all at once.

His rich dark skin and black hair, and similar golden gaze that pierced through me to my core.

He was opposite of me in every way, from his confident stance to his harsh expression.

So, to demonstrate that I meant him no harm and did not intend to defy him in any way, I came to bow on the ground in front of him.

I think that he had been a bit put off by this, but it had gotten my intent across, at least.

Then, when he had held my hand and we had vowed ourselves to one another...

I felt an odd tingling in my heart.

I didn't know what it meant to be married or what a husband or a wife was, but when he explained it to me...I blushed, feeling hot and strange.

That was something that adults did...to make babies, apparently. Did that mean he wanted to make babies with me? Were we going to have babies *now*?

If not now, when?

Was he going to make me have his babies even if I didn't want to?

I felt hot, embarrassing fear as he bathed me, looking at me with his judging eyes and ordering the servants with his authority and power that I doubted I would ever hold.

Soon enough, we had sat for the meal and now, I was feeling like I was in heaven.

How could food taste so good?

I didn't even know what the food was called or what colors they were, how they were cooked, where they came from or how they were made...

I just knew that I hadn't ever experienced anything so *wonderful*.

I felt full quickly, but when I looked at my plate compared to even children younger than I was...I had only eaten about a third of my portion, and I blushed when they looked at me strangely.

They hadn't ever seen someone so pitiful as me, I could hear in their thoughts. I was like some rescued abused animal.

"I am finished," I said, peeking up at my husband.

He nodded. "Alright. Give me a few moments to finish, and then I will take you to pick out your personal knight to guard you."

I gulped, nervous.

I was getting a knight?

I already had been given way too much.

A beautiful set of clothes, a room beyond anything I had ever imagined to share with a husband I was both intimidated and inspired by...

Even food and vitamins and medicines to fill my belly and nourish my body.

The real issue was that I didn't want a knight other than Valence. I trusted Valence, and my only other experience with a knight had been with my former guardian. I was terrified of warriors.

A few minutes passed by quietly, and then my husband dabbed the crumbs from his face before he sat his lap napkin over his plate.

He stood, and the servants bowed to him as he came and helped me up from my chair, taking me by the hand and leading me out of the dining room and through the halls.

We stopped in a large room filled with suits of armor and weapons, where knights were practicing and conversing with one another.

As soon as we entered the room, they took note of us and came to stand in a line in front of us, bowing before standing at attention.

"I have selected a group of knights to choose from for you, princess," Prince Carlisle said, gesturing to the group of knights. "You may pick any one of these knights to be your Keeper Knight."

"What...does that mean?" I asked.

"A Keeper knight will follow you around, stay by your side at all times. He will protect you and watch over you at all times. All of these knights are exceptional in skill. Sir Valence is *my* personal Keeper knight, but you need one of your own for any time that I am not around you."

"Does that mean...that I can't choose Sir Valence...?" I asked.

That bothered me. I would only want Valence as a knight, and he was saying...I couldn't have Valence. I was scared of the other knights, though...!

He laughed. "Valence is already sworn to me and sealed by the Sorcerer's seal and the Keeper's Oath. You can't just take him from me."

"Oh..."

So, it was an entirely set-in-stone kind of thing?

Did that mean that whoever I chose...would be permanent? Even if they hated me?

I looked at the knights, and each of them came, one by one, to stand before me and introduce themselves.

One, however, stood out to me.

He had dark, rich bronzy skin, but he had light-colored minty-green eyes and light, silver-toned brown hair.

He had a few scars on his arms and one on his face, but I felt the most positive energy from him than any of the others.

He was young, but he was proud and confident in his skills.

Somehow, he really reminded me of Valence, and I felt comfortable with him in the same way that I felt comfortable with Valence. They shared a similar aura.

I could sense that he was one of the stronger knights of this group, and seemed the most promising.

"That one," I said, pointing to him.

He came to kneel, reintroducing himself. "I am Sir Halo, princess Light Seer."

I smiled. "I will be in your care from now on, sir Halo," I said, bowing.

He looked at me in surprise, and I felt a rush of joy in his chest. He hadn't ever been spoken to in such a way by someone of my apparent status, and it made him happy.

"I won't let you down, princess," he said, beaming up at me before he stood.

Wordlessly, my young husband turned and led us out of the room, turning and moving through the halls until we came back to the main hall, where he turned to a door off to the side and led us through.

We followed him through another maze of halls before we reached a room that was light, full of chandeliers and many tubes of ingredients on shelves that were held up on the walls.

There were tables full of beakers, tubes and other objects.

There were thick and heavy books all over long tables strewn about.

"Axel!" My husband shouted, and I startled. "I brought her."

"Oh!" I heard a voice call out, and I suddenly saw a man with bright eyes the color of the sky and almost white hair come out, dressed in a fancy tunic and robe combination. "Hello, young Prince and Princess Seers. I am Axel Roth, and I am the Paladin Wizard of the Northern Kingdom. I have been waiting for you," he smiled at me.

His thoughts were buzzing like a swarm of bugs, but they were positive and happy and warm.

"Ni-nice to meet you," I stammered.

"You are here to seal the Keeper Knight to you, right?" He asked with a big grin. "Sir Halo is young, but shows a lot of promise! He's even been sought after to be a templar knight, and he has divine power as well as mage mana and knight aura. He is a great choice. The only knight more skilled in our palace right now is probably Sir Valence, but I would expect them to be similar, since they are brothers."

"...What are brothers?" I asked, and I flinched hard when Prince Carlisle smacked his hand to his forehead—hard.

Sir Halo and Axel both felt confusion, and they glanced at one another.

"You know how you have a mother and father?" Axel asked, and I nodded. "A brother—or sister—is another child who comes from the same parents. So, for example, take Sir Halo here. Sir Valence and Sir Halo come from the same parents. They are brothers. Sir Valence is almost six years older than Sir Halo. Sir Halo just turned sixteen a week ago."

So, that was why they had felt so similar to one another. They shared the same parents.

They were brothers!

They were young, though, to be such high-leveled knights, weren't they?

On that note, I tried to remember how old I was, but I couldn't.

"...How old am I?" I asked.

"Oh, my goodness!" Carlisle shouted, throwing his hands up in surrender and walking away. "You can get this done, Sir Axel. I'm...I'm done here. I have to get away." He then quickly left the room, and the other two glanced at one another before they looked to me with pitying expressions.

"Your Highness," Sir Axel said. "You were born in the month of Year's Fall, in the year of 501 of the Lawrence Dynasty calendar year. It is Nivis's End, of the year 509 LD. You are seven years old right now, and you will be turning eight upon your next birthday. Prince Carlisle was born exactly one year before you, on the same day, so he is eight and turning nine upon your next birthday."

I glanced at Sir Halo. "You are how many years older than me?" I asked.

He smiled. "I am almost nine years older, your highness. I turned sixteen only a week ago. Had I been sixteen in Year's Fall of last year, I would have been nine years older than you."

"Oh..." I glanced after the prince. "Why did the prince leave?"

114

They both sighed. "His highness has always been a bit abrasive. I am sure he'll come around," Sir Halo smiled at me. He kneeled before me. "Let's get this seal done, okay?"

I nodded. I didn't know what abrasive meant, but I guessed that it meant that he was angry with me. I hated that I had already upset him...

"We can only do a semi-permanent seal right now, because a permanent seal can only be performed on a teenager in great health," Sir Axel said. "This will still bond you two together, and it will work similarly to a permanent seal, but it won't take as much out of the princess or hurt her as badly."

I followed his instructions and repeated the words he told me to say, and I felt a searing pain in the back of my right hand. Sir Halo hissed a bit when the same seal appeared on him, as well.

"It looks like those pretty pictures people get on their bodies," I commented, and they laughed.

"When you are older and healthier and you can get an adult version of the seal that is permanent, it will look more like a brand or a carving...it will hurt a lot more. This will suffice for now, though." He smiled at me. "It is nice to meet you, your highness. I am sure I will see you for tutoring soon. I will be one of your teachers."

Sir Halo and I turned, and he led me out of the room and back through the maze of halls that we had to travel through to get back to my chambers.

There, he entered an adjoined chamber and I could hear him and his brother talking even as I looked around the empty room.

Well, empty of *people*.

There were so many *things* in the room that I didn't recognize.

When they came back into the room, Sir Halo and Sir Valence both smiled at me.

"I hope that my younger brother will be of great help to you, your highness!" Sir Valence said. "He's young, but he's quite skilled and a great friend. He will be good to you."

I nodded. "Thank you." I stretched, yawning a bit. "Can I take a nap...? I am tired," I said.

"Of course," Sir Valence said, and they both pulled back the blankets of my bed and helped me in, letting me get comfy and tucking me in.

I was asleep quickly, my body soaking in and relishing in the strange, odd comfortableness of the bed.

It almost made me ache more to lay in this luxurious bed...

Chapter 8

Carlisle...

"You cannot expect me to stay with this, this..." I threw up my hands. "She doesn't even know what brothers and sisters are!"

My father shrugged even as my brothers snickered in the corner of the office, sipping tea.

"You'd better adjust quickly, Carlisle," father told me, and I could feel his growing irritation. "She is here to stay, and she's been very underprivileged, abused, and hurt over her life. She's only seven. Give it some time."

"And what about social debut? Am I to attend the next formal ball with a half-wit? Or am I expected to just go alone?"

"Carlisle," mother spoke, tone disappointed. "Give her some time. She's been very sheltered. It shouldn't take long to teach her. She should know enough within the next two months to make it to the annual Veras Ball with you, at least."

I scoffed. "Yeah, sure she should. She should already be at the same level as me!" I said, exasperated. "I shouldn't need to wait for her to be trained like some kind of animal!"

"Try to have some patience. You've waited for a long time, but now she is here and safe," father said.

I could hear the underlying thoughts about his disappointment in my attitude.

"Let her have some time to learn and grow. She's not at fault for her situation and you know that," mother said.

I sighed. "Fine." I turned, going back through the halls and to the training hall. I needed to blow off some steam.

When it was time for supper, I was surprised to find that my new young wife was not at the dining hall.

"Where is she?" I asked, a bit irritated.

She was as skinny as a board, so surely, she wouldn't actually intentionally miss supper, right?

"She's still napping, your highness," Valence said, bowing at the waist. "After the sealing earlier—temporary though it may be—and being her first day here after a long trip by sea, she's just very tired. Remember, this is her first day here."

"But she—"

"The physician said that she needed the extra sleep," Halo spoke up. "I apologize your highness, but they insisted that we let her rest until she awakes on her own, as this sleeping time could be crucial to her mental development."

I sighed heavily, waving it off. "Fine. Whatever. Just leave her be to sleep, then." I rolled my eyes, before eating my meal.

When I had finished, I excused myself and went—finally—to my bedroom. It had been hours since I had been here, and I enjoyed arriving to this room to relax from a hard day's—

She was there.

*She was there, asleep in **my** bed.*

Ugh...

At least she smelled decent compared to when she first arrived, but she still had the lingering smells of saltwater and dirt on her.

I glanced over her, noting the color returning to her cheeks from how deathly pale she had been earlier, and honestly, I had to admit that she wasn't *horribly* ugly. She had a lot of potential to become beautiful one day. I just hoped that she did.

She irritated me already, but I was glad that she was at least safe, here. I knew that she would have all she needed; food, water, shelter, toilet and clothes to use...

I knew that I was being irrationally angry towards her, but I had waited all of my life to have my bride.

I grew up hearing and learning about all of the Seer couples before me, who had been raised together with one another and almost all of them had been power couples and been super close. Best friends. Closest confidants.

The only person you had to guess what they were thinking.

Would we ever be able to reach that point?

I wasn't convinced, yet.

I sighed, sliding into the bed beneath the blankets and putting a pillow between the two of us before lying down and trying to fall asleep to the soft sounds of her gentle breaths.

Days passed, and tutors were brought in for her.

A nutritionist and special meal preppers for her to be able to build strength and health quickly, as she was so emaciated.

A dancing instructor, to help teach her some expressive, fun activity to do with me...though, admittedly, she didn't do very well with this.

Everything from reading and math, to etiquettes and posture.

Fine arts to equestrian studies.

She rapidly went up in cost for her upkeep and education, and though it ate away into my personal funding and my budget as the prince, taking away the money to spend on myself, I reminded myself that it was my duty as the Crowned Prince to do these things for my Crowned Princess.

As it turned out, she was capable of understanding and retaining most information somewhat quickly, so that was at least a positive on her behalf.

Nivis gave way into Veras, and the Veras Ball arrived sooner than I would have liked.

My parents were particularly wary of announcing that the princess had been found, and advised me to wait. So, in the end, we decided to hold off for the time being.

There were rumors, of course, but none of the royal family addressed it at the ball.

I made only a brief appearance before I made my way back to the training hall, and continued my drills with my fellow soldiers in training.

I didn't care what Kinley was doing, really.

I knew she was with tutors and that she was safe, so whatever it was that she was doing was at least something productive.

I tried not to think about the circumstances of how and why she needed all the tutoring.

When I reached my chambers later that evening, I found Kinley reciting the alphabet until she noticed me.

She immediately blushed, hanging her head.

She knew that I didn't like seeing her trying to catch up to me, because it was embarrassing that she didn't already know these things.

"Hello, your highness," she said, standing and giving a small curtsy the way that she'd been taught to.

I gave her a nod. "Kinley," I said.

"H-how was the ball, your highness?" She asked, fidgeting with her hands.

She had grown increasingly timid around me, but I didn't know why.

"It was fine. I only made a brief appearance."

She nodded. "I see..." She looked around the room, not really looking at me. A common occurrence, and something that further frustrated me about her. Was I really that bad to be around?

I glanced at her stockings, which were tinged red.

She'd been disciplined by the tutor, again.

During etiquette training for royalty, a child would receive slaps of a crop against the back of the calves.

This ensured that the child had proper motivation to learn as quickly as they could so that they wouldn't have to continue getting the discipline.

"What did you mess up today?" I asked.

She glanced down and away. "I mi-misspelled your name."

Ah, she had been struggling particularly hard with that since she had arrived.

I sighed. "How many times has this been, now?"

"F-four..."

"We also need to fix that stammer of yours," I grumbled. "A princess shouldn't be a stutterer."

She blushed again, hanging her head. "I—" she cleared her throat. "I am sorry, your highness."

"Carlisle." I crossed my arms. "I am your husband. You should call me by my name, at least when we're alone."

She glanced up at me, but didn't respond.

"C-a-r-l-i-s-l-e," I spelled out slowly. "Jameson; J-a-m-e-s-o-n. Lawrence; L-a-w-r-e-n-c-e."

She gave me another curtsy, thanking me softly.

I approached her, and took her face into my hand, turning her face a bit and studying her. "You look better than you did when you arrived. You've put on some weight and you look healthier." I nodded. "It's a good thing."

"Thank you, your high—Carlisle," she said.

"Spell it," I commanded.

She blushed, and her eyes looked down at the floor. "C...a-r-l...i...l—" I gave her a look, and she cringed. "L...i-s...l...e...?" She cringed again.

"Good girl," I smiled. "Now, clean up and get ready for bed. Have you eaten already?"

She nodded. "Yes."

"Good. Do you need me to help you?" I asked her.

She blushed. She had learned quickly that my helping her get dressed, bathed, and cleaned up was all part of my duties as her husband.

It was not only accepted, but encouraged, for us to be as physical and intimate with one another as possible.

In fact, this was seen as a highly positive thing, and meant that our relationship should do well once we became adults.

"If you wish," she told me.

I shrugged, and I led her off to the bathroom.

"Carlisle?" She asked when we had entered the bath. "Do you think we'll be as close as your parents are?"

I shrugged. "Maybe. If you can learn quickly and become a good Crowned Princess, I think we have a good chance."

She nodded. "I will do my best," she promised.

"Alright," I said. "I take that as a promise."

"When can I make my social debut?" She asked. "I know why I couldn't today, but I've been studying really hard!" She told me. "I would love to see a ball."

I considered this. "When I think you're ready, we can debut you."

Chapter 9

Kinley...

Year's Fall, 517 Lawrence Dynasty

It was the Nivis ball, and it was finally time for my debut into high society.

It was a late debut, all things considered, but it had taken quite some time until they felt comfortable introducing me to the public due to some...incidents.

I had been unofficially *tested* in a formal setting—a small banquet at a Duke's estate for his daughter's tea party—and I had failed miserably.

I had embarrassed my husband badly.

I hadn't realized that I was being watched so closely, and I had taken off my shoes to step into the fountain in the garden. I was playing in the water when the servants had seen me, and gone to alert the duke and his daughter...

Then, she and her other guests had proceeded to come out and make fun of me for doing something so ridiculous and further humiliated me for crying over the incident.

I hadn't known that stepping into the fountain was so against code, or etiquette. I hadn't realized that I would shame the royal family by doing so.

When my driver was summoned two hours before the end of the tea-party to pick me up, I had seen his shock and embarrassment of having to help dry me off and lead me to the carriage to take me back to the palace.

My husband had insisted that until I had completely learned proper behavior, I not be allowed to attend any more gatherings. He was embarrassed by me, and I supposed that I couldn't blame him. He was a prince, the future king of our nation, and I was just a blundering idiot.

He had every right to ban me from being part of the social circles.

That had been three years ago, when I was thirteen.

Now, I was much calmer.

I had perfected acting aloof and detached, the way that I had been taught, and I had to keep this mask on until I was alone...when I would sit and cry to myself in a dark closet of the palace, in peace.

Due to the stress of my situation, and the depression that plagued me due to the callousness of my Crowned Prince, I spent most of my time eating in a binging manner.

I even snuck snacks into my hide-away closet, where I would cry as I ate snacks in the dark.

I sucked in as my lady's maid struggled to tie my corset into place, before she sighed. "Your highness, you truly need to stop eating so much. This is the fourth time this month that I've needed to go in search of a larger corset," she whined, going over to get a larger band out of the wardrobe.

I blushed, glancing at myself in the mirror.

She was right...

I had quadrupled in size compared to when I had first arrived here. The physician told us that I was obese, and that—at my age and my height—I should weigh about one-hundred and ten pounds. In reality, I weighed over double that amount.

A whopping two-hundred and five pounds. I carried it well; my entire body had expanded, not just my belly.

That was, however, due to strength training my Keeper Knight had insisted upon because I had been so weak before.

I regularly partook in archery and knife-throwing competitions with the knights, and I enjoyed it as a hobby. I admittedly wasn't very interested in embroidery or sewing or knitting. I didn't care about tea and tea leaf oxidation and the process of coffee making, as many women my age in high society did.

So, my arms had subsequently gotten quite thick and my thighs and legs were thick from walking and squatting a lot.

Due to the weight gain, however, I had unfortunately struggled to find clothing that fit me.

Corsets were hard to find in my size, as most noblewomen were petite and thin, and while most noblewomen found them uncomfortable to wear...

It was excruciating for me.

When my Keeper Knight arrived about ten minutes later, I was ready to go.

I glanced at myself once more in the body-length mirror nearby.

I wore a light purple, shimmering gown with dark purple and golden embroidery patterned in flowers on the bodice.

There was a deep purple satin sash wrapped and tied in the back just below my bust. One good development of having gained weight was that my bust was quite large for my age, at least, and these gowns that accentuated the bust helped out in my favor.

Sir Halo gave me a bow. "You look lovely," he told me.

I sighed. He had gotten in a habit of telling me so because he knew how low my self-esteem was about myself, and I met his eyes.

I could hear in his thoughts and felt in his heart that he was sincere. He truly meant well.

He only wished to comfort me.

I nodded. "Thank you, Sir Halo. I just wish my husband agreed."

His face got sad. "I am sure he'll see it when he matures."

When he matures...

When would that be? He was already seventeen. He was one of the most serious, strictest people that I knew.

I couldn't imagine him ever being satisfied with someone like me.

I took his arm, and he led me through the halls and to the ballroom, where the ball was already in full swing.

The announcer called out my name, and we stepped inside. Sir Halo led me down the flight of stairs, and over to my father-in-law and mother-in-law.

I glanced around, but noticed one person—a key person—missing.

"...Where is Carlisle...?" I whispered.

His parents glanced around, seemingly just noting his absence, and they discreetly called over a knight to go and check his chambers.

As I was greeting guests...and hearing a lot of mocking, negative thoughts and sneers at me and my weight, what a shame I was on the prince...how it was obvious that he didn't want to be here because he would be embarrassed by me.

That nobody would want to willingly be with someone like me.

My face flushed, and I felt the singe of embarrassment.

Was this what Carlisle normally felt around me?

This was probably why he tried to be away from me most of the time, and why he hated being around me while we were in front of others.

This wasn't the only time that he'd sought to be busy in his office or training during events. He often did this even just at dinnertime, to avoid watching me eat.

He hated seeing me eat in general. He had never explicitly *said* that, but I could see the look of disgust on his face anytime that I consumed food.

It was about thirty minutes into the ball, and Carlisle had still not arrived. I motioned for Sir Halo to accompany me, and I stepped out of the room, heading through the halls to the office.

...Not there.

I sighed, going on through the halls once more until we came to the training hall. I stepped outside into the bitter cold of the biting wind, and with a warm cloak put around me by my Keeper Knight and lifted into his arms, we stepped out into the snow.

We walked around, and then I heard it; a giggling sound, like a tinkling bell.

I had my knight set me down, and I followed where the sound had come from.

There was a dark corner of the courtyard that was covered by an overhang and a bit closed in. I recognized it as a place for the knights to strip and spray off before changing into fresh clothes.

There was a thick tarp blocking it off from my sight, but as I got closer, I could hear a small moan, and my heart began pumping wildly as thoughts trickled into my head.

My knight startled me when he grabbed my arm, and I glanced back at him.

His eyes were wide and he shook his head no, desperately.

I knew.

I knew that he was trying to protect me from what I was about to find, but something in my heart pushed me forward.

I stepped up onto the ledge up and around so that I could see behind the screened off area...and my heart dropped to my stomach.

I felt nauseated.

Pants around his thighs, hands gripping his dark hair, I saw him there, moving wildly as he thrust into a woman whose face I couldn't make out.

It could be his brother, my mind tried to rationalize.

I knew it wasn't, though. If it was his brother, I would be able to read his thoughts by seeing his body with my eyes, just as I could hear her thoughts. I was just blocking out the sound of his name in her mind.

Still, my foolish, heartbroken mind couldn't stop pushing.

"C-Carlisle?" I said, soft, and he froze mid-thrust.

The giggling-moan stopped abruptly.

He whipped his face—wide-eyed and caught—around to see me.

Tears stung my eyes.

It was him.

It was my seventeen-year-old husband, skipping my official debut into high society, as his Crowned Princess, and making love to another woman in a shed outside in the middle of Nivis.

I turned, my feet stinging from the cold as snow covered my feet even in heels, and I waded as quickly as I could through and back into the palace.

Carlisle didn't call out for me. He didn't respond, or even move.

My heart spiraled downward as the reality set in. Like I had just been dropped in the ocean, plunged into suffocating darkness. In my mind's eye, I fell into a dark chasm. I felt like I was suffocating, and like I had just been punched in the gut at the same time. The air completely knocked out of me.

He didn't even try to stop me or plead with me to stay, or pretend that he cared that I'd caught him.

I didn't mean anything to him.

I tripped, and fell to my knee on the cold tiled floor. Halo rushed to my side, lifting me into his arms, and rushed through the halls with me.

"I don't want to go back to my chambers," I whispered. "I don't want to sleep in the same bed with him."

He nodded. "Yes, my princess," he said, abruptly turning down a hall and leading me through the halls.

I was confused at first, until I realized that we were going to the Sorcerer's quarters. Relief flooded me.

I was good friends with the sorcerer. I knew that he would let me stay there until we found other accommodations.

We reached his quarters, and he was just arriving back from the ball. "Your highness?" He asked when he looked up and noticed me.

Tears trailed down my cheeks. "C-Can I stay here, tonight?"

"...Your highness, what's wrong?" He asked, opening the door to his chambers and allowing us inside.

"We just caught the Crowned Prince..." Sir Halo said, soft.

"Caught the Crowned Prince?" Axel asked. "Caught him doing what? Why would you—" he froze when he took in my face. "Oh...oh, heavens," he said, dropping into a seat nearby. "Oh, I am so sorry, princess."

I shook my head rapidly, smiling bitterly through my sobs. "I knew he didn't love me, but I...I had thought that...he would be there tonight. For my debut, as his Crowned Princess. I thought he'd be there for me. I guess that it was just foolish. Foolish of me to hope that we'd...that he'd...ever actually come to love me. I'm so stupid!"

They both came to my side, wrapping me in a tight hug while I let it all out.

"You are not stupid, princess," Axel murmured.

"You are sweet, and kind, and far better than the Crowned Prince deserves," Halo said, hugging me.

I spent the rest of my sixteenth birthday crying into the night, until I couldn't keep my eyes open anymore and I fell asleep to the sound of my closest friends discussing where things would go from here.

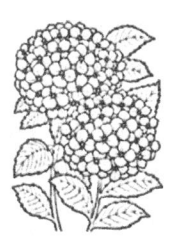

The following morning, I woke with a yawn and swollen eyes to find a spread of food on the sorcerer's table.

They both gave me sympathetic smiles, and I groaned, turning and laying back on the bed.

"Your highness...?" Sir Halo asked.

"Did..." I was so humiliated to even have to ask this question. "Did he...come to find me?"

They both cringed, but shook their heads.

So...he hadn't even cared that I didn't go to our bedroom and go to bed. He didn't care that I wasn't there.

"I'm sure you must be hungry, your high—"

"I don't want to ever eat again," I said, soft.

They both startled, glancing at one another.

"Your highness, starving yourself isn't a good way to deal with—" my sorcerer began, but I cut him off.

"My husband was—" I cleared my throat. "He...he had relations with another woman during my debut ball, on our shared birthday when I also happened to be coming of age. He skipped that event entirely to cheat on me," I sobbed. "It is because I'm a fat, ugly, stupid cow!" I wailed into my clenched fists, and they both wrapped me in a hug, just holding me and letting me cry.

"Your highness, you are not a fat—" Halo started, but I shot him a death glare. He sighed. "Okay. You are a bigger girl, I admit. But you are not ugly, and you might have been naïve and struggled along the way, but you are not stupid, and you are not a cow," he insisted. "You are a little fat, but I've seen people bigger than you, and you are young, your highness. If you get determined, if you want to lose that weight...I can help you. But I am telling you, your highness, you are not ugly. You are still beautiful, and you are one of the sweetest souls I've ever met in my life. Please...don't blame yourself for the Crowned Prince's transgressions."

That did actually make me feel a little better, because in both of their thoughts and feelings...they both truly felt that way.

They both sincerely felt that I wasn't ugly, and that I was beautiful and kind.

They couldn't fabricate those feelings.

"Thank you, both of you." I sighed. "So...what do I do now?" I asked.

"I suggest, your highness, that you go to the King and Queen about this."

"...Why?" I asked.

"Chances are, his highness hasn't told their majesties about the incident, and he hasn't been here." Axel took my hands in his. "You should ask them what to do."

I nodded, and I glanced at the table again.

I grabbed the apple sitting on the side, and stood, walking over to the door and glancing at my Keeper Knight. "Let's go," I told him.

He gave a small smile, and stood, opening the door for me and leading me out and through the halls to the office of my parents in law.

I knew that they had already eaten by this time, as it seemed to be late morning, and I knew that nobody was in the throne room unless there was business.

When I entered, my father-in-law looked up from his paperwork. My mother-in-law wasn't here.

"Where have you been?" He asked. "You rushed out last night and we didn't know what—" he froze. "Are you alright?" He asked me.

I felt my eyes burn all over again, and he stood, rushing over to me to take me into a hug as I started to cry.

Shushing and comforting, he rubbed my back in slow circles.

"What's the matter—" he glanced at my Keeper Knight, and his expression turned dark. "...No...surely, it couldn't have been him. It must have been someone else—" he glanced to me, and I let the memory of Carlisle looking back at me flutter to the front, even as I cringed. "So...it was him..." He said, considering. "And now, you want to know what to do?"

I nodded. "I...I can't sleep with and stay with someone who has cheated on me. This isn't a kingdom that allows mistresses, so..."

He sighed. "But you can't just leave," he murmured, and I could hear his underlying thoughts.

It was the first and foremost, highly crucial duty of a Seer to be with their counterpart Seer.

To love and cherish one another, and be a ruling couple.

In the history of the Seers, the only time that it hadn't gone well was when they hadn't been raised together and had killed the other, or one had been murdered, if I remembered right.

It was the most important thing for us to rule together as a harmonious, righteous couple over the kingdoms.

"But...I can't just stay with him," I whispered. "Please. Don't make me stay in the same room with him. Can't I stay in another room? Or one of the other palaces?"

He seemed to consider this, and he mulled over it in his mind as he glanced at the window, overlooking out to the estate.

There were three main palaces on the estate, as well as an annex property behind the central palace that was used for guests.

The central palace was used for the King and Queen. The western palace was used for the princes and their spouses. The eastern palace was used for the princesses—if there were any.

The royal family had a retirement villa out at the beach where they moved to once they were no longer the ruling family. So, Carlisle's grandparents and aunts and uncles lived at the retirement villa, for example, or other vacation villas in the kingdom.

"There aren't any princesses in the princess's palace, right?" I asked, hopeful. "Can't I stay there?"

He considered this. "Let me discuss this with the Queen," he said, and he motioned for me to follow him.

He led me through the hall to the end, where the King and Queen's chambers were located, and I felt my nerves grow.

I had only been in this room once, and I felt out of place here...because I knew that one day, when Carlisle and I were adults and he had become king, we would live in these chambers.

That was tradition.

We stepped into the room, and we found the Queen resting in bed, reading a book.

She looked up, and stood.

She waited a moment, reading the situation in mine and my knight's thoughts before she got a heartbroken expression on her face.

"I see," she whispered, nodding. "I suppose you can stay in the princess's palace," she said. "I am truly sorry," she told me, bringing me into a hug. "Carlisle has struggled for quite some time with all of this, and has always been a bit...harsh," she told me. "I will not force you to stay in the same room with someone who treats you this way."

"Thank you, mother," I said, hugging her.

She patted my back, before she sent for a knight to go and retrieve the Crowned Prince and bring him to the throne room.

While we were making our way to the throne room, my maids were summoned to go and pack my things.

When we arrived to the throne room, my husband stood there, and he sighed, giving a nod and looking away.

He knew why he was here.

He crossed his arms. "I see," he said. "So, she's already told you everything."

"How could you *do* such a thing?" His mother whispered, hugging herself. "To cheat on a spouse is horrible enough, but for you to cheat on her, after everything...for a Seer to cheat on his counterpart Seer, of all things!"

He sighed. "So, what is my punishment? A month in solitary confinement?"

"You aren't even taking this seriously," his father whispered, horrified. "You don't even *care* that you've seriously hurt your partner!"

Carlisle glanced at me. "*Partner*...where was she the first part of my life? Oh, that's right. *Missing.*"

"That—"

"How many years did I have to wait for her to go through training and learning for her to become a Royal Child's level of knowledge? Oh, that's right. She's *just now* there, at sixteen." He shrugged. "How many times has she embarrassed me? How many times have I heard thoughts that went like, 'oh, the poor Crowned Prince is stuck with a girl who must be humiliating to be with?' How many times have I heard the whispers and felt the stares? Even the girl from last night told me how sorry she felt for me, being stuck with...with **that**," he emphasized, glaring at me. "I let myself feel like a *man* for a change, rather than a babysitter or a parent!"

His mother shook her head, looking disgusted. "She's not the one who embarrasses and humiliates you...you are the one who does it to yourself, through your actions."

"We are giving the Princess's palace to her," his father said. "She will be moving out of your chambers, effective immediately."

He turned to me, looking shocked. "...What?"

"Did you think she'd want to stay in the same room—the same *bed*—as the man who shared himself with another woman? Who didn't even chase after her and apologize? The man who offers no apology, even now, and sees nothing wrong with his behavior?" His father asked.

"Still, to separate from me entirely—"

"You have wanted her to be separate from you for so long...well, now you get your wish. Congratulations. I hope your honor and dignity as a faithful husband and future king were worth it."

"But why would she get the princess's palace?" He asked.

"She is the Crowned Princess. You have no sisters; the princess's palace is empty. She is a princess, and she needs somewhere away from you to stay on the palace grounds."

"So?" He asked.

"'So?' She is a princess! That, and a Seer should stay in the Seer's kingdom, shouldn't they? Where else would you expect her to stay? Did you want to see her in the streets?" His mother asked.

He had no answer for that.

"You are at leisure to go to your new chambers, princess," my father-in-law said, finally.

Carlisle glared as I turned, walking out of the room.

CHAPTER 10

Kinley...

Veras's End, 519 Lawrence Dynasty

"Come on, you can do this!" Sir Halo encouraged, helping me with my weighted squats. "Keep going! You've almost got it!"

I pushed, finally making it straight with my legs not bent, and I gasped as I dropped the bar of weights to the ground. I panted, trying to catch my breath.

"Good job, your highness, you did it!" Halo grinned at me, bringing me a towel. "You reached one hundred reps!"

I smiled.

It had almost been two years since I had moved into the Princess's palace, and I hadn't seen the Crowned Prince except from a distance since I had moved.

It made me a bit sad and bitter to think about it, and what led us to this state, but I tried to bear in mind that I was well fed, I had a bed to sleep in and clothes and shoes to wear, and I wasn't being beaten.

That in itself was enough to make me extremely thankful and I felt blessed.

It was better than my childhood.

I had even lost a little of my abundant weight—about twenty pounds—in the last year and a half.

It was taking time, because I struggled so badly with eating out of stress and depression, but I was trying to get back to being thin.

Of course, my husband wouldn't know anything about the weight that I had lost.

I usually wore only baggy, modest clothes, and truth be told, I'd lost too little to really notice, anyhow.

That, and the only time we were around one another was at balls, banquets and meeting citizens for important business.

Even at balls and important banquets, he remained on the other side of the room or out of the room entirely.

There were rumors running rampant around the kingdom of the Crowned Prince's exploits.

He had continued to sleep with women, and quite popular among the noblewomen of the kingdom.

I could only cringe and seal away my heart—and shut off my mind—when I saw them fawning over and giggling at him.

Despite how he felt about me, I had truly cared for him and only wanted to make him happy.

It bothered me that he had been so dissatisfied with me, and even after everything...

I still had the inherent desire to be with him and for him to love me.

He had saved me from a life of abuse and misery and loneliness. He had bought all of my clothing—even since I had moved out of his chambers and into a palace all to myself—and had paid for all of my needs since I had arrived.

Thanks to my Knight, as well as the palace sorcerer and my maids, there was still plenty of food being brought to this palace, so Carlisle had no idea that I had lost any weight at all.

I was still far off from my goal, but I had lost a little bit of weight so I felt much better about myself already. It was working.

As Halo had told me...I just needed to trust the process.

I glanced out into the gardens from the window.

"I think that I want to take a walk," I smiled, and he grinned at me.

I stepped into the bathroom to get bathed and changed, before I came back out wearing a loose baggy dress.

Thanks to my weight, my servants no longer tried to force me to dress up or wear corsets, so I usually wore a dress that tied beneath my bust but didn't hug any curvature and didn't use a corset didn't make me look like I was struggling to pop out of my clothes.

Somehow, the corsets actually made me look bigger, almost.

I put on some sun-shades—a nifty, spectacle-type contraption that was tinted and kept the sun from hurting my sensitive eyes.

I took Sir Halo's hand, and he led me out into the large gardens that were shared between the three large palaces on the estate.

We walked, hand in hand, around the garden.

I was nearing my favorite of the flowers—the Hydrangeas with their stunning blue color—when I noticed someone there near the fountain. The fountain where *I* always sat.

My Keeper stepped in front of me. "Identify yourself," he said, tone firm and uncompromising.

"Oh, my apologies," the young man turned, facing us. He was handsome, with dark, silvery-brown hair and bright, vivid, mossy-green eyes. He was muscular, and wore noble clothing.

There was only one question on my mind.

"Who are you?" I asked, unable to keep my curiosity at bay. He was so handsome...

"I am Merik Arden, I am a Knight of the Arden dukedom," he said. "I have arrived on business with the King, but he told me to wait in the garden for a while because he was busy for a while. Who might you be?"

"I'm Princess Kinley," I said.

"Oh, that's right! You're the Light Seer Princess. I am sorry I didn't recognize you sooner, your highness."

"It's alright," I smiled. "Calm down, Sir Halo," I smiled, and he stepped out of my way. "So, what business are you here on?"

"Ah, well, it so happens that I was here because the King asked me to oversee help with the railways that are being built through the kingdom. We are helping fund it, and we are the ones who requested the construction for our business. Father gave me this project to prove my business sense because I'm getting ready take over the dukedom."

"Oh, congratulations," I grinned. "I hope that goes well."

"I also have hope that your relationship will improve with the Crowned Prince," he said, a bit embarrassed as he blushed. "There are a lot of rumors about his," he cleared his throat. "About his promiscuity and debauchery." He looked away. "My family has been on your side since we heard."

I felt my heart swell, and I blushed. "Thank you," I said. "I appreciate that."

"You are quite pretty," he said.

I blushed harder. "Oh, thank you," I said, smiling.

Even if he didn't mean it—and I couldn't read his thoughts about it—I appreciated that he tried to butter me up, anyway.

He winked at me, and turned, walking away. "I'll be around for a few months," he called out to me. "I'm sure I'll see you again."

The hours passed quickly, and I stepped outside to my garden table close by my palace, eating my supper in peace.

Once my maid had taken my dishes away, I sighed and leaned back, enjoying my tea.

"Your highness?" I heard the newly familiar voice, and I glanced over at Merik as he approached.

"Hello again," I smiled.

"What are you doing out here?"

"Oh, I eat my meals out here to myself often times, when the weather is nice," I laughed, soft. "I see the King and Queen occasionally, but I generally avoid the family meal times."

"I see," he said. "Might you like some company?"

"Sure," I told him. "Want some tea?"

"That would be great."

I sent one of the attendants to get another cup for him, and we sat there and drank tea for a while in silence as we ate some snacks.

"How long do you think you'll be staying at the annex?" I asked him. "I mean, I assume that's where you're staying?"

He nodded. "Yes, that's where I've been placed. The plan is six months, give or take, depending on how long the construction lasts."

"I see," I told him.

We continued drinking tea in silence for a while, before my maids told me that it was time for my bath and getting ready for bed.

"Well, I suppose I'd better let you get settled for the night," he said, standing and taking my hand in his. He bent at the waist, lifting my hand to press a kiss to the back of my hand. "Good night, your highness."

"Thank you. Good night, Lord Merik."

I watched him walk away.

My cheeks hot.

I jolted when I noticed Sir Halo watching me with an eyebrow raised and a small smirk on his face.

"W-what?" I asked.

He chuckled. "You totally have a crush on him," he snickered.

"Ugh! No, no I—" I paused when I noticed his expression, and I groaned as we walked through my palace. "Okay, okay. Yes, I have a crush on him. Sue me," I said, and he snickered again. I shrugged. "Can you blame me? My husband has been flaunting his trysts in front of my face, sleeping with any pretty noblewoman who will lift her skirt for him, and I—" I sighed, my shoulders drooping.

I was just a fat girl who'd never even had her first kiss...

He gave me a sympathetic expression, because he knew that already.

The last time I had seen my husband kissing a woman in the corner of the courtyard, I had told Halo that I was jealous that I'd never been kissed before.

He brought me in to wrap an arm around my shoulders, and he patted my shoulder.

"I know, your highness. Someday, I promise, you will have what you crave so badly," he smiled at me. "You're getting more beautiful by the day. Surely, he won't ignore you much longer."

"But I—" I sighed. "What if I...don't want to be his anymore? What if he's been with too many women?"

He glanced away. "...I don't know how to answer that, your highness. Realistically, that isn't going to work out well, but I just want to see you be happy."

I took him into a hug. "Thank you, Sir Halo."

Solaris's End, 519 LD

The days passed, and each day, I saw Lord Merik. Either in the gardens, or he would join me for my evening meal and tea.

It had been a couple of months since we'd met, now, and I felt myself blushing harder and struggling harder to keep my heartbeat steady around him.

He was so handsome, and his thoughts were always so kind and warm.

There was something weird about him, though. I felt like he was hiding something from me.

Every time I was around him, his thoughts were light but it felt like he was veiling something deeper.

My ability as a Seer only saw intent, emotion, and surface level thoughts.

I hoped that it wasn't anything important, whatever it was that he was hiding.

Still, I was using him as motivation to try to get fit faster. In the months since we had met, I had lost another five pounds, so that was fifteen pounds total that I had lost.

I was just thrilled to be under two hundred pounds, at any rate.

I was walking arm-in-arm with Merik one day in the gardens, when I heard Carlisle's voice.

I glanced ahead, noticing him walking with Valence while going over some papers.

Valence noticed us, and cleared his throat.

My husband glanced up at us, and froze in place. "...Kinley?"

"Hello, your highness," Lord Merik said, giving a bow at the waist. "I was just keeping her highness company," he said.

My husband smirked, raising an eyebrow at me. "So, is this your new *friend*?" He asked.

I paused. "We are friends," I smiled, acting none the wiser about his true meaning.

He chuckled darkly. "I hope you keep in mind that he should only be a friend, and not a '*friend*,'" he reminded me.

I felt a rush of anger rush through me.

Who did he think he was?!

He could sleep with anyone he wanted, but he reminded me that my friends should only stay friends?

"Is that a threat?"

"It's a warning," he told me. "I'm already stuck being married to you. Don't make anybody else be with you, yeah? After all, if you ordered it, they wouldn't have a choice, right?" He shrugged. "I would think that you'd care more about your '*friends*' than to order them to do something so..." He shuddered.

Despair spiked in my heart and poured into my body, making me feel both hot and cold as my eyes burned.

"Please pardon me," I said, turning away from him and tugging away from Merik. "I suddenly don't...feel very well," I murmured, making my way back to my palace even as my friend called out after me.

I made it into my palace before I collapsed, at least, and I gasped out for air as I clutched my belly.

"Your highness?" I heard called out, and I gasped, struggling to get to my feet.

"L-Lord Merik, I—"

"*Are you alright?*" He asked, bringing me into a hug, and the tears stung my eyes all over again.

...How...?

How did my husband make me feel so undesirable and unwanted and...and...*worthless* in one moment, and then...

Then, in the next, this man made me feel warm, fuzzy, and cared for?

I had to admit it.

After months of being friends, I had to admit that I liked—no, had feelings for—Merik. Sobs bubbled up out of me, and I felt him hug me tighter.

"He's wrong, you know. You're lovely, your highness. You're sweet, and you—forget it, I shouldn't say that."

"W-what?"

"Well, I...you wouldn't need to *order* me," he said, sounding a bit sheepish.

I gasped, pulling back and looking up at him. He chuckled, looking away, and I could picture him kissing me in his thoughts.

He...wanted to kiss me...

He wanted to kiss me?

"You wouldn't need to order me to be with you, or to...you know, *be with you*," he said, a blush tinting his cheeks.

I smiled. "Thank you," I told him, blushing myself.

"I, um...I should be getting back. I just wanted to make sure that you were okay," he smiled. "I'll talk to you later, your highness." Then he turned, walking away, and I saw my Keeper Knight step around him to come to me.

"Your highness," he said. "Are you alright?"

I sniffled, nodding, and he took me by the arm and led me through the halls to my chambers.

"I'm so sorry the Crowned Prince made you feel that way, Princess."

I shook my head. "No, it's my fault. If I hadn't gained all that weight to begin with, and if I'd been smarter and done better...maybe he could have loved me. I was such a fool to think anyone ever could," I sobbed. "My parents didn't want me. My husband doesn't want me. Nobody else wants me." I shrugged. "It's fine. That's alright. I can...I can love myself enough for everyone else," I said, hugging myself.

He leaned forward, pressing a kiss to my forehead, and I blushed thickly as I gaped up at him.

"You aren't the only one who loves you," he told me. "I love you. Maybe not *romantically*, but you're like a little sister to me."

I gave a small laugh. "Thank you, Halo."

"Seriously, though," he told me. "My older brother rescued you. I've been with you since you were seven years old, your highness. You're going to turn eighteen in just a couple more months, so...we've been together for eleven years."

I hugged him. "You're like a big brother to me, too. More so than my brothers-in-law. You, Sir Axel and Sir Valence are family to me," I said.

He smiled. "Aw, thank you, your highness. Come on, let's get you a healthy snack, hm?"

I laughed, and we went to do just that.

Chapter 11

Merik Arden...

Seed's Sewn, 519 Lawrence Dynasty

"Are you sure you can do it?" The Southern Queen asked me, hands on her hips. "You *really* think you can keep your deep thoughts veiled properly?"

I groaned, shrugging in an exaggerated way. "Look, your majesty. I got it. Keep my thoughts veiled with happy, warm, fuzzy thoughts or busy with railroad talk on the surface. Don't think about the real mission—at all—and do it instinctively once I know she trusts me enough. Plus, it shouldn't be hard to gain her trust. She's fat and lonely, and from the rumors running rampant in the entire kingdom, Carlisle cannot even hide his disgust for her." I shrugged again. "She's probably so isolated that she won't even check my deeper thoughts, anyway. The first signs of love and tenderness, and she'll melt like this," I said, snapping my fingers.

The King nodded, sighing. "Good. Be sure that you succeed. As long as Prince Carlisle is there to block our attempts to reach her, we aren't going to be get her, but from what I've heard...he's been doing our job for us."

"So, we're all in the know, right? Get her to turn against Carlisle? Make her think we love her and that we regret letting her go?"

"Right."

"Good. Convince her that Carlisle has been—because he has—blocking our letters to her and our attempts to ask for forgiveness? That we just sent her away because we were terrified that the Northern Kingdom would make her hate us?"

"Oh, and convince her that Carlisle is the source of all her pain and suffering," I added.

That should be simple enough.

Veras's End, 519 LD

She was different than I had imagined.

She wasn't just fat and ugly as I had anticipated.

In fact, she had a very pretty face, and her white hair was luxurious and shiny and her golden eyes were bright and luminous.

She was chubby—rounded and soft and squishy, yes, but she was so much more than just that.

She was softspoken and quiet, but her laugh tinkled and her dimples when she smiled were adorable.

She had a very child-like innocence about her, making my inherent mission so much easier to complete...but so much *harder*, too.

It seemed that her parents had been correct—thinking about regular business and happy thoughts on top of the deep thought in my mind kept them at bay, and that was their weakness as Seers.

A Seer could only sense intent in the moment, emotional state, and top-layer thoughts. That could be their downfall.

As long as someone knew how to veil their thoughts and true intentions, a Seer was defenseless.

I did notice, however, that my interactions with the Crowned Prince were a bit...different than the other Seers—as in, his parents and wife.

He looked at me more suspiciously, glared at me.

Days passed into weeks, though, and though he still glared at me, he never outright said anything.

I made sure to keep my thoughts light and focus on business around him. I tried my best not to think about the princess.

It amazed me how, even now, she was living in an entirely separate palace. Things were worse than the kingdom even knew, honestly.

He had isolated himself from her so severely that he had moved her into her own palace to get her away from him...?

I still couldn't understand why.

She was a little thick, but she was still pretty and very sweet. Her face was very pretty, and she had a ton of potential...

I couldn't fathom why he treated her the way that he did.

I even caught him kissing another woman one day, and when he spotted me, he just turned and walked away with the woman.

I couldn't imagine being our age and not wanting to be with a woman who had literally been my partner since birth.

That made me feel a lot less guilty for turning her against him, or pursuing her in general.

I actually didn't mind it.

The months passed by, and as I spent time with her, I came to really enjoy it.

When her husband sneered at her and told her that she shouldn't drag a man into her bed, basically...

I got angry when she ran off, crying.

He had completely destroyed this woman.

How had he done it so thoroughly?

How had he destroyed her entire spirit?

She was so timid, so afraid of love...

I had been right, after all. The most minimal amount of tenderness had her falling. Her desperation for the slightest hint of affection could and would be her downfall.

It was sad, really, how easy and simple it was.

Her blushes and the way she fidgeted with her hands and her eyes skittered away from mine each time I made eye-contact with her were all it took for me to know that she was completely enamored with me.

It had been far too simple, too easy to accomplish, and it bothered me, in a way.

I knew that her parents only wanted to use her, but I had a lot at stake in this too.

I hadn't lied to the Northern King and Queen, or to Kinley; this was a test to prove my ability to run the dukedom.

However, there was...a bit more at stake if I failed my mission.

If I did not complete my task, at least to the majority degree, then my father—who was being held captive—would be forfeit, and I would inherit the dukedom.

It had all been an elaborate ruse for me to use to get Kinley to trust me easily.

Her parents may not know her, but they were right on the money. They knew exactly how to play her, which was strange, considering that they'd never met her.

From what I'd been told, Sir Enock had been tortured into spilling all of his information about her to them before they had him executed.

Even that, though, hadn't been a great deal of information, really.

It mostly seemed to be a guess on their part, but it was terrifying how spot-on and accurate they really were about it.

Folias's Blessing, 519 LD

I was walking with her again...

Last week, I'd managed to stroke her cheek before she insisted that we stop. Today, I was hoping for something...a little more intimate.

It had taken a few weeks to get to hold her hand, and a few more to get to touch her face, shoulder or hand freely without her scampering away from me.

She had resisted for quite some time, and despite that she and her husband were certainly not on good terms, I had to admire her perseverance in trying to remain true to him alone.

It was admirable and a true testament to her loyalty, even to someone as undeserving as Crowned Prince Carlisle.

I walked with her to the edge of the gardens, hidden by rows and rows of flowers, and she gasped and gaped at me for a moment when she'd noticed where I had taken her.

She looked up at me with surprise, eyes wide.

I leaned in, ever so slowly, and pressed my lips beside her ear.

"May I kiss you?" I whispered, and she shuddered against me...before she gave the barest nod.

I leaned in, just as slowly and patiently, and I could practically see her pupils dilate as her pulse raced beneath my fingers on her neck as I brought her jaw up and her face closer.

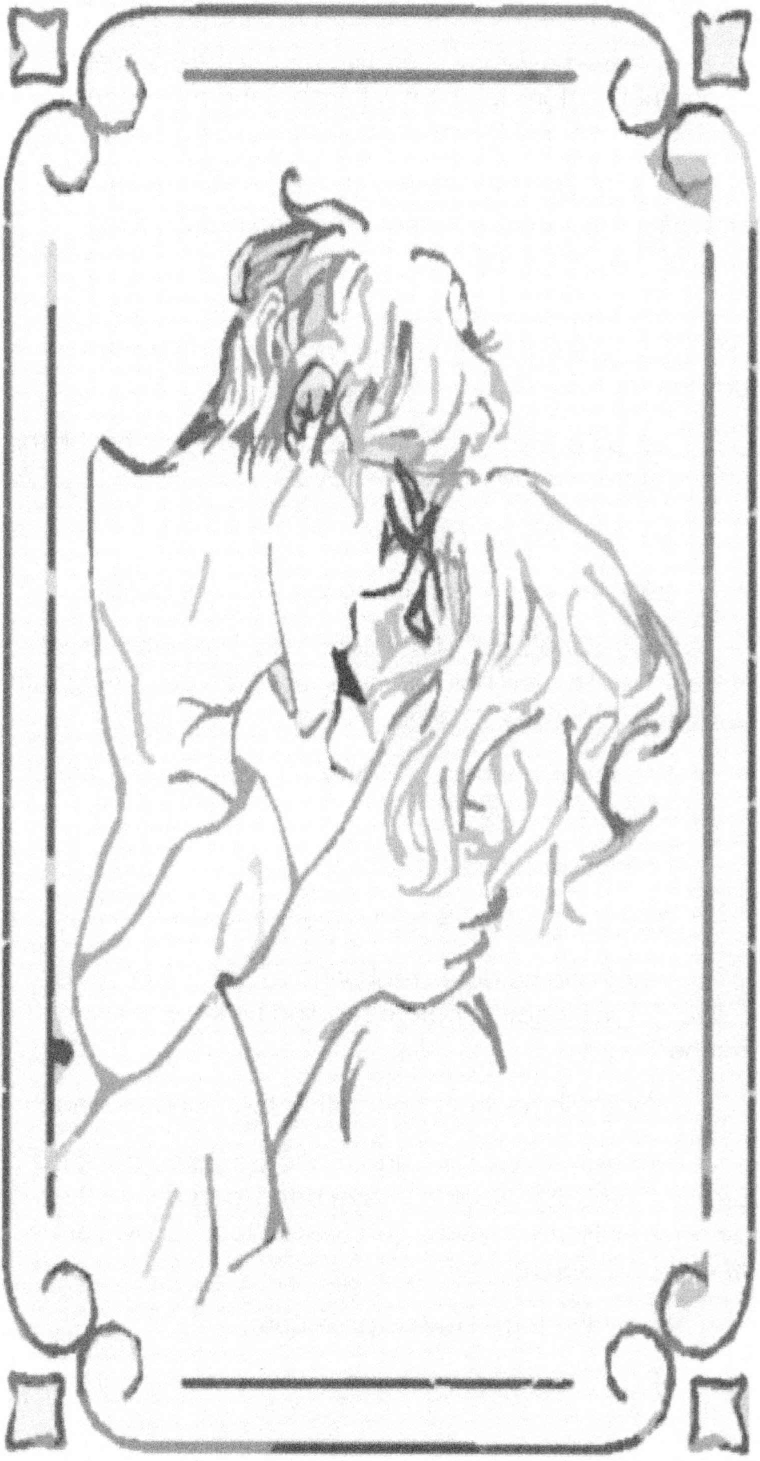

I pressed my lips to hers, and she gasped shakily.

I pressed my lips to hers two more times, before I nudged her bottom lip down with mine and moved my mouth open against her own...and she followed me.

She gasped into my mouth breathlessly as I tasted her, swirling my tongue into hers, and she moaned as I chuckled into her mouth.

I gripped her short curly hair in my hands, before stroking the shells of her ears and finally moving back to study her face.

Her pale, creamy skin was blazing red with her blush, and she stared at me with dazed eyes.

She was far, far too easy.

Truly, the epitome of being easy to manipulate...

I kissed the back of her hand. "So, I hear that there will be a Nivis Solstice ball coming soon. Are you...going with the Crowned Prince?" I asked.

She shook her head. "He hasn't gone as my partner to any formal event before."

I cringed internally.

That scumbag...he really didn't deserve her.

What had he done, really? Have a sorcerer use a spell to get her location before sending his Keeper Knight after her?

What had he really done other than fund the search?

Honestly, even if she had managed to go back to her parents, it probably wouldn't have been long before they had sent her North anyway...just twisted for their own ends, rather than being rescued.

I couldn't forget my purpose here.

No matter how sweet and innocent she was, I had a job to do.

"It is such a shame that he treats you so poorly, your highness. You deserve a real man."

She blushed, looking away. "Surely, I'm not very pleasant to deal with, though. I know that I don't have any value—"

"You do," I said, taking her into my arms to hug her again. "You are worth more than you could ever realize."

That was truth.

"Believe me, your highness, if you knew what I knew…"

"What…?" She asked, surprised. "What do you know?"

I shook my head. "I shouldn't tell you until it is confirmed, but once I have proof…I will tell you."

Oh, I would tell her.

I would tell her at the perfectly opportune time.

"I don't want to make any accusations before I have hard evidence," I told her.

Which was also the truth.

Year's Fall, 219 LD

    It was just the day before the Nivis Solstice, and I had gotten the concrete evidence I had needed; I had rummaged through the Crowned Prince's paperwork until I had found the list of orders he had given to his soldiers, and there near the bottom—listed just after her arrival here—was the order to shoot down any messenger birds from the South and dispose of their letters.

    This was the hard proof evidence that he had kept her parents' letters from reaching her, and I could see just how elaborately they had planned this.

    I remembered the order that I had received; to make sure that she turned against him, and that—if possible—I kill the Crowned Prince.

    It was funny, to me, how he had been so wary and paranoid around me for so long, but after so long of proving that I hadn't intended him any harm, he had started to drop his guard.

    If anything, he was entertained around me, now, because I actually showed interest in his estranged young wife.

    I knew, from talking to her personal Keeper Knight, that I had been her first kiss. I had suspected that was the case already, but to hear it so blatantly admitted by someone so close to her…

    I felt a bit bad.

    She deserved so much better.

I could only hope that my plans worked out the way that I intended for them to.

I met her outside for our daily walk, and I took her to our special spot—the spot by the rows of bright blue hydrangeas, although it was all just the green bush, now.

I gave her a quick kiss on the cheek, before I pulled out the rolled-up document and showed it to her.

"I found something. Your parents...they tried to reach out to you," I told her. "It seems that they were begging for forgiveness, and all of their attempts to contact you were thwarted. I found a letter," I said, pulling out the letter they had asked me to give her when the time was right.

It detailed that they had tried to make amends, that they had turned over a new leaf and regretted what they had done.

It also mentioned that they had been begging for a chance to earn forgiveness since she had arrived, and that they'd never been able to reach her.

The document I had taken from the Crowned Prince showed that his order had been made just after she had arrived, so that was the proof.

"I am sorry, your highness...I found this letter on a bird that was shot down outside of the walls, and when I found it, I sort of wondered about what it meant and what was going on. It seemed that someone was trying to keep you from hearing from them, and I wasn't sure if that was by your will or not, so I at least address it."

She paused, giving me an odd look before looking to the letter and reading over it, and then the document from the prince.

"...How did you come by this...?"

"I...I took it without permission, but only because I was worried for you," I stressed.

She looked a little suspicious, but she gave a timid nod, before turning away from me.

"Thank you," she said, taking a step to walk away before she turned back to me. "Do you have a partner for the ball tomorrow?" She asked.

I shook my head. "No, your highness."

"Will you be my partner?"

"I would love to, your highness," I smiled brightly.

I could only hope that my plans worked out the way that I intended for them to.

I met her outside for our daily walk, and I took her to our special spot—the spot by the rows of bright blue hydrangeas, although it was all just the green bush, now.

I gave her a quick kiss on the cheek, before I pulled out the rolled-up document and showed it to her.

"I found something. Your parents...they tried to reach out to you," I told her. "It seems that they were begging for forgiveness, and all of their attempts to contact you were thwarted. I found a letter," I said, pulling out the letter they had asked me to give her when the time was right.

It detailed that they had tried to make amends, that they had turned over a new leaf and regretted what they had done.

It also mentioned that they had been begging for a chance to earn forgiveness since she had arrived, and that they'd never been able to reach her.

The document I had taken from the Crowned Prince showed that his order had been made just after she had arrived, so that was the proof.

"I am sorry, your highness...I found this letter on a bird that was shot down outside of the walls, and when I found it, I sort of wondered about what it meant and what was going on. It seemed that someone was trying to keep you from hearing from them, and I wasn't sure if that was by your will or not, so I at least address it."

She paused, giving me an odd look before looking to the letter and reading over it, and then the document from the prince.

"...How did you come by this...?"

"I...I took it without permission, but only because I was worried for you," I stressed.

She looked a little suspicious, but she gave a timid nod, before turning away from me.

"Thank you," she said, taking a step to walk away before she turned back to me. "Do you have a partner for the ball tomorrow?" She asked.

I shook my head. "No, your highness."

"Will you be my partner?"

"I would love to, your highness," I smiled brightly.

Chapter 12

Kinley...

Year's Fall, 519 Lawrence Dynasty

It was the night before the Nivis Solstice ball, and I was left wondering what I was to do with this information.

Was this a security breech?

Did I need to tell someone about this?

I had to wonder how truthful my birth parents were being about their intentions, as well. Were they truly repentant?

I couldn't even be sure because I had never met them.

If they were, what was I supposed to be feeling right now?

I felt a mixture of things. I felt upset, and hurt, and bothered.

Carlisle hadn't even let a single letter in? With him, I couldn't even know if he had done it as a protective measure, or if he had done it to spite me.

After all, if he didn't want me here so badly, wouldn't it be better to send me back home to them? What did he care about what happened to me?

He had made his position on me, my feelings, and my general safety quite clear.

Did my parents...truly miss me?

Had they just been irritated because they had known that I would be sent to the North, anyway, and that they wouldn't get a chance to get to know me?

I couldn't imagine having a child that turned out to be a Seer and losing my child right away just so they could grow up in a life-long marriage to another child.

I had to imagine that it would be hard to get close to and love a child when you knew that they were going to be sent away immediately and probably raised to hate you...as they had tried to do with me.

They talked badly about the Southern kingdom all the time, but how much of that was the truth?

They even told me in the letter that they had punished Sir Enock for harming me, and had executed him.

So...where did I go from here?

I knew that I was angry at Carlisle. I wasn't mad that he had stopped the letters, necessarily, but I was livid that he hadn't ever even told me.

Nobody had told me.

I was just a girl that had been isolated in this palace to myself for the last couple of years, and had been isolated even in the main central palace while I had lived there.

My brothers-in-law weren't close to me.

My parents-in-law almost never saw me, now that I lived here. They hadn't come to see me here.

I only saw them at events, or if I went to see them for anything.

I wasn't part of this family, and despite that my knight, the sorcerer and Merik told me that I was loved and that they cared about me, and that I had value...

Everyone else, it seemed, sought to prove them wrong.

The following day, I was getting ready and met my partner outside of my bedchambers.

He looked handsome in a dark navy-blue suit with a light purple neck scarf and vest that matched the gown I had picked out.

This gown hugged my body tightly, and I was even wearing a corset! It was a beautiful, light purple with a deep, navy blue sash and navy embroidery around the train. You could tell I had lost a little bit of weight, at least, since the last time I had worn a corset.

I'd had makeup put on, and my hair done in a pretty waterfall braid around my head like a crown, all but the front.

I wore a tiny tiara that was black in my hair, though, as I knew that at any formal event, it was customary for the Crowned Prince to wear a silvery-white crown on his head.

Even though I was angry, hurt, and betrayed...I still thought of him.

Even though I was seeking to make Merik my lover—possibly—I still thought of Carlisle.

All I had wanted was to be part of his world. To belong to him, make him happy.

Today, I was determined to show him what he stood to lose if he did, indeed, lose me...and he was very close to that point.

We arrived to the ballroom, and as we were announced, everyone gaped at us as we strode into the room.

The gasps, murmurs, and whispers didn't bother me.

The thoughts running rampant about how I had lost weight since they had last seen me, wondering if I had always been so beautiful when made up this way.

I had asked the maids to spend extra time making me look nice, so it was nice that it was such a change compared to normal.

Those thoughts boosted my confidence, and I felt myself stand taller.

My brothers-in-law and parents-in-law all openly gaped at me, stunned to see me openly escorted by another man—but also to see me so beautiful. I had never been so dolled-up before.

I was certain that nobody had anticipated it.

Though, I noted with satisfaction that Valence, Halo and Axel all smirked and glanced to see how the prince was reacting to me.

I was exceedingly pleased that even though there was a woman on his arm, the Crowned Prince openly ogled me, staring at me with wide, surprised eyes. He hadn't expected for me to ever look this good...even with my being fat.

It had been two entire years since I had started this journey for my health and my self-esteem, but I had managed to lose—in total—about twenty pounds, now, and I felt much lighter in both weight and spirit.

I definitely wanted to keep this going.

Not for him or for anyone else, but for myself. I felt much better, physically and mentally.

I was still far off from my goal, but I was closer than I had been when I had started, and was thanks to Sir Halo's work and encouragement, insisting that I trust the process.

Valence and Halo had helped me to do it right.

I was still thick, but I was thinner than I had been, and I held a new air of femininity that I hadn't before. I carried myself like a woman, rather than a girl.

I smirked at Carlisle, who didn't even respond, before I turned my attention away; back to Merik.

I could practically feel the heat of Carlisle's glare burning us, but I ignored him.

This was what he deserved.

After all, I was still furious with him.

As we were sitting and chatting at dinner, where I was eating only a small salad and a boiled egg—something that surprised everyone but was a usual meal for me, now, rather than the pastas and fatty foods that I had been used to eating—Carlisle came up to me.

"May I speak to you, please, princess?" He asked.

I nearly swallowed my bite of food without chewing, and I had to clear my throat and chew for a moment before I finished my bite. I glanced to my date, and he gave me a nod.

"Sure," I said, standing and walking over to the exit with him.

We stepped out of the room into the hall just outside of the ballroom, and he looked me up and down.

"You...you look—" he scratched the back of his head. "I can't...believe that you...I..." He huffed, flustered.

Was he...about to *compliment* me?

My hopes soared for a moment. I was sure that he was about to compliment me, and I was almost ashamed at how excited I was to hear his praise. Was I really this pitiful for this man's attention...?

"You *actually* came here with another man!" He said, frustrated, and water immediately drenched the sparks of hope that had been gathering in my mind.

It was then that my anger reached a boiling point.

"How dare you...?" I asked, stepping up to him and getting in his face. "Who was it that was caught plowing his manhood inside of another woman at my social debut ball? That was on our shared birthday, by the way! *Who* has slept around the noble ladies of the court like a whore? I am sure that by now, all of the ladies of noble birth and most of the commoners around the palace have had a chance to get intimately close with you, '*your highness,*'" I emphasized. "I finally feel confident in myself. I know that I am beautiful and worthy, and *you* are *not* the one who instilled that in me. You have the nerve to get angry that I brought a date, but you yourself had a woman on your arm when I walked in!" I shouted, and he gaped openly at my tirade.

I turned, and I took a deep breath, calming myself before rushing back into the room.

I reached my table and sat once more with my closest friends and my date.

"What nerve," Sir Halo muttered. "To think that he called *you* out to seemingly scold *you*! He has no right," he grumbled.

"Your highness, please don't get upset," Sir Valence offered me a handkerchief as my eyes began to burn. "He's just...hard to deal with."

"I believe that I'll go and ask the Crowned Prince to refrain from blaming you," Merik said, standing. "It wasn't your fault to begin with. How could I not fall for you?" He winked at me.

Just as he was walking toward the Crowned Prince, however, I heard the faintest thought.

When I heard it, I thought right away that I couldn't possibly have heard it correctly.

There was no way that it was real.

I heard...

What...?

'Worst-case scenario, the princess should defend me, since I have her wrapped around my finger. Besides, she's so upset and angry at him that she might just thank me. All I have to do is angle it the right way—'

I couldn't even believe it. Was he...planning to attack Carlisle?

I couldn't understand.

I looked, quickly, as the Crowned Prince stood with his back facing our direction.

There were no people between us and the prince, as Merik approached him, and I saw Merik's hand reach for under the edge of his pants where—

There was a knife strapped there!

I didn't even think. I didn't think about it at all, because I was acting before my thoughts could even catch up.

I may be angry and hurt by him, but there was no way that I could bring myself to let him get hurt. He had saved me from abuse, and he had arguably caused me much strife and horror the last decade, but I couldn't bring myself to forsake him entirely.

I jumped up, leaping into action, and I bolted toward the two.

Both of our knights were up, but it was too late. They couldn't reach us fast enough.

"No!" I cried out in a shout, and just as the ducal heir lunged to jab the knife into my husband...

I dove between them.

Carlisle whipped to face us, gaping as he saw the scene happen even as I felt it in what felt like slow-motion.

Merik's eyes went blown wide as he saw me intercede, but it was too late.

I gasped as the dagger plunged into my shoulder, which was level with where Carlisle's heart would have been.

Carlisle caught me in his arms, and Merik stepped back quickly, hands up in surrender as the knights tackled him to the ground.

I sobbed and gripped my husband as he called my name, clinging to me and eyes full of tears.

"Kinley!" He sobbed. "Oh, no, oh, *heavens*...Kinley!"

I was amazed that he was actually concerned.

"Don't just stand there! Save her!" He shouted off at someone, tone hoarse and harsh.

I couldn't focus, but I could vaguely see Merik crying out that it was an accident as he was dragged away and I could see my closest friends swarming around me.

Then, everything turned dark.

Was this how my life came to an end?

Chapter 13

Carlisle...

It was a nightmare. A complete and total nightmare.

Not only had she shown up to the ball—looking completely stunning, despite being chubby—but she had shown up with another man!

That irked me, for some reason.

Maybe if it had been another man, it would have been different, but just a few weeks ago, I had read in his thoughts how earning her love wasn't even difficult because I was such a shitty husband...that I was just a fool who didn't realize her value.

I had realized today, however, just how much value she had and how amazing she truly was when she took a dagger through the shoulder for me.

I had dropped to my knees, taking her in my arms and pulling her into my chest...the first embrace I'd given her in many years.

I now was regretting everything that I had done to her up to this point. She had just taken a dagger for me.

She had taken a dagger for me, and I had never done anything to deserve it.

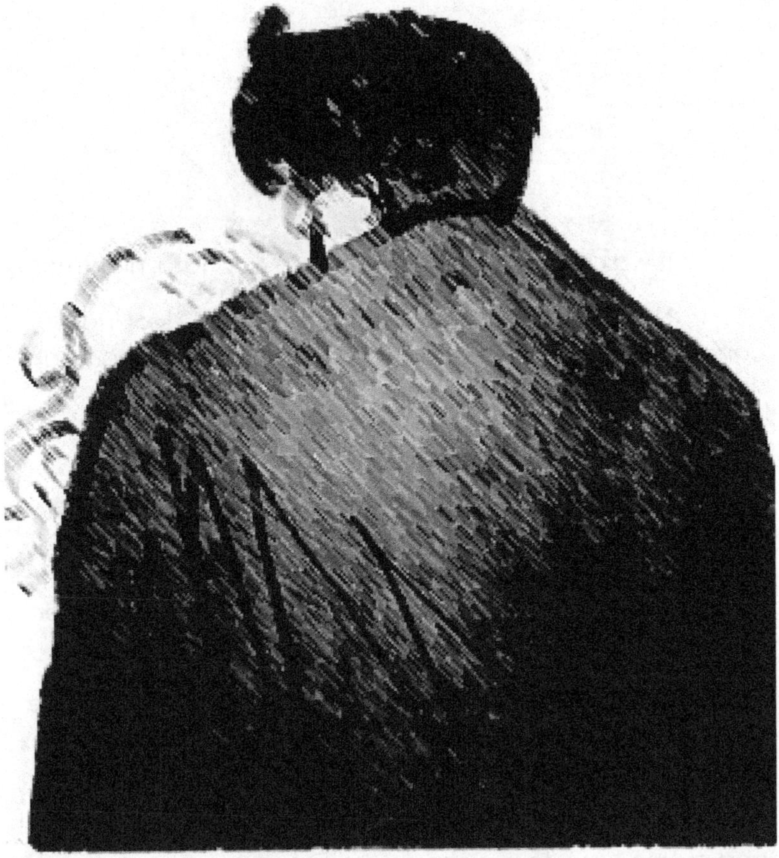

Luckily, after we had rushed her to a bedchamber and gotten her seen to, the sorcerer and the healer had told us that it was a severe injury, but it wasn't fatal.

It had missed anything vital, and my relief was so stark that it made my heart feel like it would drop out of my butthole.

They told us that she may have to re-learn how to use that arm, because the nerves were damaged, but that with the help of physical therapy, it shouldn't be an issue long-term.

In the dungeon, Merik admitted that *I* had been the target, originally, and that her parents had hired him and taken his father hostage—with the condition that to ensure his release, he was to woo Kinley and turn her against me.

The goal was to, ultimately, kill me, but if that didn't work…driving a permanent wedge between us and bringing her back to the Southern Kingdom, returning half of the power to them as it were, was a sufficient enough goal for the time being until they could use her to start a war with me.

He also informed me, under enough pressuring, that he had already informed her that I'd cut off all ability to contact her from her parents, and given orders to shoot down any of their messenger birds as they were clearly marked.

He showed me the letter that he'd given to Kinley, showing that they were trying to frame me from keeping her "repentant parents" from her to spite her and hurt her further.

My promiscuous past behaviors only helped to solidify the idea, and I felt as if I were the biggest fool.

I had played right into that plan with my actions, and they had truly read the situation and planned fervently in advance.

Anger roared through me even as the healers worked over my wife…who no longer looked quite so unappealing to me.

She had taken a dagger for me.

She had literally saved my life.

I had gotten the most minimal of scratches from the dagger, just over where my heart rested in my chest, and I realized with utter horror just how close I had come to being murdered.

This man would have killed me, if she hadn't jumped between us.

I made a decision, there and then. Though it may be completely impossible to restore my reputation and impossible to erase the past...

I could start fresh, making myself a good husband anew.

I would give up the debauchery and whoring around. I would stop drinking. I would stop all of my bad behaviors, and dedicate myself entirely to this amazing woman who had saved my life...even when I had done absolutely nothing to earn it.

I would respect this woman whom I had neglected to do so up until now.

She didn't *have* to risk her life to save mine. She could have been entirely justified to let her lover just kill me.

I could only hope and pray, now, that she would accept my affections for her...or, even if she didn't return them, if she could just let me love her and be around her, I would make myself be satisfied with that.

Days passed, and after four days unconscious...Kinley awoke. When I felt her stir, I was up on my feet at her side, and her eyes focused on me slowly.

"C...Car...?"

"Don't try to talk," I told her. "You need to let your throat adjust. You've been asleep for four days."

Her eyes went wide, and she gaped at me as I grasped her hand and held it in mine.

She looked down at my hands, and then up at my face in confusion.

"You...you saved my life, Kinley. With how I have treated you, with everything I've said and done...you didn't have to. Why...why did you?"

She glanced away. "I...no choice."

"No choice...?" I asked.

"Body...just acted," she admitted, voice hoarse and scratchy. "I couldn't...let you...get hurt."

I gave a small laugh, smiling softly at her. "So, it was just an act of instinct. That's alright," I smiled. "It is thanks to you that I lived, even at the risk of your own life. Thank you, Kinley."

She sighed, looking away. "What...why are you here?" She asked, and I cringed when I saw tears well in her eyes, running down the sides of her face and into her hair.

"What do you—"

"Don't play stupid with me, your highness," she said, and I almost bit my tongue when she turned formal on me. "You have ignored, neglected and spited me since we were children. No matter how hard I tried, you did your best to act like I was an annoying bug in your path. Why are you here, acting like you...like you care about me? Why are you pretending to give a shit?"

I startled, shocked by the curse and by her brashness.

I had never seen her so angry. I had been shocked at the ball, when she'd gotten in my face and defended herself against me, but for her to initiate an altercation against me...?

This had never happened before, and I was shocked.

"Kin—"

"If you're going to pretend you have sudden interest in me and be buddies with me until you get bored once the awe from saving your life wears off...then don't bother." She sniffled. "I didn't...save you for you to have temporary interest in me. I saved you because my body just acted. It wasn't...a conscious decision," she sobbed.

I gave a solemn nod, taking in what she told me. "Then, I will just have to prove to you that it isn't temporary."

She flinched, and turned her eyes to me. "W...what...?"

"I will change. I already have not had a single drop of alcohol since you—"

"Alcohol...?" She asked, surprised.

Oh...

It hit me, then, just how in the dark she was about my problems.

How unaware she was of the full situation I was in.

"I've been an alcoholic for a long time," I admitted. "Since just before you...just before you found me, that night of your debut ball."

She simply watched me wordlessly, in shock. I had stunned her into silence.

"I will give up the habits, and I will stop whoring around. I will respect you and earn your trust again. I will—"

I froze when she started to laugh, softly at first but then it grew until she was coughing from laughing too hard.

"That is funny," she murmured. "But I don't believe you, and I won't take that seriously. You've never respected me, and it won't be long until you lose this newfound 'respect' you magically gained just because I took a dagger for you. As I said...you are in awe and feel beholden because I saved you, much how I felt toward you because you saved me. That will wear off and you will get bored and annoyed with me yet again, and I won't be hurt by it because I will not have expected anything from you to begin with."

I nodded, taking that in. "That's fair," I conceded. "But I will prove it to you."

Then, I stood, and walked out of the room.

I decided that I would join her for at least one meal and one tea-time each day, and that I would leave gifts for her.

I would take her on nice trips.

I would gain her trust, and her affection, and I didn't care how long it took.

Nivis's End, 520 LD

Getting closer to Kinley...was *much* harder than I had originally anticipated.

She got annoyed with me quickly because I had tried to visit her for every meal time...so I had cut back my visits to only twice each day. When I cut it to that amount, she didn't act quite so frustrated, so I figured that this number of visits was acceptable to her.

I didn't want to piss her off too much. That wouldn't work well in my favor, for sure.

I visited her once in the morning for breakfast, and once in the evening for tea-time and a walk.

She didn't talk to me much, and when I tried to talk to her about anything, she wouldn't respond much beyond the bare minimum or short, curt responses.

She would just watch me with wary, collected and overtly calm eyes.

it had been a long journey in physical therapy, from what the sorcerer told me, but she had finally gained a little control over her arm. She was able to move the fingers again, so that was a good thing, and she could even grasp and hold a pen, now.

Finer movement and refined function with the fingers were still difficult, of course, but she was making progress.

I tried to talk to her about work things, personal things, and the like. I wanted to get closer to her, but she was like an iron wall.

Now that I was nineteen, my training as the Crowned Prince to take over the kingdom had truly begun in earnest, and I found my list of tasks and duties growing ever longer, but I still made sure to make time for my Crowned Princess.

I learned a few things, though, despite her refusal to cooperate with me.

She strongly favored the color purple, lavender, and the blue of hydrangeas—which happen to be her favorite flower, I discovered.

She was not fond of sweets, and preferred savory foods...though, I noticed that she didn't eat much meat.

She ate almost only fish, with a few chicken or duck dishes on occasion, and she mostly ate vegetables.

She loved strawberries and blueberries.

Her favorite thing to eat was pistachios.

She absolutely adored coffee, and the desserts she most preferred were tiramisu and coffee cake.

She enjoyed watching it snow, and would watch it for hours on end by the fireplace with a cup of warm coffee-cocoa, as her maid called it.

She enjoyed reading, as I often found her reading romance novels; especially ones steeped in history.

Her favorite of them all seemed to be about Emperor Kai Abeloth and his Empress, Nieves. She was completely fascinated by the dragons, and had seemingly dreamed of having one for her own.

Too bad that the dragons were extinct well over five hundred years ago...or else I would see to it that she got to have one.

One day, I was following her along her walk when she paused, seeing a bird that was flying overhead—unfortunately for me, the timing of her being outside and this bird from her parents just happened to be at the same time today—and she cringed when it was shot down.

"You...you're still shooting down letters from my parents," she said, blandly.

Cautiously.

"Well, I...I, um..." I sighed. "After what happened with Merik, the fact that he stabbed you because he was trying to stab me and you jumped in the way, and he admitted himself that they planned it—"

"But what if I want to see what they have to say?" I asked. "What if...what if they really do *miss* me?"

I looked into sad, scared golden eyes, and I realized something about my bride in that moment.

She truly was desperate to find love. Somewhere, anywhere.

...Even the parents who had abandoned her.

The parents who had sent a fake love interest to woo her and assassinate me, and leave her to take the blame for her lover...but she couldn't see the truth behind the plan.

She was desperate enough to seek love from even these people. Anyone.

Just not with the man who was trying so desperately to earn her love back.

She seemed to read my judgmental expression.

"If *you* can claim to suddenly make a one hundred and eighty degree turn around...then why couldn't *they*? Are *you* the only one capable of redemption, is that it?"

"No, I—"

"What if I want to know if they could love me—" she stopped dead there, looking away and wiping at her face. "Never mind. You couldn't understand. *Everyone* loves you. The entire kingdom was on your side the entire way, all the women loved you for whoring your way around the kingdom." She scoffed, and I cringed. Damn my past behavior. I knew I couldn't blame her for her anger toward me. "Of course, *I* couldn't be loved—"

"That's not it!" I said, upset and flinching at the harsh bite in her tone. "I just...don't want you to get hurt by them."

"That isn't your choice," she said. "They are my parents. It is my decision. You shouldn't—"

"I'll have the order lifted," I said, throwing my hands up a bit in surrender. "I will rescind that command."

She paused, looking me over. "Bring me that letter and maybe I will believe that."

I nodded, and trotted off to go and find the bird that had come down.

Veras's Height, 520 LD

As I had suspected, the letter was pandering to her, begging her forgiveness for the mistake and blunder that had happened.

She hadn't been the target, just me.

They were sorry, they were devastated to hear that she'd gotten hurt.

Liars, they were. They didn't care about her.

I knew enough about those people to realize that they would simply try again to eliminate me or get her to return to them to ruin our combined rule, no matter what happened to her.

They weren't bothered in the slightest about Kinley nor her safety.

Still, I kept my promise.

I had retrieved the letter for her, and I had ordered the rescinding of the original order.

From now on—as long as I was aware a letter had arrived and I got to see the contents before she read it, for safety purposes—she got each letter they sent for her.

She even sent a few of her own, against my feelings.

When I had tried to stop her, she had insisted that I wasn't respecting her feelings and thus, not respecting her, and I realized that she was right.

I hadn't ever respected her feelings before.

So, I had let it go, and tried my best to not interfere.

I had insisted, however, that I get to see each letter back and forth for security reasons, and she conceded on that point with me, at the very least.

After what had happened, I told her that she could hardly blame me for being paranoid.

She conceded with me on that point without much fuss, thankfully. She knew that I had the right to be wary of her parents, considering.

They had just tried to kill me.

In any case, I had been able to see her more often, now, and spending more time around her was…illuminating.

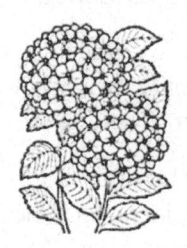

Veras's End, 520 LD

I wish that I had followed my parents' advice in the first place, and just given her the time she had needed. I couldn't begin to know how different thing would have been if I had.

She had become so lovely...

Just days ago, I had seen her maid accidently spill hot tea on her, and how had she responded?

She hadn't been angry.

She hadn't reprimanded the maid or even gotten upset.

She had rushed to ask the maid if she was alright, helped clean the mess and herself, before calmly addressing the burn on her hand and treating it together.

The way that she had handled the maid...

It was befitting of the Crowned Princess.

Who had taught her that...?

I watched her interactions with servants and knights from the sidelines, taking in how she approached them and how they thought and felt about her.

She had good standing with most of the servants who interacted with her.

About two-thirds of the palace staff did not interact with her, but for the third who did...they all thought very highly of her.

The staff who did not work with her did not look upon her favorably, and the majority of the reason for this was because I had never looked upon her favorably.

I wanted to earn her affection again, and get her in good standing with the palace staff and the royal family. I wanted her to feel at home here because I had, of course, also noticed that she had almost no interaction with my brothers or parents.

She stayed almost entirely to herself in her own palace, and though I didn't push her to move back to the central palace, I did hope that she wouldn't want to remain isolated forever.

I would have to see to it that my family treated her better from now on.

Aside from the scheduled meetings each morning and evening, I would send Valence over once each day with a hydrangea flower and a note.

The first few notes, admittedly, weren't…great.

The first note:

"Kinley,

I want to learn to appreciate you for who and what you really are. You are a sweet girl, who is kind to others. You are warm and caring and treat everyone with respect...I want to learn that respect and kindness. I want to feel it, too.

Please...give me a chance."

That note had, reportedly, been stared at with a strange expression for a long time before she had sighed heavily and folded it, putting it away in her desk.

I had just been happy to hear that she hadn't thrown it away or burned it...

That was progress, wasn't it?

One week had passed, and I had sent her a second letter.

"Kinley,

I was thinking today about your laugh; you laughed at the joke that the gardener had made, and I have to be honest with you. I want to know how good it feels to hear you laugh at something funny that I've said. I want to know what it feels like to make you feel good things.

I would love the chance, if you would allow it."

This letter, she had given a thoughtful expression, I was told.

She had seemingly contemplated this for a few moments before she shook her head, gave a small scoff, and put it into the same place she had put the first.

What did *that* mean...?

I waited another week before I had sent a third, and this time, I wanted to try a different approach...just to see how she would react.

"Kinley,

They say that 'An apple a day keeps the doctors away,' so what do they say about a fart?"

This letter, Valence told me that she had a very shocked expression before it moved to confusion...and then, she had laughed.

I had...made her laugh!

My heartrate kicked up and my chest had tightened.

Valence said that she had responded, *"Farts are good for hearts."*

I smiled.

Yes, she'd gotten it right.

Though, this got me to thinking...that was all it had taken to make her laugh.

It had just been a simple, corny joke.

Something about that made my heart ache in a strange way. If it had been that easy to make her laugh, how easy had it been to make her cry...?

How many times had I made her cry in the past? Probably too many to count them all.

Honestly, I had thrived on it for a while, like a sick bastard. I hated that I'd been that way.

A week passed, and I sent a fourth letter.

"Kinley, Sir Valence told me that my joke made you laugh...and my heart soared. But it also got me to thinking...about how easy it was to make you laugh, and how easy it must have been to make you cry. I often never paid attention to that aspect, and if I'm honest, a part of me...thrived on it. I was so angry over being trapped, so bitter over being forced. I was also far too impatient with you, when I had been praised my entire childhood for being so advanced. I was impatient for you to be up to my level right away, but that was wrong of me, and I see it now.

I want to make you feel only good things from now on. I want to love you, and you to love me."

When Valence delivered this letter and returned...he had a serious expression on his face, and I could tell that he didn't have good news.

"What's wrong? What happened?" I asked him.

He sighed, shaking his head. "She...is terrified."

"What?" I asked concerned. "What do you mean?"

He sighed. "Your highness, I'll be frank with you; she cried. She clutched that letter to her chest, sobbing, before she threw it away. Then, she carefully picked it up, folded it, and put it away before pacing back and forth while chewing on her thumb...when I asked her what she was feeling, she told me how scared she was...but she didn't tell me what she was scared of."

I nodded, taking in that information. "Do you think she's...scared of *me*?"

'*I think more so what loving you has done to her,*' I heard in his thoughts, but he was honest—though more vague—when he answered me.

"I think she is a little afraid of you, but I also feel she has the right to be...considering the past."

That was a fair answer, and I appreciated him being honest.

Chapter 14

Kinley...

Solaris's Reign, 520 Lawrence Dynasty

I was eating breakfast when, running a little late, Carlisle rushed up to sit down and start eating.

Over the last few months, he had been sending me little letters each week on top of spending time with me twice a day.

I had to admit that it was getting harder to ignore him.

My feelings for him continued to try to reaffirm themselves in my heart, and I kept trying to pull them out by the root...only to just be cutting them off just above the soil.

I had loved Carlisle...I still loved him.

I always had.

Wasn't that the very reason I had taken a dagger through the shoulder for him?

Why I had needed to go through physical therapy and had nightmares for months?

Still...

There was just too much fear in me to be willing to go to him.

Too much fear that yet again, he'd grow bored.

Fear in me that soon, he'd want to go back to whoring; that he'd be over me quickly because I wasn't experienced like he was.

I could feel him whispering niceties in my ear, but what if I gave in...and he abandoned me again?

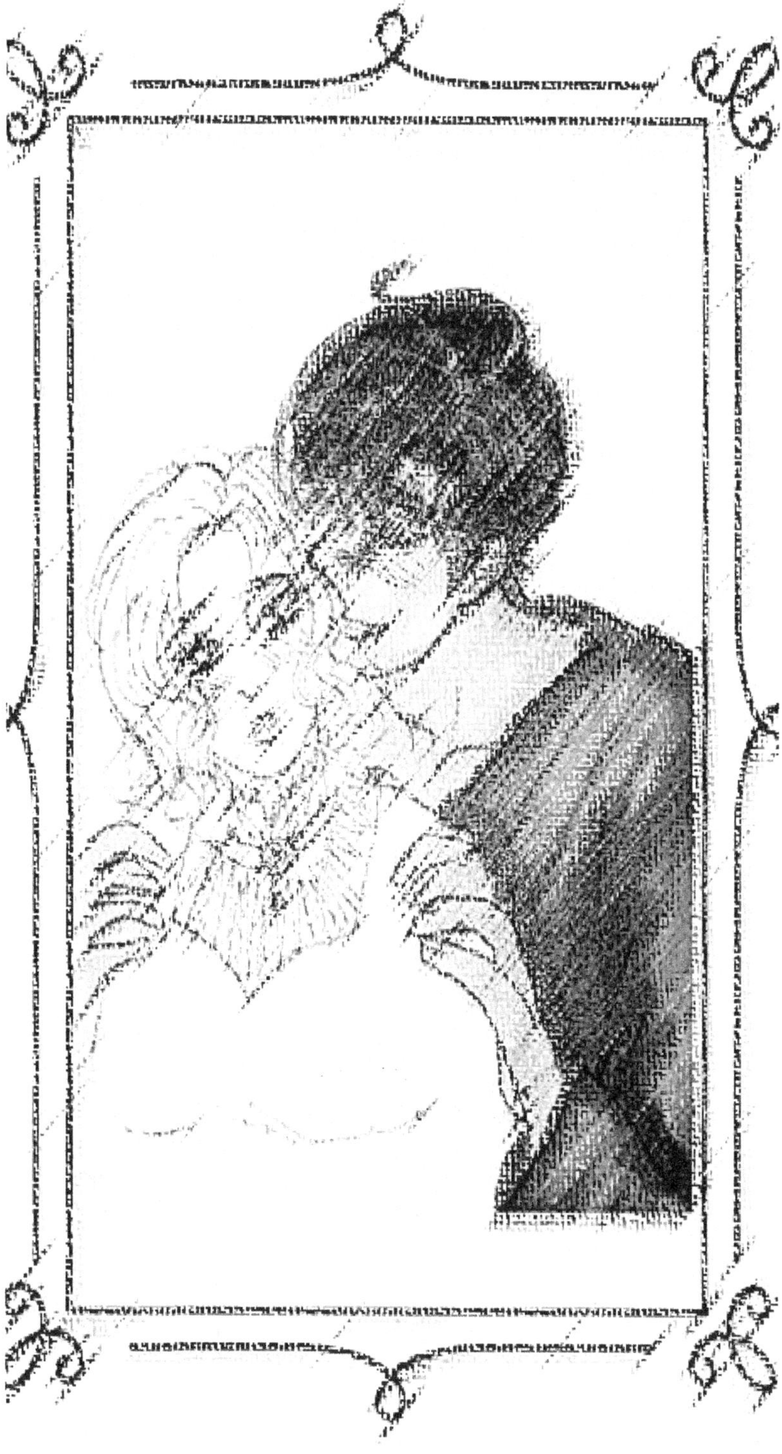

What if I opened myself up to him again and he finished breaking me...?

I didn't think that I could handle that. I'd already been broken enough.

Speaking of being broken...

My parents, in other news, had grown less frequent in their letters to me.

The last few letters had been short and irritated with me, asking so many incessant questions, I supposed.

I wanted to know about my other siblings and about them, about our culture and the southern kingdom...but when I refused to come, they got angry at me.

They blamed me for not wanting to come home.

They thought I was a fool...

Logic told me in my mind that they just wanted to hurt me or get rid of me, but my heart won out.

I wanted my family; to love and be loved properly.

Was that too much to ask for?

"You have someone asking to love and be loved now, Kinley," my sorcerer had reminded me. "I know he's hurt you before, but he's been nothing but true to his intention since the incident at the end of last year. Would it be so bad to try?"

I considered that...

It had been eight months since the incident, and I finally had almost all of the use of my arm and hand back, now.

I glanced at Carlisle, and I felt my mouth go dry as he wiped oil from his meal away from his thick lips with a handkerchief.

How would his lips feel?

His eyes shot up to mine, his mouth open a bit in a gape.

"What...?" He asked, surprised.

I startled, gasping and gaping at him. "Did I...say that out loud?" I asked, horrified when he gave a nod. "Oh, I, I'm sorry!" I said, and I stood. "I should get going, I—"

I froze when he reached out and grabbed my hand.

"Kinley, wait, please—"

"No, I—"

"Please!" He sobbed, and I gaped at him as his eyes brimmed with tears. "Kinley, please...I've done the best that I can to be true to you and prove my intentions since I vowed it to you that I would, but you've resisted me at every step, every turn. I've tried my best not to be pushy, and I've been making myself give you space, but...it isn't getting anything accomplished. You don't believe me. You don't trust—" he sighed.

"But how can I—"

"*You are right to be this way.*" He stated that, firm. Then, he sighed. "I'm sorry, I just...I...love you," he said. "And I finally see that it doesn't matter to me if you never love me again, if that just isn't possible...but if it isn't going to ever be possible, please, at least tell me so."

I considered that. What *did* I want?

Really?

How did I really feel?

Would I continue to deny him this way?

Or would I eventually give in to his wishes and let myself open to him?

There was no way for me to be positive without making that first step.

I would have to actually open myself up enough to truly consider it and take a step forward to figure it out, even for myself...and it wasn't fair to keep him waiting forever.

It wasn't fair to me, either, really. Didn't we both deserve for me to finally make a solid decision about the matter?

I needed to be smart and firm and decisive about this. That was the most important thing to keep in mind about this situation.

The fact was that being indecisive would just hurt us both, in the end, if I was truly honest with myself.

He waited patiently for me to say something, observing me quietly.

"I'm afraid," I admitted, letting him pull me over to a nearby bench, where we sat and he held my hands in his own.

"Of what?"

"What if I do, finally, let myself *feel* it? Without ignoring it, without pushing it away."

"Feel it...?" He asked.

"These little...twinges of joy and...and...*affection*, in my heart. I kept feeling little tingles in my heart whenever you sent me a letter or flowers or I saw you...I've been fighting that because I was scared, but..."

"But...?" He asked when I had stayed quiet for a long moment.

I sighed. "What if I let myself feel those things, and you hurt me again? What if I give my all, and you're left disappointed again? That would finish destroying me, and I can't do that to myself again."

"Kinley, I promise you; I will not ever *intentionally* harm you again." He smiled. "I will do all I can to respect, honor and cherish you...the way I always should have. Please..."

"And what if you get bored of me? Can you promise me that you won't neglect me again, or abandon me?"

He laughed, soft. "How could I get bored?"

"I don't see why you couldn't, so why don't you humor me and tell me why you wouldn't?"

"Well, I have so much time to catch up on, and from what I've seen so far...if I had just been patient and given you time in the beginning, if I had not been such an arrogant ass to you...maybe I would have been able to see it all from the beginning. I've missed so much because I was a pompous fool."

"Carlisle..."

"The fact is, I hurt you, and I didn't care because I was bitter...but when I saw you jump in front of that attack for me, despite all that I'd done and how I had been to you, well...it made me see you through new eyes. It took my bitterness and changed it. Since then, I have been watching you with new eyes."

I took a long, long moment to mull it over, consider it all.

"Promise me one thing," I told him, and he nodded. "Promise me that if this doesn't work...if I get hurt again...promise you'll give me a divorce, formally and legally, and let me go...don't stop me."

He cringed, and seemed to think over this condition for a few minutes...before finally, he nodded. "I promise."

"Also, I do not intend to move right back into your palace. I know that the King and Queen have been being nicer to me when I see them because you spoke to them about it, and you've warned your brothers to be nicer to me, but I'm not ready to go back to being there. I enjoy having this palace to myself and having my own space."

He nodded, looking me up and down with a contemplative expression. "Being in your own palace has done you much good, indeed. Perhaps...it is best for you to stay here for a while."

I felt surprise rush over me. "R-Really?" I asked, surprised.

I hadn't expected to get such a concession so easily and without needing to beg him for it.

He nodded. "Yes," he smiled. "You are thriving having your own space without us near you. I think it is good for you."

"But...what about when you become king?"

"When we have the coronation, father and mother—as well as my brothers—will move to vacation palaces throughout the kingdom, anyway."

"But..."

"It won't be occupied in the same manner that it is now, and so hopefully, it won't bother you so much to be there. I know you care about them, but that you aren't comfortable around them. That is fine, I understand your reasons...so I want you to know that I care first and foremost for your comfort and safety."

That wasn't the answer that I had anticipated...

I took a deep breath. "Alright, then. This was...this was a lot to take in," I admitted. "A lot to think about."

"Yes," he said. He stood, turning. "I will...give you some time to mull over our talk, and I will see you again soon. I need some time to think about all this, so I am sure that you do, too." Then, he walked away, leaving me sitting there to really take in what had just happened.

A lot had happened in the span of an hour. I had...

I could hardly believe it, but I had just agreed to give him another chance?

I had vowed not to do so, but honestly, that wasn't a rational choice in the first place. I needed to take things seriously, rather than just from a hurt child's perspective.

I had never expected myself to get back to a point where I was willing to give him another opportunity, but after months of sweet and funny little notes, little notes that promised love...I had felt myself wear down.

"Are you alright, your highness?" Sir Halo came up to me, then, sitting with me.

I wondered. Was I?

"I don't know, really," I told him honestly. "I hadn't thought that I'd ever give him another chance. It is a lot to consider."

"But you won't know unless you try to see for yourself and take that step forward," he filled in, and I nodded.

"You've always been able to see my heart, Halo," I smiled.

He smiled. "I think you're making a good decision, to be fair. I know that he hurt you...a lot. But he's trying to do better. He hasn't, according to Valence, even spoken to a woman since you took that dagger for him. I mean, spoken to a woman in that way."

"That does make me feel a bit better. I know Valence is almost always by his side."

"I think that this will be a good thing," he grinned at me, taking me into a hug.

I could only hope that he would turn out to be right.

Two days passed, and I hadn't seen him again. I was starting to feel anxious, but as I was sitting out in my garden having tea early morning on the third day...

Valence came with a letter.

I laughed, sighing at the same time, and took the offered letter from him.

"Dear Kinley,

I imagine you must be feeling a bit anxious by now...so am I. I wanted to give us both plenty of time, without seeing one another, to really have time to think over things. I wanted to be sure to give you space to think.

I hope that these past two days have been enough time for you.

If it is alright, I would like to invite you to join me for dinner tonight in the central pavilion.

We will speak then."

I smiled, and I tore off a bottom fold of the letter, asking for a pen.

When Valence brought me my pen, I wrote:

"You are right. I was feeling anxious. I will be there."

I nodded, and handed it to Valence. "Please take that to him."

He looked surprised. "You're responding this time, your highness?"

I smiled. "Yes. His first written reply from me," I admitted.

"Very good, princess," he winked at me, and off he went.

Chapter 15

Carlisle...

"That looks beautiful," I told the staff. "Thank you, everyone, for your help in preparing everything. You may all go," I told them.

Valence returned in that moment, a scrap of—a scrap of paper in his hand?

"She replied?" I asked, stunned, and he nodded with a grin as he handed it to me. I read it, and took in her script.

Her handwriting wasn't super elegant, but it was clear and easy to read...like her.

"She's...really coming."

He nodded. "Yes, she immediately started getting ready."

Getting ready...

That meant that she was getting dressed up...right?

I decided to be safe and wear a uniform that I would normally wear while performing my princely duties around the palace. It was nice and somewhat formal, but it didn't look like I was ready to go to a ball or anything.

Hours that felt like days passed by, slowly, before it became evening and the meal was underway.

I had asked the chef to cook her favorite dishes, and I would just eat whatever she herself had.

I wasn't big on fish, but I wanted to eat the same thing as her. I wasn't even entirely sure why.

"Your highness!" I heard a maid call, and I stepped over to her, leaning to where I could hear her easily because she leaned in. "You wanted the hydrangeas where?" She asked, and motioned down to her hands, to the vase I'd picked out that held bright purple hydrangeas.

They weren't common in this area, as most were blue, but I found some purple ones that I thought she might really love.

"I want them to be kept out of sight until dessert," I grinned. "When the dessert course comes, please bring them out then. Now, hurry, she's probably on her way!" I motioned for her to leave, and she smiled and rushed off with the vase of flowers.

Inside the vase, thankfully, was the soil and root. I wanted to plant the flower bush somewhere that she wanted it placed, and she could forever have her own purple hydrangeas.

"You look lovely, your highness," Valence spoke up, and I startled, turning to see her as she approached, escorted by Halo.

She was dressed in a deep green gown, with a golden ribbon sash tied around her waist and golden embroidery work. Her short hair was pulled back away from her face using hair clips, and her golden eyes shined bright.

She did look lovely, like a beautiful flower.

A lily, maybe, with her green dress as the stem, hair as the petals and golden eyes as the anthers.

She was still plump, but she had trimmed down some from her younger teen years, filling out well.

She was beautiful. It was as if her taking a dagger for me had taken the film off of my eyes and I was seeing her as she truly is...how lovely she truly is.

"You do look lovely," I smiled at her, looking her up and down and eating her with my eyes.

She blushed, pushing a strand of hair behind her ears and looking away. A very...overly-sensitive reaction to such a small compliment. How sensitive was she?

I had to wonder...how far *had* she gone with Merik, anyway?

I honestly had assumed she would have given herself to him, but with how shy and timid she acted...she acted like a virgin.

Was she, still...?

I shook the thought out of my head, rushing to pull out her chair and have her take a seat before sitting beside her. The appetizer, a trio of velvety smooth seared scallops topped with a honey Dijon avocado sauce.

After we had eaten our appetizers and talked a few minutes on how our days had gone, the meal was promptly served.

For the main course, we had grilled seasoned salmon, sauteed spinach with garlic and lemon, and honey roasted rainbow carrots.

She got excited over this meal, and I was glad that I had learned her favorites beforehand.

This meal was a big hit with her, being so healthy but deliciously seasoned.

I knew that for dessert, we'd be eating a delicious, rich, creamy chocolate mousse with cinnamon honey tuille...her favorite.

She glanced around the table, looking confused before she looked up at me.

"I...see all of my favorites, here, but I don't see yours...?"

I grinned at her. "Tonight, I wanted the focus to be on you."

"Oh," she said, blushing. "T-thank you, I'm...I appreciate that. I am very happy with the meal."

I smiled, and just watched her eat.

"W-what?" She asked, giving a nervous laugh.

"Nothing, I just...I'm happy I was able to give you a good dinner."

"I see," she smiled. She tried not to meet my eyes as she continued eating, and I could see her ears turning pink. She was embarrassed, and it was adorable.

I knew that she wasn't used to all of this attention, but it was beyond due to give it to her on my part. I could only hope that eventually, she would trust my genuine intentions to woo her.

When we had finished with our meals, we got our desserts, and the maid brought out the vase.

"Oh, oh my word!" Kinley gushed, shocked. "Is...is that...?"

"Yes," I nodded, smiling. "*Purple* hydrangeas."

I knew that hydrangeas were her favorite flower, and purple was her favorite color. It was tough to find them in the correct color, but I made it happen. For her.

"Oh, they're *beautiful*," she said. "Thank you."

We ate our desserts, before I had the vase taken inside to her chambers in her palace and I wrapped her in my jacket as we took a light walk around the pavilion.

"This evening has been just lovely," she smiled, looking over at me. "Thank you for taking such care of everything. It will be a good memory for me forever."

"Good," I told her. "I am glad to hear that." I trailed off, contemplating before I decided to just ask. "Kinley...I have a question. And if you don't wish to answer, you don't have to, since I don't really have a right to know, after all I've done, but...how...how far did you get, with, you know...how far did you get with Merik?" I finally got the question out.

She gawked for a moment, before she rubbed her arm in a sheepish way. "Oh, I...we only kissed, once."

I waited, but she left it there, and I grew further and further surprised.

"What?" I asked, stunned. "You...kissed."

She nodded. "Once."

I gaped at her. "That's all?"

She looked away, cheeks flaming, and I could hear in Valence's and Halo's thoughts that I had hurt her feelings by pointing out her inexperience.

"Nothing is wrong with that," I assured her quickly. "I just...I was surprised. You two seemed to be so close, and I thought...forget what I thought. It isn't as if I had any right to wonder about it, but I...I just was thinking about how I want to kiss you, and wondering how far you two may have—"

"*You* want to kiss *me*?" She gaped at me, and we just watched each other for a moment.

Did she not believe that I could possibly want that?

I nodded, turning her to face me. "Yes," I said, soft.

Her breathing hitched, and I could see the tears filling her eyes. "...Really?"

This was serious to her, I realized in that moment. This was important. For me to actually show that I wanted her...it was something she had so desperately needed for so very long, now, and I felt like a pig for my past actions.

*I had seen, but I hadn't **known**, not really.*

I had seen her fear, but I hadn't known her true anxiety. I had seen her sadness, but I hadn't known her self-degradation. I had known her heartbreak, but I hadn't known her hopelessness.

Now that I had seen and learned, I wanted to do all that I could to reassure her, value her, build her up, and give her hope again.

I leaned forward so slowly, and took her face in my hands.

I gave her plenty of time to back away before I, so gently, pressed my lips to hers.

They were moist and cool, surprisingly, but not in a bad way.

I pressed a few featherlight, chaste kisses to her lips before I pulled away, and when I looked down at her again, she was blushing and looked completely dazed...

In a whole other world.

I chuckled, holding her face in my hands still.

"Are you alright?" I asked, smiling.

She finally looked at me, her eyes wide and emotional.

"You...you kissed me," she whispered hoarsely. "You really did it..."

"Did you really think that I wouldn't?" I countered softly, knowing that I didn't have the right to be offended...and I wasn't.

I couldn't blame her in the slightest for not trusting me. After all, I had been cruel enough in the past to have used something like this to hurt her.

Of course, she would question if I were being honest or not in my intentions. Even now, she had a wary look in her eyes. She was afraid.

I smiled at her when she gave me a sheepish, nervous expression.

"It is alright," I told her. "You have every justification to wonder about it...my true intent, I mean. But I promised you, Kinley. I am in this, and I want this; I want you."

She blushed, looking at my lips again before she looked away, even as I still held her face in my hands.

"You don't have to believe me, yet," I said. "I will continue to work to earn my place back in your heart...because I never deserved it when I had it. Now, I want to deserve you."

Her eyes were wide and she looked like a trembling kitten, as I pressed my lips to hers again.

She couldn't understand it...

I had no right to be frustrated, because I had done this to myself. I could only continue to work toward the goal.

I pressed one final, gentle warm kiss on her lips before I pulled away and kissed the palm of her hand.

"I'll stop here for now, princess...you look like you may faint, and I wouldn't want that, so..." I grinned mischievously, leaving her chasing after me sputtering for a moment before I quickly turned around, catching her in my arms, and pecking a kiss onto her forehead.

I chuckled as she gaped at me yet again, looking at me with shock.

"That's the only kind of way I intend to trick you from now on."

She blushed, looking away again with a pout.

Moon's Dance, 520 LD

"There...is something I want to address with you," sir Valence glanced at me from the corner, holding a report in hand. "Your highness, the king and queen of the Southern Kingdom are actively bashing you around the kingdom, asking for petitions to free the princess from your care. They say that you are...controlling the content of her letters home and that you are censoring their letters to her in an attempt to turn her against them."

"What?" I asked, appalled. "I haven't censored them at all! And I have been reading the letters to and from one another, but I haven't controlled any of the content...how do they expect anyone to—"

"Their requests for petition have gotten quite a bit of traction, your highness," he told me, and I paused.

"...What?" I seethed.

He sighed. "It seems your...previous scandals are coming back to bite you in the ass, your highness. The people are bringing up that you have...been known to cheat on and humiliate and shun the princess, so that she should be returned home. The petitions have gotten over seven hundred thousand signatures so far."

"What?!" I shouted, standing so fast and hard that my chair toppled backward to the floor. "But, that's—"

If a petition got over half of the empire's signatures...it had to be acknowledged unless it strictly broke the law.

Petitions were a rare and unique tactical advantage that could be used by one kingdom against the other.

There were, currently, approximately one million, five hundred and eighty thousand citizens currently residing in the empire...so, half of that number would be seven hundred and ninety thousand.

If that number grew to be over seven hundred and ninety thousand, I would be forced to follow the majority vote of the people and send Kinley back to her parents...!

I couldn't let that happen. If she returned to her parents, they may just kill her off to keep her from being able to return to me.

I wouldn't put it past them to risk their entire family line for it.

It had been done before.

I sighed dramatically. "How far are they from being over halfway?"

"Not far, your highness."

"Bring Axel and Halo here, immediately, as well as my parents. I need to figure out a solution."

"Yes, your highness."

"So, basically, all we have to do is show her to the public and show them how happy she is...?" I asked, skeptical.

"Basically," Axel said. "If they see her sincerely happy and she starts a petition to take her parents out of power, maybe they will side with her. And because you two are the Seers, that will greatly help the cause. You two can read the top level of thought and see what you need to say to reach individuals specifically."

I could only hope that she would agree.

Chapter 16

Kinley...

Moon's Dance, 520 Lawrence Dynasty

I watched in horror as the prince cringed, his uniform shirt gripped in clenched fists. "I...know that this seems like a terrible thing that I'm telling you, but—"

"What was I expecting...?" I whispered, sad.

"...What?"

"You had me going," I said, soft. "I thought you were really sincere. But father and mother warned me that you would turn me against them, and—"

"Do you hear yourself...?" He asked, a look of hurt on his face. "Kinley, they abandoned you, and then sent someone to kill me. They're using your desire for their love against you! Kinley, I...I want to be with you. I care for you! I've been doing everything I can to prove it to you and earn my place by your side, haven't I? Kinley...they're literally making petitions to have you taken from me by force and turned over to them..."

"Are you sure?" I asked, not believing that. "Maybe they just want me to come to see them and visit," I said, crossing my arms. "You already read all of our letters back and forth! Isn't that enough?"

"But I haven't kept you from seeing them," he told me, desperation in his tone. "Kinley, please…"

I was stuck. I didn't know what to do or how to feel, and I didn't know what I actually wanted.

Was he serious?

Was *he* telling me the truth, or were *they*?

I wanted to hear the truth from them, to find out if they were lying or not.

They swore that they could love me, that they were just busy and that's why they didn't write often.

It was true enough that Carlisle hadn't kept any more of their letters from me, and he hadn't actually controlled what I had written to them, but I didn't feel comfortable going to see them when I felt that it would anger him. He didn't trust them, and he didn't like the idea of me going.

He thought they'd hurt me.

I wanted to see the good in them, and I wanted to see the good in him, too.

Over the last few months, he had done so much for me and spent so much time with me.

He hadn't ever even kissed me deeper than a chaste kiss. He had been so gentle and sweet and—

Oh, no. Oh, my goodness…

I was in love.

My heart dropped to my stomach.

This was why I had been so terrified of him to begin with, getting back close to me in my life. I knew that if I fully affirmed true, romantic feelings for him…he'd shatter my entire soul if he hurt me again.

He froze, looking me in the face.

"Kin…?" He asked, timid. "You…you just went so pale, are you—"

"I'm fine," I cut off, harsher than I intended. "Car...I need to go."

"What...?" He asked, and he lost some of the light in his eyes.

I realized what he thought that I was saying. "No, no, no," I hurried. "Not *permanently*. I just...I think it might be a good thing to go and visit them. You know, show the people that you aren't keeping me cooped up in the palace by force, and I could read their thoughts and see if they're really telling me the truth?"

He contemplated this, and finally, gave a heavy, weary sigh.

"If you really think that this is best...if you think you will be safe...then I will trust you."

My heart nearly stopped, time freezing with those words.

He...he trusted me?

He was going to trust me?

If I thought that my feelings were there before, they had solidified just now in my heart.

This man, whom had been so bitter and anguished and vexed toward me, had completely turned his feelings around and was offering me his trust.

This was monumental.

"Are...are you serious?" I asked, surprised, and he gave a single, humorless laugh.

"Yes," he nodded. Then, his bright golden gaze met mine. "But I want for you to take a squadron of knights to protect you...just in case. And, the sorcerer."

I laughed, throwing my arms around his neck. "I promise, I'll be safe! And, I'll come back safely. You'll see, Car!" I grinned up at him and then...*then, I did something I hadn't ever done before.*

I initiated intimate contact with him, and I stood on my tiptoes to press a kiss to his lips.

His eyes widened in surprise, but crinkled with a smile as he wrapped his arms around my waist and pulled me tighter, opening my lips beneath his with a push from his tongue. I gave a soft, nosey-breath sigh, melting into him as his tongue lazily traced mine.

It was slow, and hot, and heady...but patient. It was not rushed.

He pulled away, leaving me breathless, and met my eyes.

"There is...something that I want to do before you leave, however," he told me. Then, he leaned down so that his lips brushed the shell of my ear. "I want to make love to you," he murmured.

My cheeks flushed, and I jerked back to gawk at him. "What...?" I asked.

He smiled a tender, soft smile. "I want to know...that you're mine. And that you are taking me as *yours*. I want to do this before you leave, so that I have that reassurance while you're away."

"A reminder that I'm coming back," I surmised, and he nodded.

"Yes," he admitted. "I'm...I'm afraid to send you, Kin. I don't want anything bad to happen to you, and I'm scared that if I send you to your parents...you won't ever come back, for one reason or another. It took so many years to bring you here, and then I squandered away our time with my blasted foolishness," he cringed, and I could truly see the heartbreak on his features and in his body language.

He was totally defeated by his past scandals.

"Car..."

"Please," he whispered. "Truthfully, I should have been yours years ago. Always. I want you, Kinley," he said.

I felt the heat rising all over my face, my shoulders and neck, my ears...

I felt almost dizzy with the sudden rush of blood to my head.

Whether the dizziness was to blame, or the fact that I, too, wanted to be with him...I nodded, and gave him my consent.

He gasped, looking down at me in shock. "Really?" He asked. I nodded, and he lifted me in his arms, spinning me around in a circle as he chuckled and pressed kisses to my lips. "I'll see you in your chambers tonight, then, princess," he whispered against my lips, before he pulled away, walking off toward his palace as I was left standing there with Halo in the gardens.

"Did...that really just happen...?" I asked, glancing to Halo, and he nodded with a smirk on his face. "What did I just...agree to...?"

I chewed my nails as I sat on the edge of my window-seat, book discarded and my purple hydrangea nearby my seat.

I had to be honest and admit that the thought of having my body touched and...and...

The thoughts and ideas that were encouraged and spurred on by the writings in the romance novels I often read led me to feel rather hot, and I fanned myself with a folding, hand-held fan rapidly, trying to cool down.

Halo had promised me, earlier, that the Crowned Prince would stop if I asked him to, and that he wouldn't force me without my consent, but I...I wanted to do this.

I was just terrified.

I heard a small knock on the door, and I heard Halo's voice alert me that the Crowned Prince had arrived...

It was time...

I took a deep breath, clenching my silk robe in my hands as the door opened, and in stepped my husband.

He wore a robe that sat with the chest area left open, and I could see his lean musculature. His eyes were heady and warm, heating me straight through to the center, and I felt my cheeks heat.

He was watching me the way a hawk watches prey...

He stalked stealthily over to me, coming to rest on his knees between my legs.

He pressed a kiss to my hands, taking them in his as he unclenched them from my robe.

"What do you say we loosen ourselves together with a bath...?" He murmured, looking at me with an expression that dripped with sexual desire.

I swallowed thickly, not trusting my voice and nodding, and he chuckled a throaty sound before he stood and helped me to my feet before leading me through to the large bathroom.

The baths in the palaces stayed filled, like in-ground pools, and they stayed heated warmers beneath the tiles.

The water stayed rotated and fresh with a filtration and waterfall system, and there was a large fountain in the center for showering off.

There was a large wooden chest beside of the bathing pool that stayed filled with scented oils, soaps, scrubs and even some drugs.

He tugged me over to the pool, and I felt my cheeks heat as he gently pulled the sash to my robe, letting it drift open before he gingerly pushed it off of my body.

Self-consciousness and degradation boiled in my blood as his thick, heavy stare lulled over my body lazily, as if he were studying every facet and wrinkle and stretchmark.

I looked away from his eyes for a moment before he tugged on my chin, regaining my focus.

He took my lips with his, and I felt his hand grab mine and I suddenly felt something...odd. Something that I didn't know what it was, but from the romance novels that I had read over the years, I could only surmise it to be one thing.

Truthfully, I hadn't been confident that I'd ever get to experience even seeing one in real life, let alone touching one...or having one enter me...

I flushed as I pulled back, glancing down, and I saw a large bulge beneath his robe, sitting in my hand as he curled his hand around mine on the outside to cup it, holding it up.

"This is what looking at you has done to me, Kin," he whispered against my lips, kissing me again. "Look how hard you've gotten me..." He kissed me again. *"This is for you,* so please...don't doubt yourself," he chuckled.

Mesmerized, I let myself drift softly to my knees, and he watched me with eyes enraptured by my every move as I slid his robe open, taking in the thickness of him.

I only knew this as a "member" but what the novels called it, and I had no way to know what he would deem it be called, but of course I did know the technical terminology.

His penis was a good size—longer than my hand from the wrist to the tips of my fingers stretched out, in any case, but that wasn't hard since my hands were petite.

He was about two and a half of my fingers in width, and it curved upward just slightly before coming to the skin that encased the head.

I pulled the skin back, exposing the head that reminded me of a helmet, and I tentatively flicked a tongue out to lave him from base to tip.

He shivered, letting out a hissing breath and a choked back groan, and my eyes whirled up to be sure I hadn't harmed him.

When he pressed himself to my lips again, I knew that he'd only liked the feeling, and so...I went for it.

I opened my mouth, taking him in and giving a few timid strokes, bobbing my head a little on him.

The throaty, gasping sounds he made both encouraged and empowered me to keep going, and though I struggled not to gag when he reached too deep...I couldn't help but feel hot and wet, almost, from what this was doing to me.

"Kin," he murmured. "I need you to stop," he whined. He pulled me up, bringing my mouth to his again as I felt his fingers tracing the outline of my hips.

I startled a bit when he gripped my bare rear in his hand, squeezing experimentally even as his mouth trailed down to my throat.

I heard the breathy moans of a woman, somewhere, but my eyes darted around and saw no one.

It took me a moment to realize that the sounds were actually coming from me, and they went up in pitch when he took a nipple into his mouth.

I felt tingles rush through my chest as his tongue swirled around it, and I gasped and nearly came out of my skin when his teeth gently nibbled on me.

He came up me again, kissing me on the lips and leaving me breathless and breathing into him.

Then, he kissed my forehead sweetly, letting me catch my breath. Babying me into this lovemaking.

Somehow, my core got hotter all the while, and I heard him give a throaty growl as his lips moved downward again while he kept his hands massaging my breasts.

Feeling his tongue dip into my naval, before he stood, and he grabbed my hand again.

"Come," he told me, and he pulled me into the bath gently. "Let's get you calmed down a bit," he smiled.

The heat of my body clashed with the heat of the bath, and I felt extra hot as he pulled me into deeper water.

He grabbed my floral oils—made from some of my hydrangeas—and began to lather it into my skin. He scrubbed some soap into my skin next, before he finished with my hair, lathering and conditioning it before he dipped me back and let it be rinsed clean.

He made quick work of himself as he had me lie back against the tile—sitting on a ledge in the pool that was built for sitting in the water, sort of like the hot-tubs for soaking.

When he had finished washing, he came back to me, kissing me and letting his lips trail over my collarbone and my shoulders as his hands worked my breasts again.

Now, I understood what he'd meant when he'd wanted to "get me calmed down a bit".

I had relaxed as he'd bathed me, and had let myself cool down and rest as he'd bathed himself, but I could quickly feel myself heating back up now that his attention was on my body again.

I gasped when he lifted me, having me sit on the ledge of the pool and he pushed me to lie back.

"Trust me," he murmured against my breast when I resisted. "Just lie back, the tiles are warm. Just let me do the rest. I'll take care of everything."

I finally listened, and he was right; the tiles were nice and warm against my back.

I looked at the ornate ceiling as I felt his fingers press and knead, massaging my chest and my ribs, my waist and hips...

His lips pressed to my belly, again and again, and this time, I couldn't bring myself to feel self-conscious about it.

I felt his tongue tracing stretchmarks.

I felt his tongue dip into my bellybutton.

I felt his lips nip my love handles as his hands wrapped around me to grip and squeeze my butt-cheeks.

His deft hands massaged my thighs and down to my knees, before continuing down my calves and to my ankles and feet.

Then, they worked their way back up, and I was waiting for the mesmerizing feeling of those magic fingers on my hips and thighs again...

That is, until he paused for a long moment at my knees.

What was he...?

Before I could lift my head to check, I felt him push my legs apart, gently, and all of my apprehension and self-consciousness slammed into me full-force as he stared at my most intimate of places.

I started to tug away, but he held me firmly in place.

"Trust me, Kin," he reminded me, and his fingers worked the innermost part of my thighs in massage this time.

My heart thumped wildly as his fingers moved ever upward to my center, and I was gasping when I felt them touch my lower lips.

"You are so beautiful," I heard him murmur. "I wonder how you taste."

I was about to ask, when suddenly, I nearly came off the ground and I cried out in a voice I didn't recognize as his face defiled me and his tongue dipped inside of me when he'd delved past the lips.

I felt my arms fling around for a moment, seeking to grab something, but his hands shot up and grabbed mine and laced his fingers with my own to hold them tightly as his tongue plunged in and out of me.

When I had somewhat adjusted to the feeling, he moved his tongue elsewhere, and I felt a searing heat rapidly built when a sharp, panging tickle blossomed and his tongue seemed to pinpoint this one little area of nerve.

He let go of one of my hands, and I felt his fingers go to this place even as his tongue went back to delving inside of my core.

"Car-Carlisle!" I groaned, trying to keep my hips from thrusting so I didn't bother him.

"Be a good girl and come for me," he spoke just above my entrance, the heat of his breath fanning against me, before he shoved his tongue back in.

"Come...?" I asked.

I knew that word, from the romance novels that I read so often.

Is that what this was...? Was this a release about to wash over me?

I'd read about them many times, but to actually experience it was something else entirely.

To think on that, though, I realized that it wasn't actually much different than described. Every descriptive word I'd read on it matched, but this was so much more...

It was so much better.

I gasped, crying out as the burn stretched higher and the tingles got faster.

"C-Car! Car, I—it's coming! I'm coming!" I cried, and my hands shot to his hand and gripped as I suddenly shattered.

I sobbed and shrieked as the feeling washed over me, encompassed for just a few blissful seconds before the feeling cooled and the pulses began to ebb.

I gasped and flopped back on the tile, struggling to catch my breath.

My heart raced in time with the pulses, and I felt him give me one more lick of his tongue from the bottom to the top of my seam.

"Well done, good girl," he praised in a growling tone. "You were so beautiful. I could tell, that was your first time," he chuckled. "The first of many," he murmured in a promise.

I felt a tight, burning, aching feeling in my lower abdomen muscles from holding myself bound so tightly as I'd held my upward thrust during the orgasm, and my pulsing only made that ache more...but it was worth it.

I felt him lift my body and carry me through to the bedroom.

The silk of the sheets stuck to my still-wet skin and hair, and I gasped when he lifted my bottom up with his hands, shifting so that my spread thighs and hips rested against his thighs.

I watched with rapt attention as his head pressed just into my lips.

"How do you want me to do this?" He asked me, and my eyes lazily traveled up to his. "Do you want me to snap forward and give it to you all at once...? Or do you want it bit by bit, slowly, so you can adjust gradually? I've...never been with a virgin," he admitted.

I considered it for a moment.

I knew, realistically, that it was probably going to hurt either way.

Did I want to try to get it all out of the way, or did I want to ease into it?

I'd been through so much pain in my life that it seemed hardly important at this point.

"Don't do it hard, but...all at once," I told him.

He gave a nod, and took a deep breath. "All at once, then," he agreed.

Then, without further stalling and gently, he pressed it all in at once.

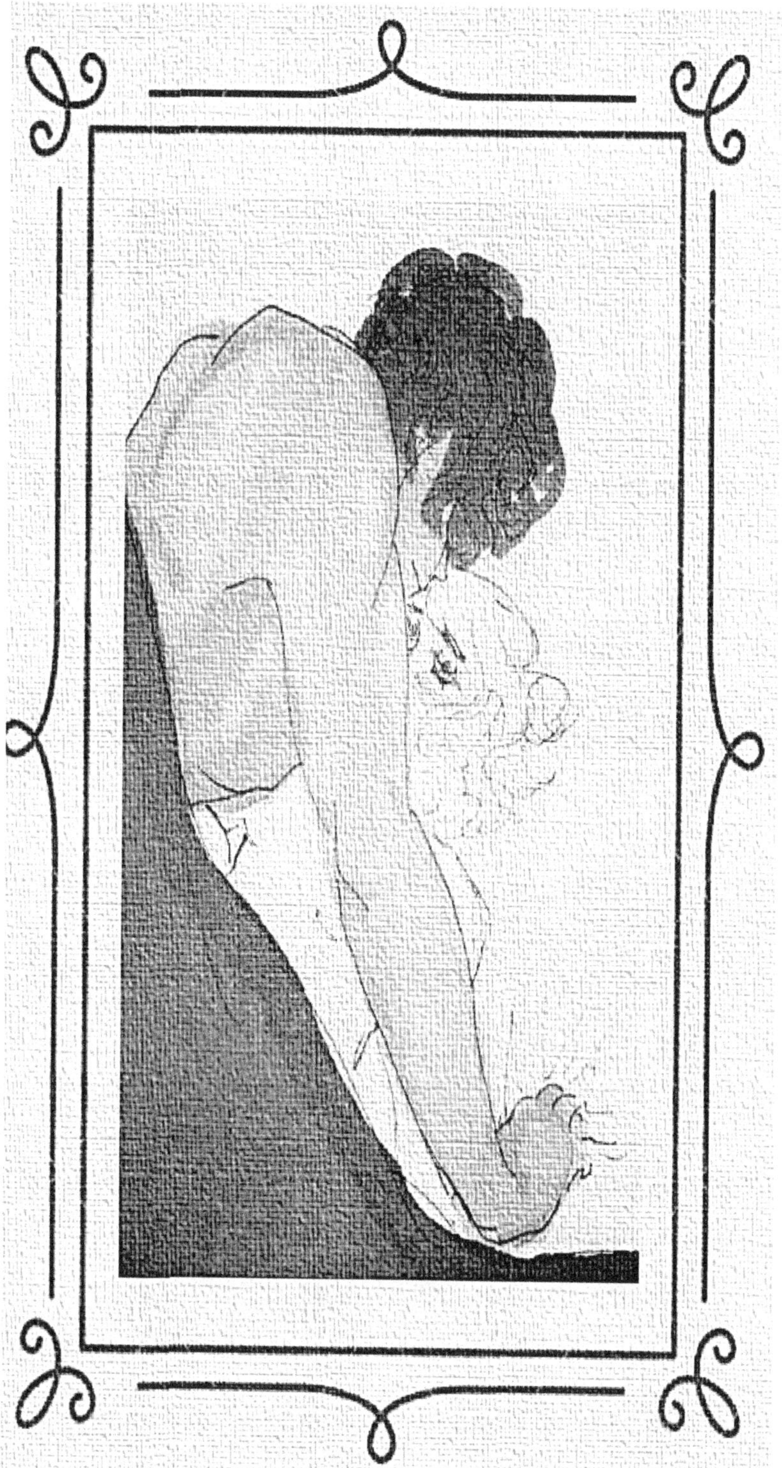

I barely felt any pain, though. Just the smallest pinch, and I winced a little.

It stung slightly and dulled into an ache, but the stretch felt more...heavy than anything else.

I felt like a stuffed chicken or something.

After giving me a moment to get used to it, I gave him a nod and he gave a few soft, easy strokes, languidly, and I started to feel good quickly.

"I'm inside you," he murmured, and I felt the heat build quickly as he kept pressing his way into me.

"You...you're inside of me," I moaned, and I felt myself pulse softly as the feeling of that second orgasm built higher. "You're really...you're really inside me!" I laughed, soft.

I felt my eyes burn.

I hadn't ever imagined I'd really get to experience this. The reality finally settled in me, though, and I felt tears fill my eyes.

He leaned down to me, kissing the tears away.

"I'm sorry, Kinley. I'm sorry that I made you wait so long, that I ever hurt you. I have so many regrets—"

"You're giving me all I ever hoped for with you now," I grinned, shaking my head. "Just...just be with me. Just be in this moment, here, with me," I started to get breathy again as he plundered deeper, and his lips melded with my own.

I couldn't tell here, in this moment, where each of us began and ended. I just knew that we were, finally, together.

Our bodies felt like one.

I started to gasp again. "C-Car, I'm—I'm almost—"

"Me, too," he groaned, and as he kissed me deeply, I felt it.

I felt him grow and twitch, hard and alive inside of my core, and I felt so warm as he shoved his head to the base of me as he gasped and groaned.

I was right behind him, breaking and falling apart beneath him as we clung to one another.

As our orgasms ebbed and receded, I cuddled into him under his body, and he turned us so that we lay on our sides. He was still inside of me and I was still wrapped around him, but he got us beneath the blanket and I felt warm and fuzzy as I drifted into a blissful sleep.

I couldn't imagine it getting any better or any sweeter.

Chapter 17

Kinley...

When the next morning arrived, I found myself alone in the bed. I felt...odd.

I wasn't sticky. I wasn't even naked, anymore.

I stood on aching legs, going to the full-length standing mirror in the corner to look over myself. I was wearing a soft robe—a fresh one.

There was a glow to my skin, and I couldn't stop grinning as I recalled the night before.

There were even fresh sheets on the bed, and when I glanced out of the window—

Oh, no.

Mortification ran through me, then.

In tradition of our people, in this kingdom, when a nobleman or royalty took the virtue of their bride, they placed the sheets on a flag-pole outside of the woman's bedroom window.

My sheet, with a spot of blood about the size of a fist and a few spots of splatter around it, hung proudly just outside of my window.

I noticed servants below glancing up at it and giggling amongst themselves, rushing around with their work.

Turning my attention back to noticing the changes around me, I also noted that I had been...ahem...

Wiped clean. I had been *wiped clean* between my legs.

"You're awake?" I heard a voice ask, and I turned with a smile to see Carlisle standing there with his eyes warm and studying me while he held a tray in his hands.

There on the tray sat a plate full of my favorite breakfast foods, a glass of orange juice, and a...pill...?

He set the tray on the bedside table, and came over to me, studying myself with me in the mirror.

"How are you feeling?" He asked, glancing up to meet my eyes in the mirror.

"I feel a little sore...but otherwise, I feel...happy."

He gave me a soft, warm smile...a smile that I loved so much to see on his face, especially directed at me.

"Good," he smiled. "I have breakfast for you, and some medication for the pain," he told me.

Oh, so it was a pill for the pain.

I was almost afraid that it was a pill to ensure that I didn't have any children...and I was thankful that it wasn't.

If it had been, that would only shatter my heart at the idea that he didn't, in fact, want children with me. We were royalty, so of course, having children was important, wasn't it?

"I've also prepared a squadron of knights to be available to leave at your notice. I wasn't sure when you wanted to leave, but they are ready to go whenever you wish."

Now, I remembered.

I had made love to him the night before in preparation to leave today. We'd had one another so that he knew that I was going to come back, and to finally give ourselves to one another.

We sat and ate breakfast together, before he helped me get dressed in traveling clothes and we walked out, hand in hand, to the courtyard.

There was already a carriage waiting for me with all of my things, and just as he'd promised, there was a squadron of knights at the ready to leave.

"Today, you are all leaving with one objective; protect your Light Seer Princess. She will be traveling to the Southern Kingdom so that she can prove to the people—and her family—once and for all that she is here to stay, and that she wants to be here. We are not holding her against her will, she is not being abused, and she is allowed to come and go as she pleases. But be on your guard," he warned. "The ultimate goal of the Southern Kingdom has always been to take over the ruling of the empire, and they will stop at nothing to achieve this goal. They may have changed, but just in case they haven't…you are to protect my Crowned Princess."

"Yes!" The crowd chorused in agreement.

I turned to Carlisle, and I reached up and took him into my arms.

He chuckled warmly, and pressed his lips to mine in a warm kiss. "Come back to me safely, Kin."

"I will, Car," I smiled up at him.

With one final kiss, we were setting out.

Sir Axel, my Paladin Sorcerer, and Sir Halo, my personal Keeper Knight, both rode with me in the carriage, while the rest of the knights rode horses around us.

It was strange…I hadn't been out of the Northern Kingdom once since I had arrived as a child, and though I had realistically known that I was allowed to leave, I just…hadn't ever considered it as being allowed.

It was an odd thing to be leaving this place that I'd once seen as a new kind of prison…but now, I saw it as home.

Oh, how the tables had turned and the times had shifted.

Our relationship had come so far in just the last year.

To think not so long ago, Carlisle had hated me and humiliated me...and now, we were together and intimate?

I wasn't sure if I could say that he was in love with me. He'd never told me he was, or that he loved me at all...but I knew that I was in love with him, and that was what counted to me.

We traveled for a few hours, before it was time to stop in a town along the road to the South.

We found an inn, and while all of us prepared our things for the stay at the town's inn, I heard the whispers and thoughts going through the minds of the townspeople around us.

'Is that the Light Seer Princess?'

'I thought she wasn't allowed outside!'

'Did the Crowned Prince finally tire of her and decide to send her away?'

Most of the thoughts were laced with concern, but there were a few others that weren't so kind.

I glanced at Halo in worry, and he gave me a reassuring smile.

"Don't worry," he smiled at me. "We know how to handle this."

Following his lead, I stepped into the inn and looked at the inn-keeper.

She was a shrewd-looking older woman, with dark brunette hair and hazel eyes. She had a beauty mark on her jaw, and wrinkles on her forehead from years of scowling. She had crows-feet and laugh lines, though.

"Welcome to The Holly Luck Inn," she said in a voice that grated on my ear, and Halo smiled at me with a wink off to the side. "How can I help you?"

Her thoughts, however, weren't so kind. *'Great, now I can tell people a real-life princess stayed at my inn and attract even more business! I wonder if she has any juicy gossip for me...maybe I could inform on her and earn some extra gold from the news outlets?'*

Halo had been right. This woman was a gossip who listened shrewdly to everything around her and used that gossip to exploit more gold for herself!

"Yes, hello, and thank you for the welcome," I smiled at her, and I decided to give her a good bit of information to happen to drop to the other townspeople. Nobody spread gossip like a town's innkeeper. "I am here to stay for a night with my knights," I informed. "We are travelling to visit my family in the Southern Kingdom, and it will be a long journey, so I want to get a good night's rest and get some supplies."

"Ah, yes, of course," she smiled, though her thoughts questioned whether or not the resounding rumors were actually false, now. "Are you moving to live with them?"

I hadn't expected such a direct question.

I shook my head. "No, just to visit. Their letters mentioned wanting to see me and for me to see my siblings, and I wrote them back that I would come visit sometime...though, of course, palace life has kept me rather busy, learning to become queen," I admitted, sounding a bit "guilty".

I could see the surprise on her face, and her thoughts lined perfectly.

She had heard—like most everyone else, I assumed—that I wasn't receiving letters from my family and that I wasn't allowed to write them back.

I could see, now, that Carlisle hadn't lied about this part of the information.

My parents were spreading lies about us; that he was keeping their letters from me and not allowing me to write to them.

"I will probably stop by here on my way back through," I smiled at her. "I plan to stay for a little while before coming back...I definitely want to get back quickly, now that our *relationship* has...*changed*," I said, letting myself picture our night together and a thick heat rushed to my face, making me blush.

She gaped openly at me, proving another point correct;

The people had been hearing that Carlisle would kick me out of the palace soon and that our relationship was terrible.

By telling her the new status of our relationship in that tone, and a blush on my face, both of which insinuated that our relationship had gained intimacy?

That was admitting that my place in the palace had just been solidified.

Her thoughts mirrored this, and she fully intended to gossip about it to her other patrons—as quickly as possible.

If anything, she was actually getting frustrated that I was taking up more of her time than necessary because she so badly wanted to go spread the news.

Halo, you are a genius, I thought to myself as I gave him a wry smile.

He winked again, giving a nod and a smirk.

The woman called over a member of the staff to show us to our rooms, and she was a bit disgruntled when I told her that I wanted a room with my sorcerer and Keeper Knight for protection purposes but finally acquiesced to my request when all of our knights glared menacingly at her.

I could hear, in her top thoughts, that this meant that the staff wouldn't be able to sneak any valuables out of my room.

A good call, on my part, to insist they were in the same room with me, then.

By the time that we had all gotten settled into rooms and it was time to go to sleep, the reception area and dining hall on the floor beneath us was buzzing with the thoughts and murmurs of the inn's patrons, and I groaned as I held my temples, a headache blossoming from the noise.

That was something that nobody considered about being a Seer—the endless thoughts of those around me.

Most of the time, it wasn't too hard to drown out. The staff in the Northern Kingdom tried to control their thought flow as much as they could, so that the Seers weren't overwhelmed.

It had taken a very long time for me to get used to that, as I discovered that once my eyes were uncovered...I could hear any top-level thoughts in the nearby vicinity to me.

When I realized that I was hearing thoughts, I had been so alarmed and thought it the oddest thing. I hadn't started hearing the thoughts and feeling the emotions of others until my eyes had been uncovered.

It was strange, and I wondered, deep down, if my parents and Sir Enoch had been aware in the beginning that keeping my eyes covered would block out that ability entirely.

If our eyes were covered, we couldn't hear those thoughts. Something about having the material blocking off our sight made it so that the power didn't work, rendering us useless.

It was funny, as I thought about it now, that such a powerful ability couldn't permeate through a measly scrap of fabric. It was laughable, almost.

This had, as was told to me, a closely kept-and-guarded secret among the royal family of the Seers.

Had it been a coincidence?

I hoped, in my deepest and most sacred of thoughts and feelings...that was the case.

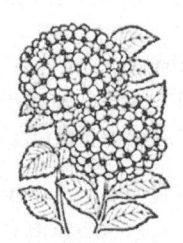

The following morning had arrived after fitful sleep, and after eating and gathering up supplies to purchase in the market, we were well on our way, with a completely new attitude surrounding us in the town.

"It is working," Halo murmured in the carriage, watching the town disappear in the distance as we rode along. "The whispers were much more positive today."

"Yes," Axel nodded. "A very proper decision on your part, princess," he complimented. "You were right. You needed to leave the palace in order to gain favor. His highness will surely hear the rumors spread, as I heard other travelers whispering about it as well as they were leaving the town. This will work."

Hope soared in my heart, and I prayed that it would continue working.

This same routine was practiced through several more towns, but we all noticed that, the further South that we travelled...the more skeptical people became.

"Their reach is much stronger in this region," Halo reminded me when I was feeling particularly stressed one night, twelve days into our journey. "I know that you don't wish to think ill of your family, your highness, but the fact is...they are purposefully spreading lies and rumors to bring you back here, permanently, and you may not want to believe it, but that won't change its validity."

I sighed, nodding as he gave me a much-needed hug.

"Yes, I know," I said, saddened. "I just...want to see for myself. I've never even seen them in person, never seen the place I was born. I would like to...at least give them a chance."

He sighed, pulling me tighter. "I will be with you each step of the way, my princess," he smiled down at me before he tucked me into bed. "We will reach their kingdom tomorrow. You'd best get some good rest."

That night, for some reason, I had strange dreams. Dreams that scared me. I couldn't help but feel a strange sense of foreboding all of a sudden, and it deeply affected my sleep.

When I awoke the following morning, I did my best to alleviate the puffiness of my eyes and take a good bath before a little pain medication, and then, we all supplied up and set out.

We were riding through the forest about two hours away from the Southern Palace when, out of nowhere, Halo slammed into me, screaming at me to watch out.

"Get back, your highness!" He shouted, covering my body with his armor-clad one. "It is a raid!"

I glanced to see that an arrow had shattered through the carriage window, and fear struck me hard at the fire that began to blossom into the carriage.

"Damn it! **Feece**!" Axel shouted, shooting out a blast of ice from his palm and dousing the flames...but he wasn't fast enough.

"We have to get out!" Halo told me. He glanced out of the broken window, looking around, and noticing the other knights fighting. He slammed the door open. "Run, your highness; run, and don't look back. I will cover you!"

"Halo, *no*!" I cried when he pulled me out of the carriage and shoved me toward the forest. I heard him urging me on in thought, pulling out his sword and running an attacker through to the hilt.

Panic overwhelmed me as thought ran through my mind at a rapid pace, and I flinched as my head felt like it would explode.

I heard Axel asking me, in thought, what in the world I was waiting for...so, I finally turned toward the forest and bolted, as instructed.

I ran for quite some time.

Eventually, I began to slow down.

I wasn't even entirely sure how long I had been running for, or how far I had come, but I did know that I was standing in sloshy, mucky mud that came up to my calves and the vines and foliage was thick and difficult to wrestle with.

I tried desperately not to be very loud, but my breath came out in heavy pants and gasps and heaves as I struggled to breathe normally again and I kept having to put force into my steps to try to get out of the mud and through the branches and vines blocking my path.

It was only exhausting me further.

I heard something rustling in the forest behind me, and I felt tears prickle my eyes as I started pushing myself all the harder.

It couldn't end this way...!

I had to get back home!

I had to get back home to Carlisle...

"Your highness!" I heard familiar voices call, and relief flooded me.

Halo and Axel! They had found me!

"Here!" I called, and I glanced behind me as best I could to see them coming out of the brush.

"Oh, heavens," Halo noted my predicament, and he chuckled as he came to help me, standing on one of the downed trees beside of me. "Here, take my hand, your highness."

"What happened?" I asked.

"Our...our squadron was all but wiped out," he admitted sadly. "Though, thanks to Axel, here, he made short work of the rest of the assailants and a couple of our men survived."

I was thankful, at least, that a couple of them had made it.

I shot Axel a grin, just before a look of horror crossed my features and fear spiked my heart as a hooded and cloaked figure, all in back, dropped out of the tree above us.

"Axel!" I cried, but as he turned, a long spear pierced him in the chest and ran him through. "*Axel!*" I sobbed as his body fell to the ground, a look of stunned shock on his face.

"Your highness!" Halo cried, trying to pull me out of the mud, but stopped and started fighting the man.

"Halo!" I cried when the man pulled out a wooden club and slammed it against the side of Halo's head, rendering him unconscious.

"*That*," the man said, mildly out of breath. "That was for my men." He looked to me, and his bright hazel eyes full of irritation as all manner of curses strung through his thoughts. "Well, well...the Light Seer Princess who starting mucking up the King and Queen's well-thought-out plans," he said.

"W-...what...?" I asked, confused as tears trailed down my cheeks.

"The King and Queen bid my platoon and I to...*dispatch* your squadron," he told me. "You've sure made a mess of their carefully laid out plans, and they aren't pleased."

"What...I don't understand—"

"Wow, you are stupid," he snickered. "I heard rumors, a few years ago, that the Light Seer Princess was said to be...a bit *slow*," he informed me. "That's why the Dark Seer Prince was so dissatisfied with you."

"But, what does that—"

He laughed at me. "I should just let them tell you," he said, and he grabbed my arm and forcefully began jerking on me.

I squealed out in sudden pain as a loud pop and a jolt reverberated throughout the arm he was pulling on, and he laughed even harder.

"Wow, you're weaker than I imagined given how fat you are. Your bone actually popped out of socket!" He laughed.

Shame and fear burned their way through me as his vile thoughts came to mind, him imagining that he was allowed to dislocate my bones one by one and torture me for days on end for all the deaths of his comrades. That was fair, I guessed...

I sobbed as I mourned for my Paladin Sorcerer and my Keeper Knight, and he dragged me away.

Chapter 18

Carlisle...

"How many days has it been?" My brother, Julian, asked me as I paced, rubbing my chin.

"Twenty-seven," I croaked. "It takes twelve days to get to the Southern Kingdom. It only takes four days for a messenger bird to get there. She should have had time to send six letters by now! My letter should have reached her by now!"

"The rumors around the kingdom have been quite positive, though," Valence noted thoughtfully. "Public opinion has gotten far better, so her idea of going to the Southern Kingdom and showing the people that she is allowed to do as she pleases—and the added bonus of mentioning your changed intimacy status and the sightings the people have had of the 'Virgin Sheet' outside of her palace window...it is safe to say that she was correct that it was the right solution."

I groaned, worried and frustrated. "Yes!" I snapped, and then I sighed heavily. "Yes, I know. Realistically, I realize that I had been wrong. Sending her was the right decision for the public opinion. All requests for the petition have ceased. But I...I'm worried. And she promised to write."

My family glanced at one another, knowing that my feelings of worry meant only one thing;

I had true, genuine feelings for Kinley.

It was no longer the way that it had once been. It wasn't admiration, or general care. It wasn't just that I appreciated her for saving my life anymore.

Our relationship had, truly, changed. I had fallen in love with this woman. Things had changed. I had changed, she had changed, the situation had changed.

What was I supposed to do now?

"Valence—"

"You wish me to go, my prince?" He asked, and I sighed out a breath of relief that I didn't even need to say the words.

"Would you?"

"Of course," he smiled, soft.

"Do not engage anyone in any way," I told him. "Keep yourself hidden; only engage if you—or Kinley—are in immediate harm, and even then...I would prefer for you to come back and seek aid. You are no longer in your late teens, but rather into your early thirties. You are my General-to-be as soon as I ascend the throne. I can't have you dying on me."

"I will follow your orders, your highness."

"Ride hard and fast...and try to make as few stops as you can. I want to know what's happening. And here—" I said, pulling out an emergency magic tool that Axel had given me the day that they'd left.

I hadn't known why or what had possessed him to do so, but he'd told me that I may need it.

This was when I felt was the right time to use it.

"This is an emergency scroll," I told him. "It can be used to send instantaneous messages when sealed. I have a scroll case, and I have the matching scroll case for the transport of messages. If you write a message and seal the scroll in this case, the scroll will immediately transport here, to me."

He gawked at it in awe, and met my eyes.

"I will find them, Prince Carlisle," he vowed.

Year's Fall, 520 LD

Another ten days passed. Over a month had passed.

Thirty-eight days total, since the princess had left for the Southern Kingdom, and I was getting angsty, but that was quickly put to rest when the emergency scroll case began to glow.

I startled, jolting, and rushed to open the thing. I pulled out the scroll and unrolled it, only to find—

Oh, God. Heavens above...

No.

No, no.

No, no, no, no, no!

"Your Highness,

I came upon a most unsavory truth; I found the caravan of the princess's squadron. All twenty knights, and Sir Axel, are all dead.

Halo was rendered unconscious and was almost dead when I found him. He had taken a severe blow to the head and when he had awoken, he had bandaged it to the best of his ability and tried to use some medicine to slow the bleeding, but he's been on his own in the forest since.

We are just two hours from the Southern Kingdom's palace.

Halo tells me that the caravan was attacked, and that they defeated the bulk of the force until a Special Forces Knight managed to come back and finish the job. He is unaware of her highness' current condition.

What do you wish me to do from here?"

Sobs bubbled out of my throat.

I knew it. I just knew it.

I had known, in my deepest gut instincts, that those damned bastards would do something like this! I knew that it had to be her parents.

No matter how much she wished to believe that they could love her, that it was possible they could be good, wholesome parents...it simply wasn't so.

"Your highness?" A nearby maid asked, bringing me some fresh water.

"Get my family together, right away, please. And then, please summon all of the commanders of the army."

"Y-your highness?" She gaped at me in shock, begging in her mind that she was misunderstanding.

"We go to war," I said darkly, and she blanched as she rushed off to do my bidding.

I took a new scroll, and wrote out a message to Valence.

"I am sending the army; we go to war. There is no way that this is a misunderstanding.

They have kidnapped my Crowned Princess, and for that...they will pay dearly.

Hold your position and nurse your brother back to health. You may join us, if you wish, when we are on our way through. For now, do not take any further action."

I sealed the scroll in the case, and it glowed again as the scroll was sent.

What a handy tool.

I wondered, vaguely, if Axel had known beforehand that he would perish during this journey...and I shook as I thought about how hurt and devastated my poor wife must be. She and the Sorcerer had been such close friends...

I hoped that she hadn't actually seen him die, but I had a bad feeling about that.

Now that I had managed to contact Valence, I stood, dressing myself in my ceremonial armor before I stepped out of the room, marching my way through the palace to meet the soldiers and my family.

They were all worried, and I briefed them quickly.

"My wife has been kidnapped and her squadron slaughtered. The Paladin Sorcerer, Sir Axel...has fallen. Sir Halo has been severely wounded. Her parents...are the perpetrators," I informed, and they all gasped and murmured before I held up my hands, getting them to quiet down again. "Make no mistake; We are off to war. This will be a difficult battle. They have been preparing for this for years. There is no other reason that they would do this, now, of all times. Mark my words carefully: They are ready for war. They know we are coming. It is up to us to rescue the Crowned Princess."

"Yes, your highness!" They all chorused, and I turned to my parents.

"I am so proud of you," my mother said, bringing me into a hug. I could see in her thoughts that she was remembering how I had once been, and how disappointed and humiliated she had been by my behavior.

Now, she was filled with pride.

"Thank you, mother."

After last well-wishes and hugs from my family, I looked my father in the face.

"If anything happens to me...if I don't make it back alive...wait for Kinley. I don't care what happens to me, I vow it now that I will send her back home alive...and she may yet have a surprise," I told him.

He gasped, grinning at me. "So, it wasn't a trick?" He asked.

I laughed. "No, no tricks."

"Good. It's about time," he winked at me. "I will look for her return...and yours. Be safe, son."

"Thank you, father."

"Be well."

Blizzard's Reign, 521 LD

Over the next twelve days, two-thirds of the army of the Northern Kingdom—about twelve-thousand men, round abouts—covered the same journey that my wife took over a month earlier.

It had been fifty-one days, *total*, since she had left for the Southern Kingdom.

It was an eerie, discomforting feeling as citizens stared at us, and our soldiers ushered them into their homes, telling them the Crowned Princess's squadron had been attacked and we were off to war.

From the thoughts, everyone wondered who was the instigator, and if this was really happening. If the Southern King and Queen were at fault.

It had been necessary for her to go...I realized that. It had drastically changed the situation. The calls for a petition to send her back to the Southern Kingdom had completely ceased. Actually, the Southern Kingdom had gone completely silent on the matter, and now I understood why.

We finally reached an inn, where Valence was waiting with Halo. They had already wrapped and prepared Axel's body inside of a coffin, and were ready to head back to the kingdom.

Or, Halo was.

"Valence," I sighed, reading his thought. "I know."

He was ready to go to war...for his princess. He'd already rescued her once, and he was ready to do it again.

"Halo," I smiled, shaking his hand and patting his shoulder. "How are you feeling?"

"Lousy," he grumbled. "The physical wounds are doing much better, but I won't be able to be on duty for a while. The physician said I have a concussion. I will need an escort with me home, but Valence has done nothing but talk about rescuing her highness since he found me..."

I laughed. "Yes, I imagine so. I will assign two knights to go back with you, and you can take the wagon that we brought. I knew that we would be taking his body back with us, so we made sure to prepare for that." I sighed. "Now, then. Sir Rayon, Sir Kieran; you two will be joining Sir Halo back home. The rest of us will head onward."

With last farewells to Halo and the other two with him, the army set out.

We were only three hours from the Southern palace, here at this inn, so I knew that from here on out, we would have to be careful. We had one last town to pass through— the very Southern Royal city in this beautiful valley that is overlooked by the castle up on the base of the mountain.

As we drew close to the city, it grew quiet. Far too eerie. There were people buzzing around, but there was almost no thought. It wasn't natural. It was making the hairs on my arms and neck rise. Something wasn't—

"Your highness!" Valence shouted, tackling me out of the way...

An arrow pierced the ground where I'd once stood, and I gaped up at the sky.

"Shields! Shields!" I called out. "Arrows from the sky!"

I watched in horror as multiple citizens were shot through, and we rushed to try to get the children safely in a building nearby, ushering people into their homes.

I could hear that they had been told that they would be fine.

They would need to keep themselves void of thought, but the army would surely rescue them.

We needed to think that nothing was wrong. I was thankful that I'd already been on high alert from the lack of thought in the town to begin with. They had been betrayed by the King and Queen of this land...and if I had anything to do with it, I would make sure there was recompense.

"Valence! Go!" I called to him. "I don't care what happens from this point; find her, and get her home. Period."

Chapter 19

Valence Trident...

Blizzard's Reign, 521 Lawrence Dynasty

I rushed through the crowd, parrying and dodging arrows. I didn't look back.

I knew that Carlisle meant business. I knew that he'd finally taken that all-important step with the princess and they had—finally—been physically intimate.

That meant that, at this very moment, the princess could very well be pregnant.

I only hoped and prayed that I found her alive and unharmed...but knowing the monsters who were her biological parents, I didn't know how much hope I could hold out for her safety.

I was stopped at the edge of the castle—the wall that blocked the castle's estate from the town below—when I saw another person there.

She noticed me, and I took notice of her outfit.

She was dressed all in black, with a leather chest-plate on. She looked like she was from a guild or something. Her thick, unruly braided hair was a rich, dark amber color and her eyes were a deep hazel-brown eyes.

"Who are you?" She asked, whirling around with a dagger pointed at me.

I held my hands up in surrender. "I am here to rescue my princess…"

She gaped at me. "You're—"

I nodded. "From the Northern Kingdom. Who are you?"

She glanced away. "My brother…he was killed when he brought the princess back alive. The King and Queen wanted her dead before she arrived, and I…" She choked up, sobbing into clenched fists. "I found his head on the spike the next day, when I went to ask where he was. He was supposed to get paid for taking out her squad and come back home, but—"

"He didn't kill her, and they can't because it'll end their family. They were expecting him to do it."

She nodded. "I…I know it might sound stupid, but I'm here to get revenge," she sneered. Her eyes flashed with anger. "I know how to get in," she suddenly told me, light coming into her face. "I already found a way in! He told me that's where he'd be…where he'd be coming from. They wanted to keep the job hush-hush, so he couldn't come out through the front door. Just in case your army came and the prince read the thoughts of the soldiers, they didn't want him to be able to identify that they'd hired someone."

"I see," I said. "Can you show me how to get in?"

She nodded. "I will," she said. "Rescue your princess, and that will get all the revenge I could deliver without me even having to dirty my hands. All they want is to torture her and—"

"*Torture?*" I gaped, and she looked away.

"I heard a woman's voice screaming…from the dungeon," she murmured. "There is a door that leads into the dungeon from the outside; it is where they take out bodies from there."

I nodded. "Please, show me the way. If I can...I will take out the executioner for you."

She gasped, staring at me in awe, lowering her weapon. "You...you'd do that?" She asked.

I smiled. "Yes," I told her.

Her eye filled with tears, and she got a determined look about her face. "Let's go," she said, giving me a nod.

We walked along the outer wall until we got to the only weakness in the wall—a drain at the base. A sewer drain.

It didn't smell the greatest, but this was more important than being prudish or picky.

This was about rescuing my princess, one of the greatest honors for a knight.

"So...how do we get in there?" I asked, raising a brow at her. "You might be small enough—might—to fit in there, but I am not."

She grinned at me like a Cheshire cat. "My brother told me a secret," she said. She approached, grimacing as she stepped into the murky, filthy drainage flowing out...and she grabbed a pole bar...

She began to turn it, and I realized that the pole had been loose!

Taking out the one pole would allow both of us to fit. It would be a tight fit, of course, but it was doable.

I was going to be able to do this.

As we both slipped in through the newly opened up space, I let my mind wander.

I reminisced about when I had first met Kinley. She had been such a sweet girl, and so timid and scared. She didn't know anything. She didn't know colors; she didn't know foods. She didn't even eat without permission.

I had watched her grow. Yes, she had grown a bit...thick...Not that this was a bad thing to be thick, of course.

It didn't matter what size someone was, as long as they weren't at risk in their health because of it, in my opinion.

However, she was an amazing young woman.

She was kind and considerate, warm and giving, compassionate and loving. To me, it didn't matter what size she was, because who she was outshined whatever she may have looked like. She was my princess, the wife of the Crowned Prince. The future king and queen.

We noticed some guards nearby, and I quietly took out some throwing knives.

They weren't alert to us yet, and there were only two, so I knew that I could get them both without catching their attention. I took a deep, silent breath...and threw both knives with pinpoint accuracy.

They made their marks on the side of the head, stabbing straight through the temple and the into the brain...and they fell dead.

We quickly, light-footed, rushed through the courtyard to the closest door—the dungeons.

There was a small, barred window. I glanced inside, and noticed that it was...strangely empty...?

My alertness spiked when a groan sounded, and I'd recognize the voice anywhere.

Kinley.

I glanced around once more, making sure I didn't see or hear anyone, I opened the door and slipped inside.

There was nobody in the dungeons.

It was eerie, almost, how there was only one occupied cell in the entire room, and there were no guards.

I slipped through softly, and I sucked in a breath as I pushed down the bile that shot up my throat.

My princess...my sweet, compassionate, wonderful Queen-to-be...was chained to a wall. She was hanging by her wrists, her body hung low as her knees struggled to reach the floor. I could see from the gnarled mess of her body that her leg was broken, her shoulders were dislocated, her body was littered with open, weeping and crusted over gashes and huge discolorations from bruising.

She had been absolutely beaten.

"Oh, heavens," the girl with me whispered. "Her clothes..."

I glanced away, noticing that she was, in fact, almost naked, and she was covered in something...

What was she covered in...?

I sent the girl over to the door to the dungeons to glance out of the small window on the door. She looked around, but there were guards down the hall. Four of them.

...Only four...?

Any attempt to open the cell—where there was a key to the gate—would be met with alerting the guards. In all likelihood, the key was with one of those guards.

"Can you fight?" I asked the girl quietly. "We'll need to get the keys."

She smiled. "I can."

Before I could stop her or say a word, she slipped out of the door and I waited in my place.

I pulled out my sword when I heard footsteps approaching, and I was surprised when I saw the girl come back into the room, a triumphant grin on her face and some blood splatter on her face, when she held up a ring of keys.

"Impressive," I smiled, sheathing my sword.

She was impressive, certainly, and I felt an interest growing in me.

She may be from an enemy kingdom, but right now, we were allies, and I wondered what could have happened if we had met under different circumstances.

We tried several keys, and I watched Kinley jerk hard, groaning and coming to as I got her unchained and brought her down into my arms.

She wearily looked up at me, and a sob of relief left her lips. "Valence!" She croaked, tears streaming down her face.

"His highness sent me," I smiled at her. "He was so worried for you. He made sure to send me, knowing I would stop at nothing to rescue you. How are you?" I asked, giving her a sympathetic glance at her face only. "What is injured? Are you in pain?"

She sobbed, trembling. "They did...such disgusting acts," she cringed.

I paused.

Disgusting acts...?

"Did they..." I cleared my throat, struggling with the question. "Did they rape you?"

"No," she whispered. "They only...used my mouth and face."

Oh...**oh**, no, no, **no**...

That was what was all over her face and chest...!

I fought back bile again, but suddenly, horns began to blare.

"What...?" I asked.

"The castle," the girl whispered. "The castle is under siege!" She told me.

"Prince Carlisle is here," I let out a breath of relief.

They had succeeded at the town below the castle. That meant that, at the very least, we should survive this.

• • •
274

I directed my thoughts to the prince, in a way that wouldn't make him angry and lose focus.

'I've reached and freed Kinley. Focus on this, I will get her out of here.'

Of course, I couldn't hear a response from him, but I knew from previous experience that he must have been listening for my thoughts as soon as they arrived to the castle.

"Let's go," I told the girl, and we got Kinley unchained.

I sighed, and I met her exhausted eyes.

She knew. From the look that ran across her face, she absolutely knew.

I had to reset her bones.

There was simply no way that we could travel for two weeks back to the Northern Kingdom with her in this condition, and if we left her bones unset, it could lead to an entire array of other horrible issues.

She nodded. "Just...do it quickly, please," she pleaded with me.

I gave a tight nod, and with assistance from my ally at my side, I quickly slammed them back into place. She bit into a thick, rolled up scrap of fabric the girl had offered, and tears rolled down her face.

As we got her stood up and leaned against the girl, a startling realization hit me. She had lost some weight. Around her ribs had slimmed quite a bit, and just below her ribs was a swollenness about her belly.

It was a little different than her usual thickness, which was more toned. This was looser, a bit swollen.

She must have heard what I was thinking, because she began to sob and reached a gentle, cupping hand to her belly. I could see the confirmation on her face, in her body language.

Pregnant. My princess was *pregnant*.

It was still somewhat early, it had to be.

As I recalled, she and the prince had been intimate in the middle of the prior Folias's Blessing, and it was now Blizzard's Reign. It had happened right before she had left.

The fruit of their growing love. Pregnant, but there was no glow. No joy.

She had been beaten and tortured.

It would, frankly, be a miracle if the baby even survived all of this.

I glanced to my ally. "Get the princess out of here. I will proceed on my own. There is some unfinished business that I have to attend to," I practically snarled.

She, thankfully, didn't argue. Considering that the princess was obviously pregnant, and her current condition, she could see rationally that the princess needed to get out of here immediately.

I stepped up to the princess, and I gave her a gentle hug before I pressed my forehead to hers. "I will see you soon, princess." Then, I pressed a kiss to her cheek and then kneeled to press a kiss to her belly—to my young prince or princess—before I stood and walked away.

I walked out through the door to the dungeon, and as I made my way through the maze of hallways, I came across fewer soldiers than I had anticipated.

Most of the ones whom I did come across immediately held their hands up in surrender, and didn't try to fight me, oddly.

What...?

The only thing I could figure—

Just then, I reached the throne room, and I could see why the soldiers outside were standing down.

The Dark Seer Prince stood there over the King and Queen of the Southern Kingdom, both on their knees, staring down at them with disgust.

Surprisingly, he turned to me. "Kinley?"

"Safe. Rescued...with *big news*."

He turned to me, fully, reading my thoughts. Suddenly, his eyes went wide, and he gaped at me.

"Preg—" He paused. "Pregnant. She's *pregnant*?"

I nodded. "She is pregnant, your highness."

"Oh," he said, breathing out a shuddering breath. "Oh..."

"I need to make a request, your highness."

"Valence," he groaned, glancing at the king and queen. "I wanted to—"

"*They beat her*," I seethed. "They let the torturers—" I choked off. "They *ejaculated* all over her."

"What?" He raged, glaring down at them.

"Please," I asked him.

He turned toward me fully again. "Valence—"

He didn't get the full sentence out, however, before the queen stood, grabbed a nearby soldier's weapon...and stabbed the prince in the back of the ribcage area.

He shouted out a cry as all of our soldiers rushed to his side, even as I swung my sword and decapitated the queen. When the king leapt up to rush me, I quickly did the same to him.

Our soldiers rushed to get the prince laid down, leaving the knife in the wound and calling for a healer.

This couldn't have been more dangerous.

Legend told of a serious repercussion of a member of the royal family attempting to kill one of the Seers; their entire family line would die in succession. Only the direct link—parents and children.

If the Dark Seer Prince died due to the Southern Queen killing him...Kinley and her siblings would all die.

This was a direly important situation.

We worked over him, and when the healer arrived, we received good news; the knife had not pierced anything fatal. It was purely in the flesh.

Knife removed and wound cauterized, the prince—whom remained unconscious—was carried out on a stretcher.

I knew that, in the prince's absence, I was the highest-ranked soldier of his army. I turned to the other soldiers of the Southern Kingdom.

"In the light of what has happened…we will convene with the Northern King and Queen to choose what will happen now. The Southern Prince is too young—and too closely related—to the Southern King and Queen, these…traitors," I spat in disgust. "Tonight has proven that this family is not cohesive of comprehensive enough to run the Southern Kingdom. You will need to remain on standby, but for now…all of you need to convene to your personal homes except for the former king and queen's children and their servants."

Everyone began to file out, even as my prince was carried out on a stretcher.

With Kinley waiting outside on a stretcher of her own, both of them were then placed in a carriage for safety before we set out for the Northern Kingdom.

Chapter 20

Carlisle...

Nivis's End, 521 Lawrence Dynasty

I was drifting.

Floating.

I was in a row-boat on a calm, gentle lake, deep in the mountains. A beautiful sunrise on the horizon coming up behind the mountains. The water clear, stunning blue.

The clouds above fluffy, silver on one side, bright golden on the other side...reminiscent of Kinley's hair and eyes.

Kinley...

My pregnant wife...

Feeling slammed back into me as I sucked in a breath, and I suddenly heard a voice. For the first time in my life, however, I wasn't bombarded by thoughts the second that I started to come into consciousness...what...?

I couldn't understand. Had my gift left me?!

Panic set in, and I began to pant.

"Easy," my ears finally honed in on the voice that had been speaking to me.

Valence.

"Easy, your highness. Easy," he said. "We took a step to help block out the voices so that whenever you started to wake, you would not be slammed by the voices."

"H-how...?" I croaked.

"We actually got the idea from the Crowned Princess," he said, a smile in his voice. "She told us during a moment that she was awake. Though, she hasn't been awake much since we returned."

I groaned.

"Yes, your highness, don't worry. We have a servant already getting pain relief for you, and her highness is right beside of you."

"Is she awake?" I asked, wondering why I hadn't heard her yet.

"No," he said. "This pregnancy has been wearing on her, with what she went through. The physician put her on high-risk alert, and put her on strict bedrest."

Fear began to burn bile in my throat.

"The Crowned Princess has been waiting for you," he said with a smile in his tone again. "When she is awake, all she talks about...is you, and how excited she is for you to wake up."

The fear simmered down, and though the worry was still ramping up in my mind, warmth and affection began to pour in, too.

It was humbling to know that my wife was happy about being with me, about being pregnant with my—our—child.

It was an honor to know that this woman was the same one I had put through so much, and that even through all of this...her heart was receptive to me.

She was opened to me, and we had reconnected.

Several days passed, and I blinked awake.

I hadn't been able to be awake at the same time as Kinley, yet, but I had been awake and up a time or two.

I was still recovering from the stab wound.

The blindfold had been removed from my eyes, and I could hear thoughts buzzing around in the distance. I hadn't known that cutting off the eyes with a measly cloth could cut out all of the thoughts and feelings around me, and it gave me an entirely new appreciation for my bride.

She had been blindfolded for the first seven years of her life, almost, and to think that she had been cut off from such an important part of her identity...

It was humbling, to say the least of it.

Everything about her humbled me, now.

I had learned that one of my brothers had been sent to the Southern Kingdom to become king there, and there were already young noblewomen being considered to be his bride and become his queen.

It was sort of ironic that my younger brother had become a king before I had, but that was just how things had turned out.

As I opened my eyes, I looked in awe at my bride. She was lying there in the sun on the bed, the light illuminating her beautiful silver hair and her pale, creamy skin. She looked like some otherworldly creature.

Her eyes fluttered open, and I felt my heart flutter in my chest as our eyes locked.

"Car," she breathed, a smile lighting her features.

I glanced over her, looking at her swelling belly and her soft, happy features. She was positively glowing, so radiant that my heart thudded hard in my chest. She smiled at me with twinkling eyes, her hand reaching toward my face.

"Kinley," I murmured, and I smiled brightly at her as I reached my hand out and up, stroking her cheek before it slid down her neck...her collarbone and shoulder...

Down her arm, and down to her hand to hold there.

We lay there, simply holding hands and staring at one another as her eyes filled with tears.

"You...you came for me," she whispered. "You came to save me."

I gave her a confused look. "Of course, I did..." I told her. "You are my wife..."

I leaned over, scooting closer, and I gently pressed my lips to hers.

"I love you," she whispered, and I felt my stomach churning and my heart racing.

"I love you," I told her, holding her gaze. "I love you, Kinley." I sat up a bit, and pulled myself close so that I could hold her in my arms.

Together, we chuckled and cried softly as we held one another.

Solaris's Reign, 521 LD

I paced outside of the room, waiting for news.

I had been in the room, but the crying and screams had made me pass out, and I had been promptly asked to leave the room so that my wife could focus.

She had been in labor for fourteen hours, and there wasn't a lot of progress.

I did know, from the rising pitch and octaves of the cries, that she was going to give birth soon.

I paced and waited, paced and waited...

Finally, I heard it; the cries of a newborn.

I turned, rushing into the room, and bypassing the infant for the moment, I took my sweet wife into my arms.

She was tired and worn down. She was struggling to catch her breath. She was sweaty, and her hair was a matted mess—though, it did smell good with her shampoo, in any case.

The nurse brought over the infant, and we both gasped in awe at the child. He was placed right into Kinley's arms, and her eyes immediately filled with tears.

"Oh," she murmured, seeing his bright silvery-gray eyes and his white hair. "He's stunning."

I grinned at her. "Yes...yes, he is."

"What will we name him?" She asked.

I considered that. "I think we will name him something that one of our ancestors had been named. He has dark, silver-gray eyes, just like him, and white hair close to silver. He looks just like the wizard from the history books," I grinned. "Winter. Winter Nias Karlyn Lawrence."

Her eyes filled with tears.

I remembered that, from history discussions over the last few months, her favorite figure from our history books had been the sorcerer, Winter.

He had made all sorts of records and history in the past, centuries and centuries ago.

She was so happy with this name.

Epilogue

Epilogue – Winter Lawrence...

Veras's Height, 529 Lawrence Dynasty

"Come on, come on!" I called, kicking the ball away from my cousins.

My uncle and his children had come to the Northern Kingdom so that his newborn son—only six months old—would be paired with his bride right away.

It was strange, to get a baby sister that I knew about ahead of time, but to know that she would immediately be heading South to become the Crowned Princess there.

My *cousin* was the Light Seer Crowned Prince—born in the Southern Kingdom, a male Seer, for the first time in generations. The new Dark Seer Crowned Princess, my baby sister, had been prophesied to be born exactly six months later...to the day.

It had come true, and my mother was in the middle of giving birth at that very moment.

I was a little sad that I wouldn't get to know her very well, and that she wouldn't live with me, but still...

I was happy, though, to have a close relationship to my cousins.

This was my first sibling, and they were taking her away, after al...

I needed all the cousins that I could get.

We were in the middle of our game when the nurses came to fetch us, and we were ushered in to the room where my mother was waiting.

In her arms, she held something that nobody had expected; a pair of *twins*.

One had the Seer's eyes; bright and golden and shiny. A pretty, beautiful black-haired girl.

The other had the same dark, silvery-grey eyes that I had, with black hair.

My skin tone was dark, like my father's, but this child's skin tone was white and milky like mother's.

Both twins were stunning.

"Cashmere and Castiana," my mother deemed them. "Castiana, the Dark Seer Princess, and Cashmere, the first princess of the Northern Kingdom."

Everyone smiled and congratulated my mother, and my new baby sisters were gently placed in my arms.

I was a proud big brother, in this moment.

Over the course of our lives, we would travel back and forth between the kingdoms to visit one another, and for the first time in generations, the new ruling Seer couple would rule in the Southern Kingdom.

My mother and father would have only one more child; another daughter, with father's rich dark skin and mother's white hair, with my eyes.

She would be named Cottonia.

I would be the ruling authority in the Northern Kingdom, as the only heir to the Northern throne, and I would marry a duke's daughter and settle down at the age of twenty-two.

We, together, would have four sons.

Father and mother spent the rest of their days happy. Content to just walk around the gardens and smell the hydrangeas.

The vision of my father, standing behind my mother with her arms in his hands, watching my mother even as she was watching over my baby sister and the gardens.

The vision of my mother with a smile on her face...

I was happy.

It was a peaceful life.

Bonus Chapter 1

Bonus Chapter 1 – Valence...

Blizzard's Reign, 521 Lawrence Dynasty

"So, now that your princess is safe and my brother is avenged...what now?" Valentina asked me.

Valentina, I found out, was the name of the woman I had met outside of the Southern Kingdom's castle. Oh, yes, the irony of how similar our names happened to be wasn't lost on me at all.

I glanced her way, and I blushed. She was wearing a tunic and skin-tight leather pants, with her leather armor still on and blood-splatter stained into the leather, but her dark amber hair was in a neat and tidy braid now and her dark hazel eyes were shining.

"If you would be interested, I...um...I think you would make a good addition to the royal guard, and..." I cleared my throat. "I would love to take you to dinner sometime...if you, ahem, would be interested in that...?" I asked, timid.

She grinned at me. "Really?" She asked, much more open than I had anticipated.

I nodded. "Yes," I said, nervous anticipation building in my gut.

"I would like that," she smiled.

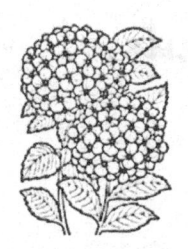

Solaris's Reign, 522 LD

"I am humbly asking for permission to marry," I told the King, bowing low.

He had a considering expression, but Kinley looked on with a wide and happy grin on her face.

"I think you have earned it," she told me. "Let him go ahead and marry, Car," she smiled at him.

He huffed, grinning and rolling his eyes. "You have our blessing, Valence," he smiled, glancing at me before going back to kissing the Queen.

I had purposefully wanted to ask while they were getting heated up, because I knew they would want to push out an answer quickly so that they could get back to focusing on one another. It had always worked before.

I rushed through the palace and out to the temple, rushing to ask the head priests to perform a ceremony quickly.

Valentina had told me, quite clearly and repeatedly, that if we married, she didn't want a ceremony or a big deal made of it.

She was, in fact, a bit of a trickster, and so she wanted to get married without anyone aware and pop the news onto people...

Who was I to deny her request?

She was already waiting with the priest when I found him, and I started to laugh softly.

I had told her that I needed the King and Queen's direct permission and blessing to marry, as the head of the Royal Guard and the Keeper Knight of the King.

She must have gone straightaway to the priest because she anticipated that I would get the blessing.

So, there and then on that blaring hot day in Solaris's Reign...

I made Valentina my wife.

We had already...*ahem*...gotten physical with one another, several times, in the training hall's broom closet between training sessions. I was so thankful that she had joined the squadron...

Now, however, we were legally married and I would be able to love her in the comfort of a bed, in actual bedchambers.

A miracle, to say the least.

Her insides squeezed me like a vice as I surged into her, and she clung to me as I thrust my way in her heat...

For the first time, I let myself go within her...and it was everything I had never known that I wanted until that point.

Finally, at the age of thirty-five...I was finally married...and I was happy.

Days later, I watched with my wife in joy as my Queen danced the night away with the king, and her bright smile and excited eyes when she glanced our way and asked us to join them meant everything to us, because she knew...they knew we had married.

The fact that they knew that I was happy and married made it all the more sweet and precious to me.

Bonus Chapter 2

Bonus Chapter 2 – Halo Trident...

Solaris's Gifts, 526 Lawrence Dynasty

I was on an errand for the Queen when I first saw the love of my life.

I was grabbing a specially made gown for the Queen; the queen was very into the fashions of this boutique, but she wasn't feeling well that day.

When the butler came and told her the order had been finished and was ready for pickup, she asked me—very pitifully—if I would mind grabbing it.

Of course, I didn't mind. It also gave me the chance to get my brother and sister-in-law a gift for their upcoming child.

Yes, Valence was going to be a father in a matter of weeks, now. Their first child.

Valentina, the poor girl, had grown quite large and miserable with the pregnancy, but she was excited.

I stepped into the boutique, and I saw her at the counter assisting a particularly volatile young man raging about wanting to return a gown his lover had ordered—and put under his name to pay for—and his wife finding out.

The man grabbed her arm, and I felt fury rise as I rushed over.

"Stop, in the name of the—" I began, but I froze still when she hoisted him up by his collar, dragged his body over the counter, and slammed him down so that his head bashed on the counter on the way down.

"Do not ever put your hands on me—or any woman, for that matter—in a threatening way, you filth!" She snarled at the man. Then, she lifted him by his collar again and roughly shoved him out toward the door of the store. "Get the hell out!"

I watched in awe as she put this man in his place.

Then, her furious glare leveled on me. "What? You think I need a man's help? A poor, pitiful little woman needs a big, strong hulking man to help her, right?!" She seethed, and I held my hands up in surrender.

"No, miss, but I—"

"But what?!" She screeched.

I cleared my throat. "I am from the palace. I was going to place the man under arrest for touching you in an aggressive way, seeing as I am a knight from the palace."

She glared me down, noting my armor, and huffed, crossing her arms. "Well, I can handle myself just fine without your assistance," she told me.

I grinned at her. "Yes…yes, you can," I winked at her.

"So, why are you here?" She asked in a huff.

"My Queen has ordered a gown, and I am here to retrieve it for her. She was feeling unwell, so she sent me in her place."

"Oh!" She gaped, suddenly looking embarrassed. "I should have made the connection…" she grumbled, rubbing her arm and looking uncomfortable.

"Nothing to worry about," I smiled.

When she handed me the gown box and I turned, I gave her another glance and a big grin before I left.

Over the next two years, I would return every day with a beautiful flower. She would refuse to tell me which was her favorite, so every day, I brought a different kind with me.

It was a late afternoon in Seed's Sewn, of the year 529 LD, that I would find her being held against the wall in the back alleyway behind her store, fighting off a man who was attempting to force her into a carriage.

I rushed with my sword and tackled the man, arresting him, and would find out later that he was her fiancé.

She was a landlord's daughter—not a noble, but a high-ranked commoner among the common folk. She was rising in the ranks due to her highly popular clothing boutique, and as the daughter of a very reputable land-lord, lower-ranked noblemen were showing interest in her as a marriage partner.

With her light brown hair and bright, stunning green eyes, it was no wonder to me why she was such a high commodity, of course. I had been smitten from the moment I had first set eyes on her, in any case.

She would, painstakingly, thank me and in a very awkward, uncomfortable manner...invite me to come to her house to let her cook for me.

That day, I learned that her name was Britannia, she was only two years younger than I was, and she had hated her fiancé from the start.

As a landlord seeking to rise in rank, however, her father had been unable to refuse the viscount's marriage proposal for her, and she had said nothing because she knew that her family was seeking to use her matrimony to gain a new foothold in the noble community.

She confided in me that his arrest surely wouldn't deter him, and she was terrified of facing him—or her parent's disappointment for fighting against him.

She admitted to me that they would fully expect her to let herself be assaulted, if that were something that he wished to do. That she needed to be prepared for that event, take it gracefully and willingly; gladly, even.

Sick bastards.

I pleaded her case to the King and Queen who, in their wisdom and with their Seer eyes, gave the girl the title of Count.

Britannia thanked me by inviting me out to dinner again...and again.

Finally, I asked her, and on that fifth date...?

I asked for her hand in marriage.

Not for a political arrangement, because I was happy with my current rank and status...but because I loved her.

She admitted, softly, that she loved me too, and a month later, we were wed.

It took six months after being married for her to trust me with her entire self, and it was the most blissful thing I had ever encountered.

Finally, at the age of twenty-six, I wed the girl of my dreams.

Within another year, I would father a daughter named Harmony, who would look exactly like me, and two years later, a son named Samson, who would look just like his mother.

Our children would grow up with the royal children and their cousins, and we would all live happy, healthy lives.

A journey that had started so turbulent and terrifying, so harsh and lonely and afraid...ended on such a high note.

The King would live to the age of sixty-four, before he would pass in his sleep from unknown causes.

He wasn't really that old, but the physicians just said that it had been his time, they supposed. There was nothing wrong with him, health-wise.

The Queen would live to the age of seventy-eight, and pass from sickness—though, thankfully, she passed in her sleep and unaware.

It was a peaceful life, though, and for that...I was thankful.

—Fin—

Extra Content

Author's Medical Corner:

Believe it or not, a unique but common mental disorder was mentioned in this novel!

These two phenomena are called "Ambivalence," and "Philomisia."

Ambivalence is the extreme hatred toward someone you love, and can be treated. It is a stem off from depression and has several different causes and factors that can be involved. Philomisia is the hatred of love, in general. Our Male lead in this novel suffers from both conditions.

In each of my novels, I try to not only entertain with amazing, vivid storytelling—and fluster, with hot and vivid steamy smut scenes—but I also try to throw in real-life physical, mental and emotional conditions that exist, that many people may not be aware of or ever think of.

In this novel, there are no physical illnesses or disorders mentioned, but it does touch on difficulty to lose weight. Our mental/emotional references are Ambivalence and Philomisia.

I hope that you enjoyed this segment of the medical corner!

Here are some reference materials that I used from Google!

⌂ 🔒 google.com/sear 🎤 [9] ⬆

Images   Videos   News   Shopping

Feeling Love and Hate at the
Same Time - Exploring your mind

❓ About featured snippets   🏳 Feedback

People also ask   ⋮

**What is it called when you hate
someone but you love them?**   ⌃

While hate is essentially on the other
end of the spectrum of feelings,
emotional ambivalence happens and
it is not uncommon. As it's
happening, you may not realize that
you are indeed in the midst of loving
and hating a person all at the same
time. Feb 14, 2021

🔖 https://shemenajohnson.com › mixe...

Mixed Emotions: Can love and hate
co-exist? - Shemena Johnson

MORE RESULTS

Emotional ambivalence is defined in the Oxford dictionary as: **the fact of having or showing both positive and negative feelings about somebody/something.** At times in our lives, it is likely we will all experience emotional ambivalence. Mar 15, 2023

https://www.livability.org.uk › blog

Emotional ambivalence - Livability

Images   Synonym   In relationships

The emotion that's standing in the way of your healthy change: Ambivalence

MORE RESULTS

What causes emotional ambivalence?

Issues surrounding intimacy, separation, trust and self-confidence are commonly at the root of chronic ambivalence. Treatment that focuses on resolving these internal conflicts should help one to develop the courage to take action, make decisions with less fear, and have a "go for it" attitude. Jul 26, 2013

MT https://mainlinetoday.com › health
Dealing with Uncertainty: How to Cope with Ambivalence and ...

MORE RESULTS

| Images | Synonym | In relationships |

What is an example of an ambivalent emotion?

Is emotional ambivalence a disorder?

People who routinely experience ambivalence should also seek a doctor's advice, even if it does not accompany other symptoms. **Ambivalence may be related to a mood disorder such as depression.** Early diagnosis and treatment typically lead to better outlooks for individuals with schizophrenia or a mood disorder. Jul 19, 2022

https://www.medicalnewstoday.com › ...

Ambivalence: Is it a symptom of schizophrenia?

MORE RESULTS

Images   Synonym   In relationships

https://www.medicalnewstoday.com › ...

Ambivalence: Is it a symptom of schizophrenia?

MORE RESULTS

Is ambivalence a symptom of depression?

==Prolonged ambivalence has been associated with post-traumatic stress disorder, obsessive-compulsive disorder, depression and addiction.== Aug 4, 2021

https://www.washingtonpost.com › ...

When feeling ambivalence is unhealthy, and what to do about it

MORE RESULTS

| Images | Videos | News | Shopping |

What does it mean when you hate someone you love?

Does BPD make you hate your partner?

What is Philomisia?

Philomisia is the noun for **the hatred of love**. The person would probably be called a Philomisiaist or a Philomisist.

https://www.quora.com › Is-Philomi...

Is Philomisia a correct word for one who hates love? - Quora

MORE RESULTS

Extras:

Name pronunciations and illustrations:

Kinley: Kihnn-lee. Light Seer Princess

Carlisle: Cahr-lie-ull. Dark Seer Prince.

We hope you enjoyed The Royal's Saga, Book 4:
The Hidden Queen
Please join us for the next installment of The Royal's Saga: Book 5 –

The Conquering Empress...

Coming soon!
Scheduled to be released Tuesday,
October 31st, 2023!
Available for pre-order now!

Book Excerpt to follow

Kristen Elizabeth

The CONQUERING Empress

3RD AND FINAL REVISION
EXTENDED AUTHOR'S ART EDITION

Book 5 Excerpt
<u>Viorel</u>

<u>Solaris's Reign, 790 Imperial Lunar Year</u>

"It is time for you to marry. Your mother grows weaker, and your destined bride has just come-of-age. The Day-Giver king is getting restless, ready to send her here. You need to prepare yourself, because she will be coming soon. The Seal has chosen, but we only prolong the wait for you. It is time to bring her here."

"How old is she?" I asked. I hadn't been paying attention when he'd spoken to me.

For her to have been chosen this late after my seal had been chosen, she must have been much younger than me.

I had already gotten my Seal six years ago.

"Turned thirteen this month," he said. "You will be nineteen in just a few days...We may not know why your empress had to be chosen so late, but you won't be expected to be intimate until she gets her courses, so I will concede on that point, at least. The Seal has a reason behind all, son."

I groaned. "Father, I don't want to marry," I said, irritated. "I don't care about that. The Seal isn't all-know—"

"*You don't have a choice!*" He shouted. "You are lucky that the Seal chose you. What if your little sister had been married off to one of the Day-Giver's princes? Then, the Day-Giver king would have become the main ruling Emperor, and our kingdom would rely on their scraps. That cannot happen. The north should be above the south; it is in nature itself!"

"Father—"

"You are the one whom was chosen by the Seal. You also happen to be the Crowned Prince, the oldest of my sons. She is the only daughter that Day-Giver king produced, so she is the one the Seal has chosen for you."

"But father—"

"We *need* to be in control of the Daylight that she will produce. We need to hold the power. And you know what? It doesn't even matter if you don't like her! In fact, never do! Never like her if you don't wish it! Do you know what you can do if you *don't* like her? Bed her to ensure that the line passes to an heir through her, and then find *queens*."

Queens…?

"In the olden times, emperors who disliked their empresses would ensure that her prestigious bloodline produced powerful, strong heirs for him—the more, the better—and then he would take queens on the side with whom he could truly enjoy himself. You know how our system works. While the children of the queens cannot inherit the throne if your empress has given you an heir, she can adopt the children of queens even if she cannot give you a proper child to rule. The empress sits next to the emperor and holds power, but the *queens* are there to give you pleasure, son."

I considered this.

I hadn't ever really agreed with the polyamorous system our empire had in the past…

It seemed like so much extra work.

Father, unfortunately, failed to realize that it wasn't just marriage and the Seal that I hated the thought of.

I hated the thought of becoming the emperor, in general.

I was the oldest of the children, so I was already expected to rule this kingdom even if I hadn't been chosen by the Seal.

I didn't want that responsibility.

If I could, I would hand over that role to one of my younger brothers.

Father thought that my only issue was being stuck with only one woman...and that just wasn't it.

Since the Seal system had been implemented many generations ago, the men had gotten greedy; their chosen loves weren't enough anymore.

My father had my mother, the empress whom was a Day-giver...and he had four queens from other kingdoms.

Once he got tired of one, he would marry another and pay attention to her for a few years, before he found another queen to marry.

My father had four other children.

Two from the first queen, a boy and a girl. Those children were raised by a nanny and rarely ever seen, save for at formal events, and they would never rule the country...

Unless, of course, I were killed or I passed away. Then, my mother—who was no longer capable of giving birth to children, due to her health—would have to adopt the son as her own, giving my father an heir.

One child from the second queen—a girl, doomed to be used for political gain like the rest of the siblings.

The last child came from my mother, the empress...the only other full-blooded imperial child.

He was young, still just a few years old.

My younger brother wouldn't be old enough or ready to try to rule over anything for quite some time, but in the event that I remained healthy and nothing happened to me, he would become and arch-duke in the empire and rule over his own lands.

Father was a prime example that you didn't have to love—nor respect—your empress.

"I guess we'll just see," I said, groaning. "But just know; I do not want this. I do not intend to have heirs right away, and I would prefer not to have to see her at all. I have no interest in these things. I have my studies in swordsmanship and sorcery, after all."

"Yes, yes," he said, waving me off and paying me no mind whatsoever. "You wish to be the most famous sorcerer knight there ever was, I know."

I rolled my eyes, stepping back out of his office...but he was right.

My sorcery was nothing to scoff at, and that's what I really wanted to be doing.

Not playing "emperor and empress drama games" with some little girl six years younger than me.

Moon's Dance, 790 Imperial Lunar Year

The girl trembling before me continued to eye her father, the king of the Day-Giver kingdom, even as she stood in front of myself and the priest, giving vows in marriage.

It was obvious to me that she'd had just as little choice in this matter as I'd had, and I didn't know if I was sympathetic or annoyed—it felt like a combination of both—but bitterness burned my throat.

I lifted her veil, and I saw her glowing, striking golden hair with streaks of the lightest blonde, and her bright blue eyes that shined like the piercing blue sky

She *was* rather pretty, though she was a little on the thin side. Her arms seemed like bone and skin, and her hands were cool to the touch all but her seal on her right hand, which felt hot to the touch as my thumb grazed over it.

I saw that she, indeed, shared the same seal that I had, on the opposite hand as my own.

It wasn't a mistake, no matter how it annoyed me.

She felt as if I would break her if I touched her, and contrary to what her father *may* have thought, *I* didn't actually find that attractive.

My own sister—half-sister she may be—was well-built and thick. A bit fat, actually, but compared to this girl, she was a healthy, vibrant beauty full of energy.

She seemed livelier than this pitiful, sickly girl.

I realized, however, that the quick darting of her eyes revealed more than just *nerves*...

It seemed...she seemed *afraid* of her father.

If nothing else, I was thankful that I seemed to be getting her out of an abusive situation, and that was enough for me. It was the only amount of kindness that I intended to give her.

I didn't know her, but we were going to be together the rest of our lives.

She would be supplying all of the daylight to my kingdom for the remainder of her life, so I guessed that I could at least be civil.

I was thankful that I would not have to touch her for a while, but that would also mean that my mother would die...and it was an event I didn't look forward to.

Folias's Blessing, 791 Imperial Lunar Year

My young wife stood in front of me at the end of the bed, waiting for me to move.

She had started her monthly cycles and my mother had died, and thus, it was time to consummate our marriage and become the emperor and empress. She had finished bleeding just days ago, a week after she had started and long enough for the kingdom to mourn.

Light emanated from her and she practically glowed with her newfound power.

Rather than radiating darkness the way that I did, she radiated light.

Her skin was well-tanned and much darker in comparison to my light, pale skin, but I pressed forward.

I was thankful, at the bare minimum, that she had put on a little weight since she had arrived to my kingdom a year ago. I heard from her attendants that she struggled to eat the larger portions she'd been being given, but she was finally starting to gain a bit of weight. She wasn't like a twig anymore, though she was still under the weight I would like to see her be.

I made myself hard and felt her up a bit before I pushed her face-first into the bed.

When I lubricated her and entered her body, she still hadn't been prepared well enough, and I cringed as I listened to her sobs and pleas for me to hurry and finish...though, I was vaguely surprised that she wasn't begging me to stop.

If she had...I would have.

Her screams and sobs were hard to listen to, and I told her—much more harshly than I had intended—to be quiet. Her resulting cringe and pushing her face deeper into the bed had me struggling to focus on finishing the task at hand.

I finished as quickly as I could, given the circumstances, and stepped over to the kings. I watched the sheet with the insignias of our kingdoms get stained, before I heard a sniffle.

I glanced over to my wife, and it took everything in me not to make a scene at her crumpled body in the floor.

I directed the attendants to see to her before I quickly made my way out of the room as soon as I could manage to, trying to ignore her glowing blood on my body even as my newfound power of darkness radiated from me in a fog of wisping black energy.

That...had been *awful*.

I couldn't see myself ever wishing to bed that girl again. It had been a dreadful experience, and I was sure she likely felt the same.

Had I been wrong to try to stay away from her all this time...?

I thought I was doing her a favor.

She had felt nice and tight, had been warm and her body welcomed me...though, I knew that she wasn't aroused and had no feelings for me, and she hadn't actually welcomed me.

It was a difficult scenario. I didn't know what I was supposed to do, and father only advised me to do whatever I wanted. I was the future emperor—now emperor.

I tried my best to put the events from this day out of my mind, and I made my way to the throne room to proceed with the showing of the bloods and the coronation to officially and legally be known as the emperor.

The following morning, even as the sheet from our consummation hung on my throne in the throne room, I didn't see my bride.

I inquired about her, only to find that she had been offered breakfast in her room...and she had refused, before sending the servants away.

"I'm sure she'll get over it and come around," father said, rolling his eyes. "She's just sulking. Your mother did the same."

The mention of my mother being in this kind of condition left me feeling some kind of ill.

Blizzard's Reign, 792 Imperial Lunar Year

We cheered and toasted, lifting our glasses after a successful negotiation with another nation, when I saw a young king from another kingdom lean forward and press a kiss to his queen's lips...

A nation where polygamy was banned, and the king chose from a selection of noblewomen to become the queen.

He chose the one he liked best and began to court her, and when they were ready, they married.

A system like that...may not be quite as terrible.

History had shown that our kingdom didn't seem to run well under any system, so something radically different seemed best.

Speaking of queens and wives...

I glanced around, and realized with a start...my own bride was not present.

"Were the wives not supposed to be part of the negotiation?" I asked my father, and he startled, glancing at me.

"Do you not even realize that there is daylight outside? Have you not been paying attention in your schedule information? The updates on the que—I mean, empress?"

I didn't understand. "What does—" and then it hit me. "Oh..."

"She is giving her light for our kingdom, of course," he said, as if it were the most obvious thing that she absolutely should be doing. As if being here, with me, in a meeting for the rulers and their ruling queens, were an unthinkable thing.

I sighed, looking outside at the light that sat over the city, lighting up the place with a brilliant light.

She seemed to be doing well, at least, to give off such a bright light...but perhaps my opinion was affected by the fact that mother's light had been dimming for quite some time before her death, and the light outside had been growing dimmer as a result.

Had the sun always been meant to shine so brightly?

When the meeting was finished, it was time for the night to be coming out, and so the light was becoming dim and shining in a way that looked like sunset.

I was coming through the halls when I saw a couple of maids crossing through to another corridor, helping a stumbling girl that looked a lot like—

Wait...

I startled as I got closer, seeing that my bride was barely moving as the maids each let her wrap an arm over their shoulders, helping to carry her to her chambers.

"What...*what* is going on?"

"Oh, nothing for you to worry about, your majesty. Her majesty is simply tuckered out from giving light today. She hasn't quite adjusted to it yet, so she is a bit weak." They turned, continuing on their way to my bride's chambers.

Why did they seem to cavalier about this? This wasn't normal!

This...wasn't *normal*, was it?

They said that she wasn't adjusted yet...did that mean that giving daylight was so strenuous and tiring that it took months of being this worn out to suddenly adjust...?

I glanced to my butler nearby, who bowed.

"What is it, your majesty?"

"I would like to see my bride...what was her name, again? I would like to see her giving her light tomorrow."

"Empress Katria, your majesty. We can go see her tomorrow."

I gave a nod. "Yes...*Katria.*"

...
....
......
....
....
....
....
..................................**Want to keep reading?**

Be sure keep an eye out for the release of
The Royal's Saga, Book 5: The Conquering Empress!

It only gets better from here, and let us not forget: STEAMIER.

...Y
U...
...M

Books by Kristen Elizabeth

>The Royal's Saga<

The Apathetic Knight, Part 1 – The Crowning
The Apathetic Knight, Part 2 – The Burning
The Apathetic Knight, Part 3 – The Freezing
The Villainous Princess, Part 1 – The Trapped
The Villainous Princess, Part 2 – The Freed
The Disregarded Dragon
>The Hidden Queen<
The Conquering Empress
The Abandoned Prince
The Decoy Duchess
The Empathetic Brother
The Anonymous Writer
The Luxurious Slave
The Incensed Guardian Novella
The Royal's Behind the Scenes Finale Novella

The Shifter's Saga

The Rejected Lady Book 1: Parts 1 & 2
The Rejected Lady Book 2: Parts 3 & 4

…Further titles coming soon!

The Lover's Saga

Titles coming soon!

The Spell-Caster's Saga

Titles coming soon!

The Dreamer's Saga

Titles coming soon!

The Queen's Saga

Titles coming soon!

The Knight's Saga

Titles coming soon!

The Immortal's Saga

Titles coming soon!

The Villain's Saga

Titles coming soon!

The Children's Saga (PG13)

Titles coming soon!

Acknowledgments

A special thanks to my proof reader & good friend, Trisha, for reading through the novels and helping me with the grammatical and spelling aspects. Without your help, there were a lot of mistakes that would have made it into the books, and you encouraged me a ton. Thank you for your interest and investment in the story! I love you.

A thanks to the Ghost-Writer who helped me with some editing, some of the ideas, and some of the bonus content added to the original story. You rock, and I appreciate that. Thank you so much!

A special thanks to those who supported my work, including but not limited to, Sammie-Anne, Shannon, Amber, and so on. Several people who really encouraged me to write, publish and seek higher things. You guys inspired me to make this possible. I appreciate it so much. Special thanks goes to my most avid of fans, including Christine, Jeanna, and a few others who had been following my work and have gone to extra measures above and beyond to support and read my works.

All of you aforementioned people make writing the books so much more exciting so that I can see your reactions and give you good books to read!

Thank you all for being amazing. Without you, there is no way I would have gotten such a great start!

A special thanks to my husband, Reece, for allowing me to take so much time to write and keeping everything running, and not complaining a ton.

You wanted me to pursue my goals, and I needed that extra push because I'm bad about procrastinating on things. I love you, handsome ;)

Lastly, I want to give a special thanks to my mom. You don't read my work or really think this will go that far, but you love me and try to support me the best you can. Thank you for everything, and I love you.

Thank you all so much <3

About the Author

Kristen Elizabeth is now on social media! Follow on Instagram and Tiktok! Handle for both apps is

lovelymadness92

She also has an author's page on Facebook! Check her out at

Kristen Elizabeth
(Lovely Madness Fantasies)

Follow for more bonus content, updates, and publishing schedules!

Kristen spent the majority of her life emersed in arts and music, and used writing and reading as an opportunity to escape from the trauma and depression that spiraled out of control from the background that she crawled out of.

Writing, arts and music opened up an entirely new world for her, and she kept herself surrounded by it to avoid the stress and anxiety that was forcing down on her.

Kristen, herself, is also on the Autism Spectrum, and wants to share her unique worlds with those around her.

She hopes someone out there will enjoy her creations as much as she does and use her creations to escape from the mundane everyday life.

Kristen's biggest goal is to fit somewhere outside of the norm, and to broaden horizons in the world of fiction.

Life isn't always happy endings, sunshine, and rainbows.

Sometimes, life is an utter freakshow and things don't work out the way you hoped.

That's something that Kristen wants to bring to her writing.

Let Kristen help you fall into her world of Lovely Madness ;)

None of this happens without the readers! Please help me by sharing and spreading the word means so much to me!

Thank you so much!

I hope you tune in for Book 5:
The Conquering Empress

Author Q&A

Q: Where do you get the ideas?

A: I am autistic, so my brain is almost constantly running at warp-speeds with ideas. I have over one-hundred novel ideas right now, currently, and over seventy started.

Q: What is your writing process like?

A: My process is simple—I get a new notebook, and begin writing down basic ideas in the beginning. Once I have an idea I like and that I would like to expand on, I begin the process of "storm-boarding." This is where I lay out my main Female Lead, Male Lead, trope ideas, general ideas, an antagonist or issue, and how they get past it. Then, I lay out charts of family trees, timelines, tie in histories...it can be a length process, and that is what takes the longest.

Q: What is the fastest you have typed up a novel?

A: A week. With every book, I write the first three chapters before I move on to the next story, and write the first three chapters...that way, when I go back to finish the story, I simply re-read what I have so far, and I just let it flow out of me. I don't usually read over it or check it until I am going through for editing purposes. I do, however, keep my basic storm-boards in mind and try to keep things as close to the written layout and ideas as possible, without deviating.

Q: How many books did you publish the first/first and second editions for?

A: Books 1.0, 1.5, 2, 3, 4, 5, 6, 7, and 8...so, total, 9 books published. I stopped publishing to revise the books and create the special Author's Art Edition of the saga.

Q: How many books are in this saga?

A: 13 novels, and 2 novellas.

Q: Will all of your novels tie in together the way that 1.0 and 1.5 are?

A: That is my intention, currently. In this saga, it will mention other characters from the saga in each book, but years do pass between the settings of each book, so it isn't quite a, "I'm the Female lead, meeting the Female lead of this novel."

About this Book

The Hidden Queen, firstly of all, is a self-publication made possible by Amazon Self-Publishing KDP.

The author spent close to a year putting together this novel. The original drafts and stormboards were crafted in five-subject notebooks, before being made into manuscripts.

Most of my typing is done between 8pm and 12am, as my children are the light of my life and I do not take time away from them to work. (When they are in school, of course it is a different matter, though, and I have normal working hours until they get home.) Overall, typing up the story took about six months.

This work is entirely fiction, and is entirely original material from the author.

The original 1st edition of—

"The Royal's Saga, Book 4: The Hidden Queen was published on March 7th, 2023.

It had a hydrangea flower photo as the cover.

The original book 230 pages long!

The 2nd edition was a revision for extra editing, with a cover change, as well. The 2nd edition had 264 pages.

Finally, last but not least, this new edition of The Hidden Queen – Author's Art Edition is the final release of the self-published version of the novel, and at over 350 pages long, that is over 50 pages of added dialogue and author's hand-drawn art featured!

No other release of this novel will take place unless it is brought into a publishing house and released with tons of new features.

Thank you again to all of you readers!

You are amazing, and I hope you enjoy the rest of the novel series!

Please review the story, and please share with friends! One of my biggest dreams is to see people unboxing my story and enjoying the worlds that I take them to within it.

Much Lovely Madness to you all!

#TheRoyalsSaga

#TheHiddenQueen

#SteamyRomance

#KristenElizabeth

#LovelyMadnessFantasies

Kristen Elizabeth
Letting you fall into a world of
Lovely Madness

Reader's Observing Questions:

Q: Who was your favorite character? Why?

Q: What do you think will happen in Book 5, The Conquering Empress?

Q: How did this book make you feel?

Q: Were you surprised by the ending of this novel and how the story turned out?

Q: Were there any predictions you made about this book that did come true?

Q: What did you think the novel would be like, based on the cover and preview in Book 3?

Q: Do you want to read Book 5? Because it will be released soon!

I hope you enjoyed the book! I hope you keep following the journey that this story takes!

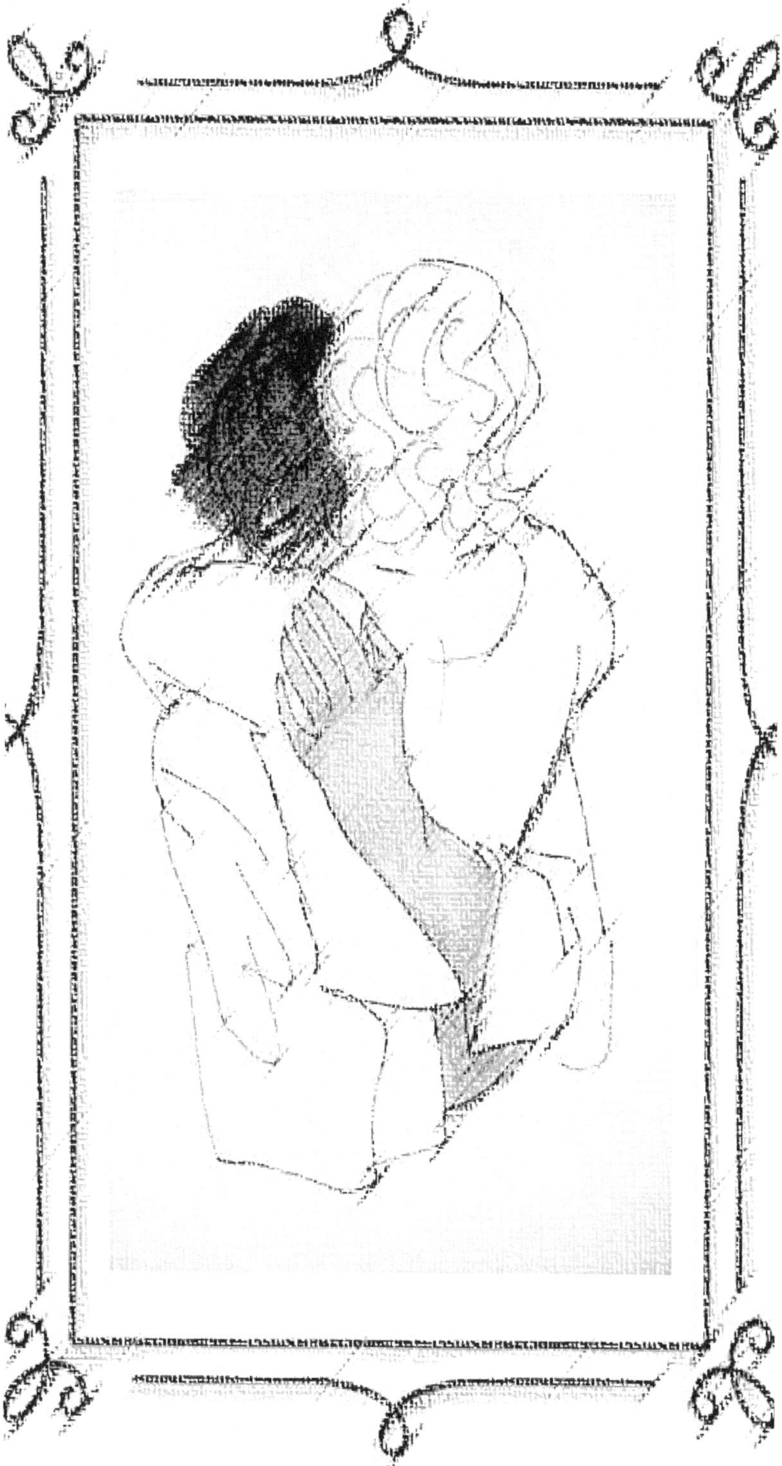

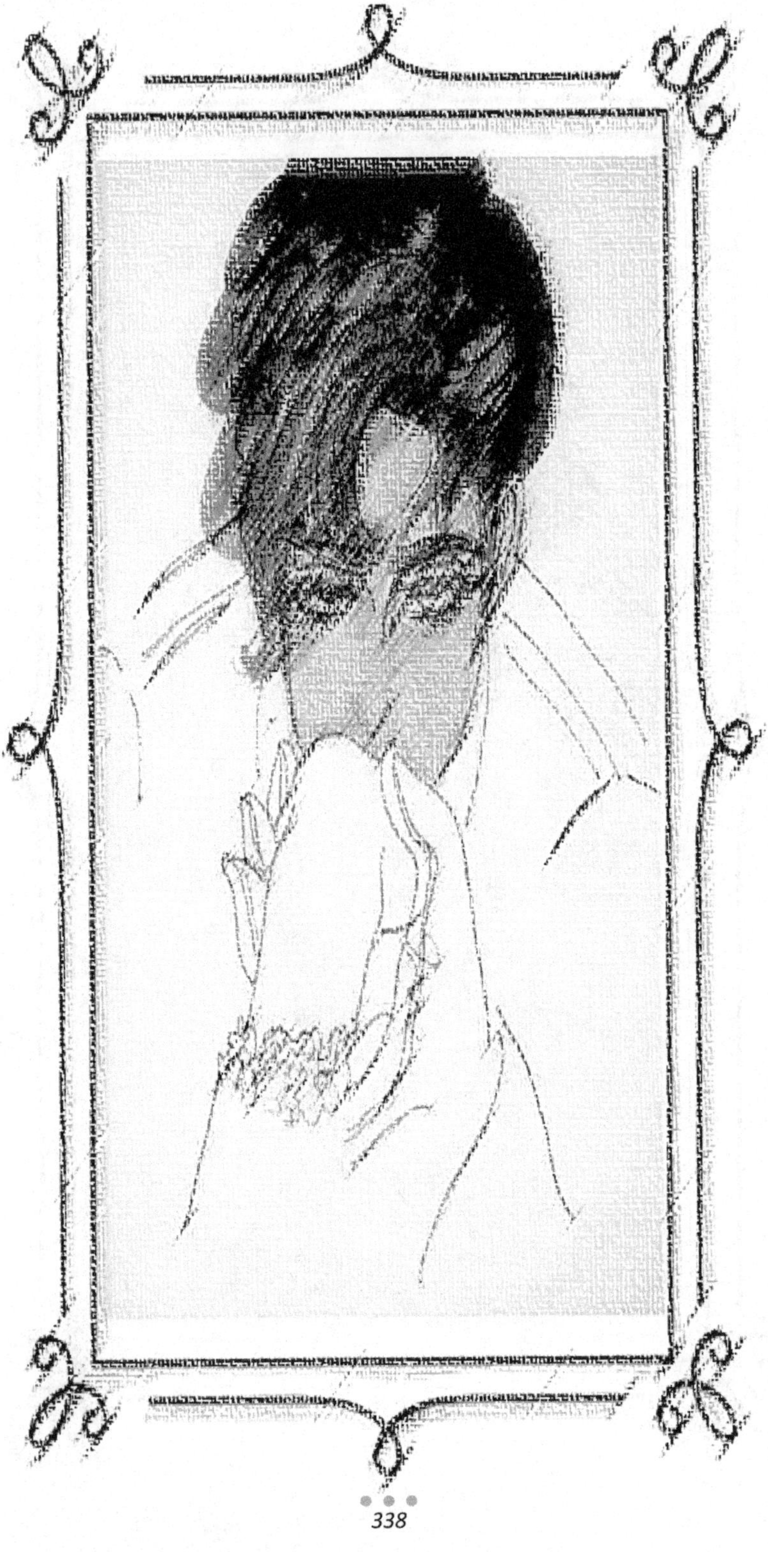

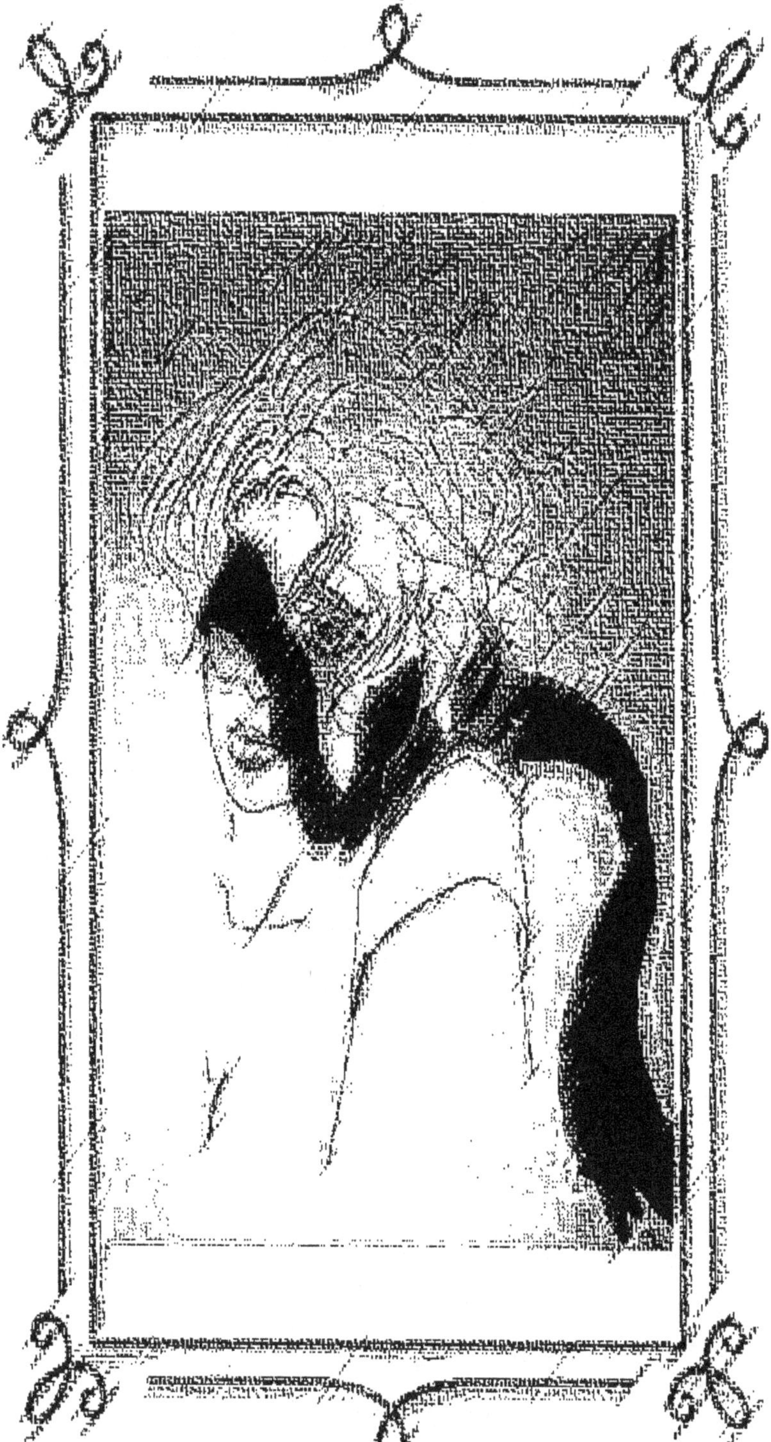

Special Bonus Note:

Kristen Elizabeth
The Royal's Saga

In honor of Relaunching
The Royal's Saga,
I will be Rapid-Realeasing the novels throughout the remainder of the year 2023, in anticipation of the release of
The Shifter's Saga
Coming January, 2024!
Follow me for more!
@ lovelymadness92
Insta & tiktok!

Lovely Madness Fantasies

Kristen Elizabeth

FANTASY ROMANCE AUTHOR

Final Remarks

Thank you so much for reading Kristen Elizabeth's novel world of Lovely Madness

The Royal's Saga, Book 4:
The Hidden Queen
3rd Edition; "Author's Art Edition."

Made in the USA
Columbia, SC
27 May 2024